I've travelled the world twice over,
Met the famous: saints and sinners,
Poets and artists, kings and queens,
Old stars and hopeful beginners,
I've been where no-one's been before,
Learned secrets from writers and cooks
All with one library ticket
To the wonderful world of books.

© JANICE JAMES.

MADELEINE

Matt and Tess Severn returning to England after a long absence in America were desperately hoping that Madeleine would not be home when they went to visit Tess's mother. Madeleine, Tess's identical twin, from whom they had fled seven years before . . . Tess and Madeleine had the faces of angels, and yet there was a sweetness in Tess's expression that was strangely absent from Madeleine's eyes . .

Books by Bernard Taylor
in the Ulverscroft Large Print Series:

PERFECT MURDER
MADELEINE

BERNARD TAYLOR

MADELEINE

Complete and Unabridged

ULVERSCROFT
Leicester

First published in Great Britain in 1987 by
Severn House Publishers Ltd.,
London

First Large Print Edition
published September 1989
by arrangement with
Severn House Publishers Ltd.,
London

British Library CIP Data

Taylor, Bernard, *1934–*
    Madeleine.—Large print ed.—
    Ulverscroft large print series: mystery
    I. Title
    823′.914[F]

    ISBN 0-7089-2064-0

Published by
F. A. Thorpe (Publishing) Ltd.
Anstey, Leicestershire
Set by Rowland Phototypesetting Ltd.
Bury St. Edmunds, Suffolk
Printed and bound in Great Britain by
T. J. Press (Padstow) Ltd., Padstow, Cornwall

This is for Sue

This is for Sue

1

"**D**ADDY, you're driving on the wrong side of the road."

Robbie, like his two younger sisters, spoke with an American accent. Matt caught his eye in the driving mirror above his head. "No, Robbie, that's the way they do it in England."

"It's scary."

"You'll get used to it."

Monday, June the 20th, the day of the Severns' homecoming. The sun gleamed on the bonnet of the hired Cortina estate car as Matt eased its nose out into the traffic and headed for the M3 motorway. Above, the sky was almost totally free of cloud, only the faintest wisps drifting slowly, lazily in the blue. The trees and hedges that lined the road were rich in their greenery; a green that only England seemed to have.

Matt sighed, settling into the seat. So far the return had gone well. The flight had been smooth and comfortable, the children had been well-behaved—considering the time it had taken—and the Avis hire-car booked from Los Angeles had been ready and waiting when they'd emerged unscathed from the Heathrow customs. Also, they would be going home later in the week; to their *own* home, in Ashford Barrow, and, beyond that, the new TV series was waiting. They were, it seemed, all set. Then why, he asked himself, was there, beneath the surface of his calm, that vague little feeling of disquiet?

"Where are we going now?" Susie's small, strident voice came from the seat immediately behind. Tess, next to him, turned slightly and said over her shoulder, "I told you. We're going to visit your grandmother."

Glancing in the driving mirror Matt watched briefly as Susie nodded, her chestnut-coloured hair bouncing beside her cheeks. She'd reached five years of age that past spring.

Robbie turned to her and said, "Can you remember Grandma?"

"Yes, of course I can."

"So can I," Laura chimed in. She

couldn't, though, Matt was sure. She'd had her third birthday only the week before and had been little more than a year old the last time Ellen, Tess's mother, had visited them in America. Laura, like Susie, had been born in California. Only Robbie, just over three months short of his eighth birthday, had ever experienced anything of England. But he, though born there, had been taken abroad whilst still a baby, so his firsthand knowledge of Britain was no greater than that of his sisters.

Susie's question as to where they were going enabled Matt to put his finger on the cause of that little nagging unrest inside him. It was because now, today, before going on to their own home, they were going to visit Tess's mother—and the last time he and Tess had been together in her house Madeleine had been there as well. That meeting with Madeleine: it wasn't something that he or Tess would re-member with any kind of pleasure.

"I'm tired." This was Susie, for whom the adventure of travel had gone. "I want to go home."

"We're going home," Matt told her, "when we leave your grandmother's."

"I mean our *real* home—in Laurel Canyon."

"We've got a different home now," Robbie said. "We're not going back to California anymore."

Laura spoke up defiantly at this. "Yes, we are, aren't we, Daddy? We are, aren't we?"

"No, Robbie's right. Our home is in England now."

"Is it a long way," Susie asked, "from Laurel Canyon?"

Matt glanced at her face in the mirror, her wide blue eyes with the concern written in them. Then Laura's face came more into view as she leaned forward. Her hair was a little fairer than Susie's, but of the same texture. Straight and heavy, it hung untidily now about her cheeks. The blue ribbon Tess had tied there had gone.

"Is it, Daddy?" she asked. "Is it?"

"Is what what?"

"Is England a long way from Laurel Canyon?"

"Yes. A very, very long way."

"Well, then," Susie said, "how are we going to get to Disneyland?"

4

Robbie answered her. "We won't. They don't have Disneyland in England."

"Is that true, Daddy? Don't they have Disneyland in England?"

"No, I'm afraid not."

A little silence, then Laura's voice: "Is this England? Are we at England now?"

"Yes, we are."

"I don't like it."

Matt suppressed a smile. "You will. Give it time."

"No. I just like Laurel Canyon."

After some further murmurings amongst themselves, the children fell quiet. Matt's mirror told him that Robbie was sitting gazing out at the passing scenery while Susie and Laura, eyes closed, nestled close together. Robbie, looking up, caught Matt's gaze in the mirror and grinned at him before looking away again. In Robbie Matt saw himself as a child, the same dark hair inclined to curl in the same way; freckles across the small, blunt nose; bright, dark eyes and wide, gap-toothed smile. As a child's face it was almost a cliché.

Shifting his focus, he glanced across at Tess and, keeping his voice low so as not to disturb the girls, said: "What are you thinking about?"

"Oh," she shrugged and smiled. "Nothing in particular. Just about being back."

"Are you *glad* to be back?"

"Oh, yes."

Oh, yes, she had said. But had there been the slightest hesitation before she had answered?—as if she could have qualified her positive reply? He let it ride. He knew that as far as the respective countries went Tess felt as he did. They'd loved their home in California, yet at the same time, in spite of his success there, they'd never really settled. Not truly. And if seven years hadn't been enough, well . . . But then, they'd known at the start that the arrangement wasn't ever meant to be a permanent thing; they'd never regarded it as such. They'd simply gone there because of the opportunity presented, an offer he couldn't really refuse: a good part in a good film, and one that had promised to bring him some of the recognition he'd been seeking. And after that film there had come other film and TV offers, and so he, Tess and their growing family had stayed.

Now, breaking into his thoughts, Tess was saying quietly, "I doubt that *she'll* be there, will she?" and he realised with a little sinking of his spirits that she meant Madeleine.

"No," he answered. "Isn't she supposed to be going off some place? That's what your mother said, wasn't it?" He realised that there had been that little preoccupied shadow behind Tess's eyes for some time now. He had seen it there even on the flight over. Madeleine was in the back of her mind just as in his own.

"Who won't be there?" came Robbie's voice, and Matt thought how remarkable it was the way children were so attuned to the slightest wave of disturbance that threatened to ruffle their security.

"No one you need be concerned with," he told him, then glanced at the boy's reflection as he weighed the words, gave up, and turned to look from the window again. After a few moments Matt said softly to Tess, "Anyway, for God's sake, it's been seven years now."

"Seven years. That's a long time."

"Yes. Seven years without a word from her."

"What did you want from her—regular chatty letters?"

"Well, no, but—well, just the odd word from her would have shown that . . ." Her voice tailed off. "Oh, I don't know. I just thought perhaps there might have been something over the years, just to show that . . . that the past is past . . ."

"Now wait a minute," Matt said, "you talk as if you've been waiting for her to forgive us. No. If there's any forgiving to do it should be the other way around. We've done nothing to her, no matter how she might view it all."

"You're right, of course. And that's the trouble—the way she views it all." Tess frowned. "But a person can't hold a grudge for *that* long, can they?"

"No, of course not."

"No." She shook her head. "But there's been nothing from her. Seven years and no word at all from her. Not a Christmas card, a birthday card. Nothing."

"All right, so she was upset at the time, but—"

"Upset!" Tess's voice was laden with irony. "Upset."

"Yes, to say the least, I guess." Matt

shook his head. "Ah, forget it, Tess." He reached over and pressed her knee. "Come on—it's finished."

"Yes." She nodded. "I suppose I'm just getting neurotic. You're right—it *is* finished. It is."

The car wound on through the Hampshire countryside. They'd be there soon, Matt said after a while, and the girls became alert again.

"Is Grandma's house like our house in Laurel Canyon?" Susie asked.

Robbie answered, "The house in Laurel Canyon isn't our house anymore."

Tess said, "I'm looking forward to getting home. *Really* getting home, I mean —to our own home."

They'd let the house in Ashford Barrow through agents while they'd been away, and a couple of months ago when it had become empty again Matt had flown back from California and, in preparation for the family's arrival, had spent the best part of a week arranging for it to be cleaned up and painted, and all the furniture taken out of store and put back where it belonged. He had returned to Los Angeles for the remaining time leaving their neighbour, Dave Kinsell, looking after the place and keeping an eye on the work in progress. Since then Dave had reported that the work was finished and the house ready for the family's return, and now Matt, like Tess, looked forward to the time when they'd be back there. And they soon would be. Everything was working out perfectly. The only faintly dark spot on the horizon was Madeleine, and, Matt told himself now, she was only there as a result of his paranoia.

He had met Madeleine before he'd met Tess. That was nine years ago now. He'd been appearing in a television commercial for some tour company's package holidays in Spain. Madeleine had been another of the performers. She'd been a model then, and had been chosen simply to look decorative, unlike the actors, Matt among them, who had roles to play. An assortment of characters was needed: a mother and father in their late thirties, a small child, an elderly couple, a teenage couple, and a pair of honeymooners. It was a typical bread and butter job, and designed simply to show that the holidays on offer were ideal whatever the age group. Matt, at twenty-seven, was cast in the part of the young husband on honeymoon, while Madeleine, at not quite twenty-four, was to play the bride.

The filming had all worked out very well. One week in a Majorcan hotel and the whole thing had gone according to schedule. Madeleine had done the little that was required of her: looking stunning sitting beside the pool, dining with Matt on the hotel's terrace backed by a flaming sunset (which had actually been a sunrise), and walking hand in hand with him on a moonlit beach.

They'd become fairly friendly during the week on the island and on the last evening, with the filming all behind them, they joined the rest of the production company for dinner and afterwards for a drink at the hotel bar. Then they had gone off alone for a walk along the beach, returning to the hotel at about one o'clock. There, after another couple of drinks at the bar Madeleine had discreetly gone with Matt to his room. And so they'd spent the night together.

There had been nothing memorable about that night. There was no great passion, other than the passion of the moment, of the night, of two people who find one another attractive and spend a few hours satisfying the desires born of the meeting and the time. It was no more meaningful for Madeleine any more than it was for Matt himself, he was sure; there were no profound silences, no vows of undying love, no vows of love at all, or even of friendship.

When morning came Matt said perhaps they could meet again some time, maybe get together for a drink or dinner some day in London, and she had said yes, perhaps they could, but her heart had not been in the acceptance any more than his had been in the invitation, and that was the end of it. There was no exchange of phone numbers; nothing. In no time they were each drawn back into the business of getting on with what had to be done, of packing up, leaving the hotel and getting to the airport.

Matt remembered that on the plane she had sat with some members of the production crew while he, along with some of the other actors, had sat slightly apart. Then on landing at Luton airport they had said goodbye and parted, two people going their separate ways, two people who had found a brief, comforting diversion in one another's company for a time and which time was now over. End of story. That, Matt had assumed, was that.

It hadn't quite worked out that way, though.

A couple of months later while in Soho on business he made his way to a small Italian restaurant he sometimes visited when he was in the area. Finding on his arrival that the place was full and that there would be a little delay before any space would be free, he moved over to the minute bar to have a drink until one of the tables became available. And it was then, just after he'd been served with a vodka and tonic that, glancing over the other diners there, he saw the familiar face.

She was sitting alone at a table in the corner, just beneath the shaded window. He had hardly thought of her since their casual parting at the airport. Still, although he had no particular reason to want to renew their brief acquaintance it had been pleasant enough, so there was no reason why they shouldn't meet again on friendly terms. Besides, at any moment she was bound to see him, if she hadn't done so already.

Holding his drink he stepped between the tables, seeing her glance up at his approach. When he smiled at her he expected her to smile in return. She didn't, though, and he could see no hint of recognition in her eyes. When he came to a stop at her table her expression was one of slight puzzlement, as if she was trying to remember where they'd met before. He said, still wearing his smile, which was beginning to feel a little strained, "Hello, again. How are you?"

And then she smiled, a rather warmer smile than he remembered. "I think you've made a mistake," she said. "I *think* so—or my memory's not as good as I thought."

As she spoke it seemed there was something about her that wasn't quite the same. It was nothing he could put a name to, but he felt she had changed in some subtle way.

"You've forgotten," he said, "and so soon. Doesn't your memory go back as far as the summer?"

She nodded. "Yes, you *are* making a mistake. We haven't met before."

"But—"

"I think you're mistaking me for my sister."

"Your sister . . ."

"Madeleine. She's my twin."

Her twin. "Well, that explains it," Matt said. "I supose this happens to you all the time."

She smiled. "Sometimes. And to Madeleine, too, I expect."

"Yes, I expect so." He felt foolish standing there and after another moment said, "Well, I'm sorry to have troubled you," and turned to head back to the bar.

She said quickly, "Haven't you got a table?"

He stopped and turned back to her. "No, not yet."

She indicated the seat opposite. "Well, it's all right with me if it's all right with you . . ."

He sat down facing her and they introduced themselves. Her name was Teresa, she said, though she was usually called Tess. She wore a grey wool dress with a red silk scarf at her throat. Her blonde hair was about the same length as Madeleine's, falling to just above her collar, but styled more simply, looking more casual, its loose waves framing her face more softly. The subtle differences in her features, though, he couldn't see at that time—he was only aware that the differences were there. It was rather uncanny; there was Madeleine's oval face, neat little nose, wide blue eyes and wide smile, and yet the sum total was not quite the same.

As they ate Matt told her about his work as an actor and she told him of her own job doing promotional work for a London publisher. She was emotionally unattached, he learned, and lived alone in a small flat in Wandsworth. Her father was dead, and her mother lived in Hampshire. She didn't see much of Madeleine, even though they both lived in London. When he asked why he had found her eating alone she shrugged and said, "I was hungry", which he thought was a suitable answer to a pretty stupid question.

As the meal progressed it became clearer to him that the most obvious difference between the two sisters was in their personalities. Tess had a particular sense of humour that he had not noticed in Madeleine, and altogether a freer, warmer aura about her. In his memory, as he sat there, Madeleine came to him as being somewhat fey and ethereal, while in contrast Tess seemed more pragmatic and down-to-earth and to possess a contagious sense of fun. It didn't take him long to realise that, apart from the reflection-like qualities of their appearances, they were totally unalike.

And he realised something else by the time lunch was over. He wanted to see Tess again. Very much.

When he asked her if they could meet again, though, she hesitated. "I don't poach, you know," she said.

"Poach?"

"I mean if you're seeing Madeleine, then that's it."

He wasn't seeing Madeleine, he assured her. He'd already told her how Madeleine and he had met and briefly worked together, and that, he went on to say—of course leaving out any mention of that last night in Majorca—was all it had amounted to. And in truth that was so; it hadn't

17

meant anything more to either one of them.

Now Tess pondered the situation for a moment and then smiled. "All right," she said.

Ellen Rayfield, Tess's mother, lived on the outskirts of West Priors, a small village of just over two thousand inhabitants set in the heart of the countryside between Andover and Basingstoke. Her home was a large, sprawling Regency house which had been in the Rayfield family for three generations. The house was set in over nine acres, most of which had been left as rough meadow and areas of copse. Ellen had been brought to the house as a bride and now, with her husband long dead and her two daughters grown and living away, she remained there alone but for the companionship of the resident housekeeper. She, Jane Merrill, a little woman of fifty-eight, widowed and childless, had been with Ellen since before the birth of the twins, and was regarded almost as one of the family.

Matt drove the car through the village and past the church just as its clock's hands touched eleven-forty-five, and then turned into the winding drive that led up to the house. Soon afterwards he pulled up the car on the forecourt close to the porch and even as he and Tess and the children piled out there was Ellen opening the front door and beaming her welcome.

Tess threw herself into her mother's arms and they held fast to one another, tears of happiness on their cheeks while the children watched, a little apart, a little awed. Then Tess stepped back to where they stood in a tight little group, held out her arms behind them and said, "Aren't you going to say hello to your grandma?"

Shyly they did so. First Susie, then Robbie, and then last of all Laura who clung for some moments to Tess's skirt before hesitantly moving forward to be embraced by the gentle, smiling woman who held out her arms to her. After Matt and Ellen had embraced, Jane appeared and with her, too, there were embraces all round. Afterwards Tess and the children went into the house and Matt took up the two overnight cases and followed after them. While he carried the bags upstairs Tess and the children went into the large sitting-room where they sat beside the elegant French windows that looked out on to the smoothly cut lawn.

A few moments later when Matt rejoined them they were deep in conversation, catching up with the news of the past two years; the time that had elapsed since Ellen's last visit to them in California. Matt, having seen Ellen on his recent trip over, when he'd come back to see to the house, was content to leave the two women to it; content just to sit back and relax and share in the happiness of their reunion.

Ellen was a tall, upright, grey-haired woman whose slender build belied an energy that seemed boundless. Now in her sixties her days were spent on her beloved garden, on various committees in the surrounding areas, in her work as a local magistrate and in the St. John Ambulance Brigade. She was warm-hearted and generous, and Tess, watching her with the children, found herself regretting the years they had been deprived of each other's company. But now, she said to herself, they were back, and back to stay. And, living not too great a distance away from each other, her mother and the children could soon begin to make up some of the lost time.

"Which one is you, Mom?"

It was Robbie's voice, and Tess turned and saw that he was looking at a silver-framed photograph of herself and Madeleine, taken when they were eleven. He had only seen his aunt when he was very small and much too young to remember the meeting, and in the intervening years she hadn't figured in his life at all. Now, standing before the photograph he just stared. "Are they *both* you?" he asked.

"No." Tess smiled. "Just one. I'm the one on the right."

"Then who's the other?" asked Susie.

"My sister," Tess answered.

Robbie nodded, saying, "Oh, yes!—your twin sister. Aunt Madeleine." He paused, then added, "Is she dead?"

"Good heavens, no!" Tess smiled and frowned at the same time. "Why on earth should you ask that?"

"Well, you never talk about her . . ."

Jane came in then to say that she was working on lunch, and would the children care for a soft drink in the meantime. She didn't need to ask the question twice and at once the children swarmed towards her.

When they had gone from the room Tess said to Ellen, "Do you see much of Maddie?"

Ellen nodded. "Oh, yes. Every two or three weeks or so she drives down from London. Sometimes she'll stay overnight but usually it's just to have lunch with me or to spend the afternoon."

"Is she still doing the same job—her secretarial work for the oil company?"

"Oh, yes."

"She doesn't miss her modelling?"

"It's been so long since she gave all that up."

Matt got up from his chair, moved to the window and stood looking out. "Does she know we're coming back to England today?" he said.

"Oh, yes, of course," Ellen replied. "I told her."

"And does she know we're coming here?" Tess asked.

"Yes. She was down a week ago. I told her then that you'd be coming here before going home. But she's gone off to Yorkshire. I told you—her boss is taking part in some convention or something, so, of course, she's got to be there as well."

Matt, leaving Tess and Ellen to talk undisturbed, said some few words about looking at the garden and went from the room. He found the children in the kitchen where they had just washed their hands and where Jane was giving them glasses of Coca-Cola. He poured a vodka and tonic for himself and then led the way out into the sun. There he sat on a patio chair while the children drank their drinks and then rushed off to explore. He called after them not to go too far and then put back his head and closed his eyes. It was so peaceful. All he could hear were the desultory murmurings of the children set against the constant background of the sweet sound of the birdsong. He thought back to the guarded talk of Madeleine in the house; guarded as far as he and Tess went, anyway. They had always played down their estrangement with Madeleine in front of Ellen, so she had been kept pretty well in the dark. Both he and Tess were agreed that it was necessary for Ellen to remain ignorant of the true situation. That way she could keep the affection of both her daughters and not feel she had to split her focus. And anyway, she would never have understood Madeleine's behaviour, he knew. Come to that, he now said to himself, he never understood Madeleine either. She was quite beyond him.

Not that he had always thought so. During the first weeks with Tess he had imagined that the earlier relationship with Madeleine might lead to some little embarrassment where the two sisters were concerned, but he hadn't ever foreseen it as anything of any importance—anything more than a little temporary awkwardness; anything that a little commonsense wouldn't quickly dispel. He had been wrong, though.

Later, looking back, he realised that all the time during those early weeks Tess had been apprehensive about Madeleine; an apprehension apparent not so much in what she had said, but more in what she had done. He remembered how she'd put off introducing him to her mother, knowing, of course, that Madeleine would then learn about them; and how, when he had finally come to the house to meet Ellen, Tess had first made sure that Madeleine wouldn't be present.

He had met Tess in the October and his first meeting with Ellen had taken place about two months later. He and Tess were so much in love with one another by that time, and he knew beyond doubt that he could be happy with her; that he would be. He had known his share of women over the years, but he had never known anyone like Tess. She had brought into his life so much that he wasn't aware even existed. For one thing she'd brought a sense of purpose, and with it had come the realisation that, alone, he'd been missing out on so much. All told, though, it was simply her—Tess. She had come into his life and that was enough. Her very presence there created needs in him which only she could fill. Once she was there in his life he wanted her to stay.

During the first night that Tess and he had spent together (on their third meeting) he had briefly found himself looking back to the night he'd spent with Madeleine in Majorca. It was strange, though, despite the similarity in their appearances, that was where any likeness began and ended. Perhaps the essential difference was in Tess's warmth and her eagerness to make him happy while at the same time she had so positively sought pleasure for herself. He couldn't be sure; all he knew was that just before they finally went to sleep in one another's arms in the small hours of the morning he felt so warmly and surely the sense of his well-being; it was as real to him as the scent of her, the feel of her smooth, silky skin under his palm and the softness of her hair against his cheek. Wonderfully tired, satiated and at peace, he had fallen asleep quite quickly . . .

It wasn't until after they had begun to discuss marriage plans that he told Tess how he had once slept with Madeleine. He'd put it off, he supposed, for fear of upsetting the applecart. But it had to be said, he knew; if not it would surely weigh on his mind, and he wanted not the slightest shadow between them. Selfish, perhaps, to risk giving her pain in order to gain his own peace of mind, but there was more to it than that; there was always the chance that she would learn of it from Madeleine at some time in the future, therefore it was better that she knew of it first from him.

When it came to the telling, though, he hadn't been content just to tell her the simple facts; he'd had to explain to her that it had meant nothing, that it had been meaningless—for Madeleine as much as for himself—but Tess had interrupted, stopping him, placing her forefinger on his lips and telling him that it was part of the past and to let it remain where it belonged. He had never loved her more than in that moment.

Later that evening he had found her unusually quiet and looking a little troubled. He knew somehow that she was thinking about what he had told her.

"Does it make a difference after all?" he asked, and dreaded what her answer might be.

She looked across the table at him, a sad little smile lifting the corners of her mouth. "Oh, no. Not to me. Not to me at all." She paused. "But perhaps it will—to Madeleine."

They married in February, four months after they had met. Madeleine was still away, living and working in France, where

27

she had been for some time. Tess phoned her there and told her once the wedding was planned. It was the first she had spoken to her of her association with Matt. Madeleine, making some excuse, didn't come to the wedding.

After lunch Matt saw the children back into the garden and then returned to the sitting-room where Ellen was pouring coffee. When she handed out the cups Tess and Matt gave her the little presents they had brought and watched as she opened the packages, beautifully gift-wrapped as only the Americans knew how. Ellen was just admiring the Pierre Cardin silk scarf that Tess had chosen when Robbie came running in, his voice high-pitched with excitement.

"I thought for a minute it was you, Mom," he said. "I was certain it was you."

"What are you talking about?" Tess asked him.

"Aunt Madeleine. She's *exactly* like you."

Tess started to agree with him; yes, Madeleine did look just like herself, and

28

then stopped and stared at him, the realisation dawning.

Robbie turned and gestured towards the front of the house. "She's here," he said. "Aunt Madeleine—she's just arrived."

2

SILENCE fell suddenly into the room and for a moment it was almost as if the people there had stopped breathing. The only sound appeared to be coming from the old grandfather clock, its usually unnoticed tick now seeming to boom out into the stillness, while Robbie looked at each of the adults, as if wondering whether he had said something wrong. And then Tess gave a short, hollow little laugh and the spell was broken.

"Madeleine," she said, "she's *here!*" And although she smiled broadly there was no hiding the flash of panic in her eyes, and the sound of it in her too loud, too happy sounding voice. She half rose from her chair with her words and as she did so there came the sound of footsteps in the hall and then Madeleine was there.

Like Tess, Ellen and Matt stood up. Tess could feel the smile on her face fixed like cardboard. She watched Madeleine as she paused for a second in the doorway, swept the company with her glance and then came on into the room. She was wearing a white blouse, light denim skirt and sandals, and carried a bag slung from a strap over her right shoulder. She looked very beautiful.

"Hello, Mummy," she said as she crossed the room. She put her arms around Ellen, embraced her and kissed her on the cheek. Then, smiling, she released her and turned to face Tess and Matt. "My God," she said, "but it's been so long."

And then she was moving to Matt, stretching up to kiss his cheek, while Tess, watching, found her brain conjuring up the scenes from their last meeting, in that same room all those years ago, recalling the things that Madeleine had said. Tess had hated her for that; for the unhappiness she had brought.

And now here Madeleine was again, putting her arms around her and kissing her. And then, looking directly into her eyes, her smile trembling slightly, she was saying softly, "Welcome home, Tess. Welcome back."

And all at once Tess felt that her own

smile was no longer strained. Yes, she said to herself, everything was going to be all right. She had worried unnecessarily and it was all going to be okay. She had so dreaded this first meeting after such a long separation, fearful that Madeleine would provoke some scene or cause some upheaval to spoil their homecoming. But it was all right. Clearly, Madeleine was holding out the olive branch, and she, Tess, eagerly took it and held on. Forget what's gone before, she said to herself. *She* wants to and so can we. The past is past; let it remain so.

"Thank you, Maddie," Tess said, "it's good to be back."

With the ice broken everyone seemed to relax. Madeleine asked if there was coffee going, and a minute later was sitting down with a cup in her hand, saying that her boss hadn't been able to attend the convention after all and that consequently she'd been set free for the rest of the day. "And as I so wanted to see all of you," she said, "well—here I am."

Robbie, during all this, was still there, leaning against the arm of Tess's chair while he watched his aunt with an expression of wonderment on his face. This woman, his Aunt Madeleine, was so like his mother that he seemed unable to take it in. And then Susie and Laura came into the room and joined him in staring at the newcomer.

Madeleine, seeing their expressions, chuckled and shook her head in sympathy. "Poor children," she said, "they must be quite bewildered, poor things."

She reached out, took Robbie's hand and drew him closer. "So you're Robert," she said, "the young man of the family."

He nodded and whispered shyly, "Yes." Then, smiling at her he added in a rush of enthusiasm, "Mommy and Daddy are going to buy us a puppy as soon as we're halfway settled. Will you come and see him?"

"Oh, I'd love to," Madeleine said. "You just tell me when and I'll be there." She turned to the wondering faces of Susie and Laura, and with a little laugh said, "But why are you all looking so surprised to see me?" Turning to Tess she added, "You'd think from the looks on their faces they didn't even know I existed."

"Oh . . ." Tess waved the idea aside.

"You know children. Besides, you must admit it's got to be a bit of a shock for them—seeing us side by side for the first time."

Madeleine nodded, then beckoned to Susie and Laura. They went to her, Laura shyly, but Susie more readily.

"You're such pretty little girls," Madeleine said, "and I hope that now we've finally met I shall see something of you. You must get your mummy and daddy to bring you to see me in London. You'd like that, wouldn't you?"

Shyly they nodded. Then Madeleine said, "And soon, I suppose, you'll be off home to Ashford Barrow."

More nods.

"Are you looking forward to that—to going there?"

"Yes," Susie answered, giving the lie to all that she'd previously said, and then Tess interrupted to say that it was nearly quarter-to-three and she thought the children ought to have a little nap—even if just for an hour—and catch up on some of the sleep they'd missed.

When there was a groan of protest at this she added, "Well, you can go out and

34

play for another twenty minutes or so, but then you *must* come in and get just a little rest."

They needed no further telling and in a few seconds all three of them had gone out into the sun again. When the sounds of their voices had faded away Madeleine turned to Matt.

"I missed seeing you when you were back here a couple of months ago," she said. "I got home here and Mother told me you'd been to see her."

He spread his hands. "Oh, it was a very quick trip. I was only in England for a few days." He was conscious of having to justify his actions.

Then Ellen, as if he was in need of support, said, "He only came to get the house in order for when Tess and the children got back." She turned to Matt. "That reminds me, the house agent sent me another set of keys to the house after you'd gone back. They're on the hall table. Don't forget them when you go tomorrow."

"You're going back tomorrow, are you?" Madeleine asked.

"Yes."

"You haven't seen the house since it's all been done up?"

"No." He began then to tell her something about the work he'd commissioned in preparation for the family's return: the improvements, the painting and decorating in the colour-scheme Tess and he had chosen, the new pieces of furniture and the items he'd bought to supplement their own things that he had taken out of store. He told her how the Kinsells had been looking after the house while it was empty and keeping a watchful eye on the various jobs that had had to be done. And it was all so much idle chat, he felt. Madeleine couldn't be interested in hearing about it any more than he was in talking about it. And he didn't really know why he was doing it, except that perhaps it was a way of getting through the time, of covering the difficulties of the meeting.

He was quite relieved when Susie and Laura came back. Laura went over to Tess who took her up on her knee while Matt asked Susie where Robbie had got to, and Susie said she didn't know, that he had gone off on his own. She'd hardly finished speaking when Robbie came into the room, all excitement, and eager to show them something that he had discovered outside.

Matt got up, took Susie's outstretched hand and with a murmured "excuse us" followed Robbie out into the back garden.

It was so good to be freed for a while from the atmosphere indoors. He fervently hoped that Madeleine didn't plan on staying very long. Their own stay wasn't going to be any fun if she did. While he was relieved that she'd been so friendly and seemed anxious to avoid any unpleasantness, at the same time the desired sense of well-being couldn't be summoned up at will.

Following Robbie, Matt and Susie turned to the right and took a path that led up behind the garage. Matt could guess where they were heading. There, not too far from the house, and screened by shrubbery, stood a tiny thatched cottage. Very old, it was the simplest construction, little more than a one-up, one-down.

"Does anybody live in it?" Susie asked in a hushed voice as they approached.

Matt shook his head. "No, no one."

"What's it for?"

"It's a house. It stood here on the land long before Grandma's house was built."

"Did you know it was here?" Robbie asked.

"Oh, yes, I remember it from years ago. It looked a little smarter then. Now it could do with a lick of paint."

On tip-toe, Robbie peered in at a window. "There's a lot of stuff inside," he said.

Matt moved to join him. "Yes, but nothing much of any value, as far as I can remember. Just a load of junk and stuff, I think."

"I can see furniture, and some boxes . . ."

"Is it used for anything now?" Susie asked, and Matt shook his head. "I don't think it's been used for ages. I believe your mother and your Aunt Madeleine used to play in it when they were children."

His words sparked off more interest in Susie and she said excitedly, "Oh, can we go inside?"

Matt shrugged. "Well, I don't suppose it would do any harm to look." He moved up the two steps to the front door. "That's if it's not locked, of course."

"It is," Robbie said.

Matt tried the door. "I'm afraid you're right. Ah, well, never mind . . ."

"Can't you unlock it, Daddy?" Susie asked, who thought adults were capable of solving any problem. "You can, can't you?"

Matt made another attempt to turn the ungiving handle. "No, I'm afraid not. But maybe tomorrow we'll get your grandma to see if she can find the key."

"You don't need to wait till tomorrow," said a voice behind them and, turning, they saw Madeleine coming towards them, her strap bag over her shoulder. As she came to a halt she said to Matt, "I decided it was time I got going again, so I came to find you to say goodbye."

Matt said, "I was just saying that you and Tess used to play here when you were children."

"Oh, yes." Madeleine smiled and nodded. Coming closer she stopped by a little stone frog that sat about a yard away from the door. She lifted the figure and there Matt saw the door key. Madeleine took it up and held it out to Robbie.

"There you are. Now see if you can open it."

Robbie inserted the key in the lock, turned it and then turned the door handle. Then he looked across at Matt and grinned as the door swung open.

Madeleine nodded encouragingly at him. "Go on in," she said.

Matt followed Madeleine and the children inside. He had forgotten what it was like, but now, seeing it again, he knew instant recognition. It was all just as he'd remembered it. There was the old fireplace, looking just the way it had so many years ago, and still with the little stack of logs beside it. There, too, was the flight of open stairs leading to the room above. The movable contents of the place, too, were just as he recalled, and he stood in the dim, dusty interior and looked around him at the old pieces of furniture, the boxes of discarded toys, the warped, broken-stringed tennis racquets, the boxes of old books and home movies and the dusty, rejected framed pictures.

"It's a mess, isn't it?" Madeleine said, though the children thought otherwise.

"I think it's *great!*" Robbie said enthusiastically.

Susie quickly chimed in, "Oh, Daddy, can we play here? Can we?"

"I'm sorry," he answered, "you'd get too dirty—and besides, it's time for your nap."

She met his words with a howl of protest. "Oh, Daddy, *please.* I won't get dirty, really I won't."

"No." Matt shook his head. "Maybe tomorrow. Anyway, we'd have to ask your grandma. Then if it's all right we'll get your mother to put you in some old clothes. Then maybe we can come back and have a real look around."

While Matt was speaking Robbie had climbed over the back of an old sofa, completely disappearing from view. Now, just seconds later, he suddenly reappeared, standing up behind the sofa's back, holding in his arms a huge doll.

Although Susie laughed when she saw it the sound she made seemed born more out of fear than delight. But then a moment later she clapped her hands together and cried out, "Oh, it's a doll! It's a doll!"

"Of course it's a doll." Matt laughed. "What did you think it was?"

Before she could answer Robbie said scornfully, "She thought it was a body." He turned to her. "That's what you thought, isn't it?"

"No, it isn't!"

"Yes, it is."

"It's *not*." She shook her head vehemently. "Daddy, make him stop."

As she finished Robbie lurched forward over the back of the sofa and, holding the huge doll, thrust it out towards Susie. She screamed, stepped back and reached out for Matt who patted her shoulder. "Okay, knock it off now," he said to Robbie. "That's enough."

And then Madeleine's voice came as she gathered Susie in her arms. "Shame on you, Robbie, to scare your little sister so." Then to Susie she said softly, comfortingly, "There's really nothing to be scared of. It's just a big, silly old doll, that's all. It used to be mine when I was a little girl."

She reached out, took the doll from Robbie and brought it closer so that Susie could get a better view. "There, you see? There's nothing to be scared of, is there?"

She smiled as she looked at the doll. "I called her Bella, which means 'beautiful'. Though I think, now, that I could probably have chosen a more suitable name for her. She's not exactly beautiful, is she? In fact, I suppose she's really quite ugly." She paused. "Oh, but I did love her."

Matt, looking down at the doll, wondered how on earth anyone could love such a thing. It was probably the ugliest doll he had ever seen, and he was hardly surprised that Susie had reacted to it as she had. The doll was a great gangling thing, almost as tall as Susie herself. It was dressed in a sort of diaphanous nightdress, which was covered by some old dressing-gown that looked as if it might have belonged to either Madeleine or Tess in their childhood. Its head was painted like a store mannequin of years past, with red-painted cheeks and lips, and high, arched eyebrows. The eyes were disconcerting; they were not looking in quite the same direction and had a rather baleful stare. The face was framed by a wig of blonde hair. The doll was grotesque, Matt thought.

"Come on," he said to the children,

"we've got to get back to the house. Your mother will wonder where we are."

Madeleine handed the doll back to Robbie, and holding it in his arms he climbed out from behind the sofa and moved to the door.

"Where are you going with that?" Matt asked.

Robbie turned and said, smiling, "I want to show Mommy."

"What for?"

"I want to give her a surprise too."

"You mean give her a scare. You think that's a good idea?"

"Maybe just a *little* scare, then?"

Susie moved to the door. "I shall tell Mommy," she said, "then she won't be scared," and she skipped down the steps and ran off towards the house. Robbie turned and followed, hampered by the cumbersome doll.

As Matt watched the children vanish beyond the shrubbery Madeleine said, "Oh, dear, I hope I didn't start something."

Matt shook his head. "No, I don't think so."

Madeleine looked around the dusty

44

interior. "It really is a mess, isn't it? I haven't been in here for years and I'd forgotten what it was like."

Suddenly something caught her eye and she stooped and peered into the shadows. Matt watched her as she bent lower, reached in under an old dining chair and straightened with something in her hand. She gave a little wondering shake of her head. "I can't believe it," she said. "After all this time."

"What have you found?" he asked, and she opened her hand to show, on her palm, a ring with a double band and two semi-precious stones.

"I lost it years ago," she said. "And I never knew where." She turned it over in her fingers. "It's my Marie Antoinette ring." With a little twisting movement she pulled the ring apart, making two separate rings. She held them out to him.

As he took them he said, "Why do you call it your Marie Antoinette ring?"

"In my teens I read about Marie Antoinette and her love affair with Count Fersen. She had a ring like this, a ring that became two. And she kept one half and gave the other to him—or maybe it

45

was the other way around. I've forgotten. Anyway, it was engraved, *Everything leads me to thee*. I remember that. Later, when she was in trouble and needed his help she sent her half of the ring to him as a sign . . ." She sighed. "Oh, so beautiful and so sad. I used to imagine I'd meet someone like Count Fersen someday." She gave a little laugh. "The things you think of when you're young."

Matt looked at the rings. They were of gold, each with a little red garnet in a decorative setting. He pressed the two settings together so that they locked to hold the two parts as one and then handed the ring back to her.

Madeleine said, "Oh, I so wanted a ring like hers—Marie Antoinette's. In the end my father bought me this. I suppose it was the nearest thing he could find. It was much too big for my finger, but I wouldn't let him have it back to be altered. That's how I came to lose it, I suppose." Now she eased the ring onto the third finger of her right hand. "It fits me now," she said.

She looked then at her watch, said, "Ah, well," and moved to the door. Matt followed her outside, locked the door behind him and replaced the key under the stone frog. Then as he stepped to her side she turned away from the path they had taken from the house and started off to the right. This way also led to the house, but it was a longer route, going through the flower gardens and by the lawns. Side by side they made their way by the privet hedge towards the rockery, and as they came to it Madeleine moved slightly ahead, came to a halt and turned towards him. The way here was narrow. On either side the ornamental stones were covered with ferns, marigolds, forget-me-nots and nasturtiums. Behind her the huge weeping willow cut off Matt's view of part of the house. Unable to go on, he, too, had stopped.

Madeleine stood facing him as he smiled questioningly at her. She said: "I wanted to see you before I go . . ." Then she looked away, as if finding it difficult to continue. She turned, bent slightly, plucked a marigold from among the stones and held it to her nose. "Hardly any smell," she said, and Matt wondered where all this was leading. Then she went on quietly, avoiding his eyes, "I just wanted to say I'm sorry. About everything."

"Oh, please . . ." He waved away her apology. "Please, let's forget it."

"I wish I could," she said. "Oh, I was so wrong to act as I did. Causing that awful scene just before you left all those years ago. And then the phone calls . . ."

"It's over now, Madeleine," he said. "Forget it."

She shook her head. "All that bother I caused . . ."

Bother she called it. "Forget it," he said again, and added, lying, "we have." He went on, "It's a long time ago now. We can all be friends again." *No*, he said to himself, *never*. Friends, never.

"Sometimes," she said, "I look back on that time and wonder what I could have been thinking of." She shook her head as if in wonderment at her memories, then gave a deep sigh. Looking at her sad, so beautiful face, Matt felt some pity for her.

After a moment she went on, "It wasn't me. I mean it wasn't really me. Something got into me, I suppose. I was angry, hurt . . ."

Why? he thought. Why should she have

been angry and hurt? She'd had no reason to be. She had never been betrayed.

"You've got beautiful children, Matt," she said after a moment. "Robbie, Susie, and little Laura. Beautiful."

"Thank you." He smiled. "We are very proud of them. Naturally."

"Naturally." She nodded. "I'd love children like them," she added.

"Oh, you'll have them," he said awkwardly. "Some day."

"Some day?" She raised her eyebrows. "I shall be thirty-three in September. I'd better hurry up and find a husband before it's too late."

"Oh—it's not too late; you mustn't think such a thing."

"I didn't say it was," she said. An edge had crept into her voice. "I said, *before* it's too late."

"Yes."

A silence fell. Matt wanted to leave, but the right moment wasn't there.

"Tell me," she said, "what was your reaction when I appeared a little while ago? You weren't expecting me, were you?"

"Uh—no. No, I wasn't. We weren't."

"I'll bet you thought: Oh, Christ, no, not that bloody woman. Here she comes, ruining our homecoming. Ruining our visit to Tessa's mother. Is that what you thought?"

He grinned weakly. "Of course not . . ."

"No?"

"Well," he said, "we were surprised to see you. Ellen had told us that you were busy on your convention . . ."

"Oh, yes." She nodded. "You must have been so relieved to have heard that. What did you do—time your visit to make sure you wouldn't have to face me?"

"Come on," he said, "let's not get into all that."

"I'm not getting into anything." She turned from him and looked at the flower in her hand. After a little silence she said, "I wanted to see you before I go. To—apologise."

They were going back over old ground now. He was silent, wary of saying the wrong thing.

She went on, "Anyway, I shan't be staying. Now that I've seen you—and Tessa—I'll be on my way again."

"Are you going back to London?"

"Yes. To my little flat. You must come and see it when you're up in town. It's quite nice." She looked up at the sky. "This sun is beautiful, isn't it? But I suppose you're used to it like this in California, aren't you—a lot of sunshine."

"Yes, but it's not always as pleasant as this . . ."

"Remember that week we had together in Majorca?"

That week they'd had *together?* He said nothing.

She continued, "I often think of that. The weather was wonderful, wasn't it? And you remember how we'd walk out on the beach in the evening? That shoreline was so beautiful. I'd love to go back there sometime."

He didn't know what to say. She was making it sound as if they'd frequently gone off together. One walk along the beach was all they'd had. What was she doing, hinting at a past togetherness that had never existed? He watched as she looked down at the marigold in her hand, raised it, put her thumbnail under the flower's head and, with a neat little movement, flicked the blossom off and up so that it formed an arc through the air and fell among the stones of the rockery. She tossed the stem after it, looked at him and then stepped forward, hand held out. "Well . . . goodbye, Matt."

He took her hand. "Goodbye, Madeleine."

"I won't be coming back into the house, so please say goodbye to the children for me. I've already said my goodbyes to Mummy and Tess."

"Yes, I will."

"And bring the children to see me sometime."

"Yes."

And she still stood there. "Oh, dear," she said, giving an arch little giggle, "Tess will be wondering what we're up to, won't she? All this time alone in the garden together."

He gave a brief, humourless chuckle and took a step forward.

"Yes," she said, taking the hint, "I'd better get off and let you go, too." She still didn't move, though. Then into the silence she said, "Who'd ever have thought we would be so formal with each other." She laughed, rather too loudly. "We could at least give each other a little farewell kiss." She stepped towards him, put her hands lightly on his shoulders and quickly he bent his head and kissed her lightly on the cheek.

And then suddenly her arms were around his neck and her lips were pressed against his. When she broke away from him he tried to make light of the situation and gave an awkward laugh. It was a mistake.

"What are you laughing at?" Her voice was cold. "Is something funny?"

"No. No, of course not."

"No. No, of course not," she mimicked him. Then she added scornfully, "I'm sorry I'm such an embarrassment to you. I am, aren't I?"

"Oh, please, Madeleine," he said wearily, "let it be."

She gazed at him with a slight frown, then said, "Your children . . ."

"What about them?"

"They looked at me in the house as if they'd never heard of me. As if they didn't know I existed."

"Oh, they knew all right. Of course they did."

She nodded. "Yes—*just*, I expect. Didn't you ever talk about me while you were over there?"

"Yes, of course." A lie. They had rarely talked about her, he and Tess. Madeleine had been one of those subjects they'd tacitly agreed to avoid; a subject best not talked about. And so, of course, the children had been hardly aware that they had an Aunt Madeleine, an aunt who was their mother's twin sister . . .

"Yes, of course," Madeleine mimicked him again. "You really expect me to believe that? And when Robbie came in, saying he wanted to show you something, you couldn't wait to get out, could you? You think I didn't notice. You must think I'm stupid. And now you can't wait for me to go, can you? Am I ruining your visit? *Am* I?"

He didn't answer.

She glared at him, her words measured. "You *prick*."

He stared at her for a second, then took a step to move around her, but she stepped in front of him, blocking his way. "You can't take it, huh?" she said. "You getting out?" She gave a smile that became a sneer. "Well, at least you've only got to go back to the house to get away from me. The last time you left the country."

"I don't think you and I have anything more to say to one another."

"No? You might not have anything to say to me, but I've got a few things to say to you."

"I don't think I particularly want to hear it, so if you'll just stand aside . . ."

"When I'm ready." She was looking at him as if he were a specimen of some digusting germ. "What's so special about *her?*" she said. "About her—Tessa. Is she different in some way? Is she different from me?"

His lips felt tight with anger. He nodded. "Yes, she is. I'm only just beginning to find out how different."

"No." She shook her head. "She's no different from me. Except perhaps in her smugness." She glared at him, and then all at once her tone changed and she said sorrowfully, "I was so—so fond of you. So fond."

"Oh, come on now."

"I was. And I was attracted to you from the start."

"No one would ever have known it."

"Don't you make fun of me." Her voice was ugly again. "Don't you spoil my memories of that time."

"Madeleine," he said clearly, "get it into your head—there are no memories to be spoiled. We worked together for a week and at the end of it we had a—a brief little fling together. That's all. There was nothing more."

"Nothing more to *you*, perhaps."

"Or to you, either. You know that. Don't make it into more than it was. It was pleasant at the time, but that's all. And when that time was over, the whole thing was over. For both of us. You didn't want to prolong it anymore than I did."

"Don't try and speak for me. I gave you a woman's most sacred possession."

He stared at her in amazement. "*You what?* Jesus Christ, don't give me that bullshit. A woman's most sacred possession! How do you spend your time —reading Victorian novels? What is all this melodramatic crap?" He laughed. "A woman's most sacred possession? You

56

didn't give me anything you weren't perfectly ready to give!" He glared at her scornfully. "Why don't you go back to London."

"I'll go when I'm ready and not before. This is my home, not yours. It's my mother's house, not yours."

He shrugged, looked at her for a moment, then turned, heading for another path that led to the house. She ran after him, overtook him and stood in front of him again.

"You dropped me," she said. "When you were finished with me, you just dropped me."

"Madeleine . . ." He tried to keep his voice low, calm. "You must understand, once and for all. Get it into your head. Get rid of that fantasy you've got going on in there and face the truth. I didn't drop you. I didn't have you to drop. For God's sake, we spent one night together. *One night*. I hardly think one night constitutes a love affair."

"You didn't give it any further chance."

"I didn't want to. And neither did you. You know that. There was no point in it for either of us."

"You didn't give it a chance. *Her*, though, you did. It was different when *she* came on the scene."

"Yes, it was. It was."

"Yes!" She said the word triumphantly. "Yes, it was different then. And you only met her through me. If you hadn't met me first you and she would never have met."

"Probably not. But that's the way it goes. Nothing happens in isolation. Everything we do is the result of something else, either of our own actions or someone else's." He realised even as he spoke, though, that she was taking nothing of it in. He might have been talking to a brick wall.

"You *married her*," she said, and it was as if she was accusing him of some unspeakable crime.

"Yes," he said. "I married Tess. And it's time you accepted the fact."

"But why did you? Why? Is she better in bed?" She paused. "Is that it?"

He turned his back on her, moved back along the path towards the rockery and walked on in the direction of the lawn. He had just reached its edge when he heard the sound of her running feet behind him,

58

and then she was overtaking him again, turning to him and throwing herself at him, arms reaching out, wrapping around him.

"I'm sorry, I'm sorry, Matt! Forgive me," she cried, and he saw tears streaming down her cheeks. "I didn't know what I was saying. Forgive me."

"What's the point?" He took her arms away. "I'm sick of your apologies, Madeleine. They're meaningless."

"But I mean it! I do mean it. You don't know what it was like, having you marry Tess when you'd started off knowing me. You can't imagine."

"Obviously not." He spoke coldly, unmoved by her tears. "But whatever you felt it's time you got over it. Tess and I have been married over eight years now."

"Yes, yes. You're right, and I'm sorry. I am."

"Yes? Well, if you're really sorry, sorry for all the hurt you've caused then—"

"I am, I am," she said, interrupting.

"If you are, then there is something you can do . . ."

"Tell me what it is. Just tell me."

"Just stay away from us. Stay the hell

59

out of our lives. Just keep away and don't bother us again. *Ever.*"

He stepped past her and moved on towards the house. From behind he heard her voice, her anger mixed with the sounds of her crying.

"You bastard. You prick. You bastard."

With the sounds of her words fading behind him he went into the conservatory. The first thing he saw there was the doll where it lay sprawled in a wicker chair. He glanced at it and went on into the house, moving through the hall. He wasn't ready to face Tess or Ellen right now. Reaching the library he went in and just stood there, aware of his heavy breathing and the pounding of his heart. After several minutes had gone by he heard footsteps descending the stairs and then the door opened and Tess stood there. She looked at him, stepped into the room and closed the door behind her.

Moving towards him she asked, "What are you doing here?"

He shrugged. "Nothing."

"I saw you come in. I saw you from the bedroom." She paused. "And I saw you exchanging a few words with Madeleine . . . What did she have to say?"

"Oh, nothing of importance. She just came to say goodbye." Changing the subject he said, "You put the children to bed?"

"Yes." She nodded. "I just took their shoes off and covered them up with a rug. They're so tired. Still, even this little rest will help them."

"Yes . . ." His thoughts were still preoccupied with Madeleine. She had said she was leaving, but she had not. He could see her VW Golf still on the forecourt.

"Robbie brought that doll back with him," Tess said after a second. "Awful ugly thing. I made him put it outside in the conservatory."

Matt nodded. "Yes, I saw it there as I came in."

"I think his idea was to give me a bit of a fright—so Susie told me, anyway. And I must admit, it did give me a bit of a start when he came in and pushed it under my nose." She gave a little shudder. "I just find it so repulsive. I always have. Ever since the day Maddie got it. I've always hated it. She used to torment me with it. It used to give me nightmares."

She reached out and took Matt's hand. "Anyway," she said, "it's no good standing here being negative." She turned and led the way from the library. "Come on, let's go and join Mum."

As they moved out into the hall Matt heard the sound of a car starting up at the front of the house and he stepped back into the library and glanced from the window. As Tess stood watching him he, in turn, watched as Madeleine turned her car on the forecourt and sped away along the drive. He turned back and moved towards Tess, breathing a sigh of relief. He could relax now that Madeleine was gone.

3

WITH the children asleep, and while Ellen was in the kitchen giving Jane a hand with the children's supper, Matt and Tess went out into the garden.

They walked in silence for a little while, then Tess asked, "Did something happen this afternoon?"

"What?"

"With you and Madeleine."

When he hesitated she added, "You might as well tell me, Matt. I know something happened while the two of you were outside. As I told you, I saw you from the window, when you were coming back to the house." She paused. "And I saw you before then. You walked into my view just beyond the willow tree and I saw Madeleine come up to you and stand in front of you. I could tell something was happening. And then, of course, when I came downstairs and found you in the library I could see at once by the look on your face . . ."

He told her then of what had passed between Madeleine and himself and as he spoke Tess remained quiet, her mouth set. When he had finished she felt the pricking of tears in her eyes. "I was afraid it was something—something like that."

They came to a stop and he drew her to him and held her close. "Don't think about it any more," he said. "She's gone now and that's that."

"Yes." Her reply was muffled against his shoulder. Then she drew back her head and looked up at him. "Thank God she's gone. Now that you've told me this—well, I couldn't have stayed if she'd been planning on staying as well."

She thought again of the things he had told her, of the bitter words Madeleine had said, and her mind immediately went back to the previous time she and Matt had met Madeleine. It had been in the second year of their marriage and just a few weeks before they had left for California. With their departure so close they had wanted to spend a little time with Ellen and so, taking Robbie, who was less than three months old, they had gone to spend Christmas with her.

Up until that time they had seen Madeleine only very infrequently, which few occasions had occurred at Ellen's house. Madeleine had always been polite and pleasant, but they had never felt comfortable with her; they had always felt that her friendly attitude had been applied purely because of Ellen. But at least she had made some effort, whatever her motive was, and they had gone along with the charade.

Then, driving to Ellen's that Christmas and knowing that Madeleine would also be there, they had hoped and believed that somehow it would all come right, that they could truly become friends. After all, wasn't it the time of goodwill, and wouldn't they shortly afterwards be leaving the country?

It hadn't worked out the way they had hoped, though. No matter how they tried, there had been no relaxing for them while they were there in Madeleine's company, and in the end they just looked forward to returning home. And then, just as they were on the point of leaving there had been some trivial incident that had released the flood of Madeleine's anger—anger that until that moment she had kept hidden behind her façade of distant friendliness.

Tess could still recall vividly how she and Matt had stood there, Robbie in Matt's arms, while Madeleine had launched into her tirade. Ellen had been upstairs at the time and as Madeleine had kept her voice low she had heard nothing of what was said. For all Madeleine's lack of volume, though, she had managed to get over her message very clearly. It had come pouring from her, all the poison of her bitterness. Her voice dripping with hate and resentment, she had railed at them in a harsh, piercing whisper, calling them every vile name she could think of, vowing to them that she would never forgive them for what they had done to her, and that if it was the last thing she ever did she would repay them for the hurt they had caused.

Throughout it all Tess had stood wide-eyed, horrified. She thought she had known Madeleine, but watching her and listening to her that December afternoon it was as if she were seeing her for the first time. A couple of minutes later when Ellen had come down with the little gift she had bought for Robbie she found them all standing pale-faced, tense and silent. Somehow Matt and Tess had managed to recover some of their composure and, after kissing Ellen and thanking her, had left the house. In the car on the way home Matt had sat looking grim-faced out into the darkness while Tess had wept.

And that had not been the end of it. From that time until their departure in January they had been subjected to a number of telephone calls from Madeleine, each one more abusive than the last. After the first one Tess had been afraid to answer the phone and in the end all she could think of was the time when they would be getting away from England altogether . . .

And now they were back, after all these years—and in spite of their absence and their hopes, it seemed as if nothing what-ever had changed.

How Madeleine must have been seething all the time they'd been away, Tess thought. "It's unbelievable," she said to Matt. "We've been gone so long and she still feels exactly the same way. You'd think it all began just weeks ago." She shook her head. "She seems to make up her own truths. She lives with her—her fantasies—and in the end comes to regard them as real."

Matt said wearily, "But for God's sake, she's got to face reality sometime. She can't go on like it."

"It's not only that, though," Tess said, "—her inability to accept the truth; it's something else. That awful resentment she has—she seems to foster it, to nurture it. And she doesn't change. She's always been like it, even when we were children. She was never happy with what she had; she always wanted what was somebody else's. And of course the somebody else involved was usually me. I don't know—it always seemed that the very fact of something being mine made it far more desirable to her—as if she was never able to see its worth until I saw it. Like you. She never wanted you till I had you." She sighed. "Ah, well, it'll all get sorted out, I suppose." She turned in the direction of the house. "Come on. We'd better get back and see to the children."

After Matt had awakened them the children got up and played for a time in the garden close to the house. Then Tess called them in to eat the supper of cottage pie and salad that Jane and Ellen had prepared. It was nearly six o'clock by the time they finished eating, and half an hour later while they sat in front of the TV Tess went upstairs to run the water for their baths. She was just coming back down the stairs when Matt came into the hall. He looked up at her and she saw the expression on his face. "What's up? What's the matter?"

He said nothing, but glanced back over his shoulder and then reached up to her. She took his hand, moved down the remaining steps and let him lead her into the library. There, keeping his voice low, he said, "She's back."

"What?"

"Madeleine. She's come back. Just a second ago while you were upstairs. She's here now—sitting in there with your mother and the children."

Tess shook her head in bewilderment. "But what for?"

He shrugged. "To stay—so it seems."

"Oh, God." Tess groaned. "Did she say how long for?"

"No. She just breezed in and said she'd decided to come back and spend some time with us."

"But what about her work?"

Matt waved a hand impatiently. "Who cares about her bloody work. She's come back, that's the important thing. And you know why she's here, don't you? She knows we'll be uncomfortable with her here, and that's what she wants. She's determined to try and spoil it for us—our being here with your mother."

"And she's done it. She *has* spoiled it. I can't stay here now. I want to leave."

He nodded. "That's the way I feel, but we can't start like that on our first day back—running away from her."

Tess wearily shook her head. "I can't cope with this. I want to leave. I'm sorry."

"Look," Matt said, "I know you're tired. I'm tired too. And the children. We're all tired. But your mother will be so hurt and upset if we leave just like that . . ." He put his hand on her shoulder. "Look, we'll go in the morning if you still want to, all right?"

Tess thought of Madeleine again, and then of the home that was waiting for them. "No, *now*," she said. "Let's go now. Let's go home to Ashford Barrow. I hate hurting Mum like this, but I can't help it. We'll come back and see her another time, soon."

"But what about the children—they're just about to go back to bed and—"

"They'll be all right," she said. "And it will be better for them to be out of this atmosphere." She looked at her watch. "Let's go home. It won't take us long to get there. Please. Okay?"

He nodded. "Okay."

She moved back into the hall and started towards the stairs. "I'll go and pull the plug out of the bath and repack the children's nightclothes." Halfway up the stairs she glanced back down at Matt. He looked up at her for a moment, then turned and moved away in the direction of the sitting-room.

As he went in Ellen looked at him, her

expression bewildered. She was well aware of the undercurrent, but hadn't a clue as to what was going on. Robbie, shoes off, was lying on the rug watching the television while Susie and Laura lounged on either side of Madeleine's chair as she sat making cat's cradles with a piece of string. Fascinated by her deft fingers, the two girls hardly looked round as Matt entered the room. Madeleine did, though. She glanced up and gave him a hesitant little smile.

He ignored her and said to Ellen, "Ellen —could I have a little word with you—in private?"

As Ellen got up, Madeleine said with a note of solicitousness in her voice, "Would you like me to leave you alone for a few minutes while you talk?"

Matt shook his head, moving back towards the door, Ellen behind him. "No, that's all right, Madeleine. It won't take a second."

In the library he told Ellen that they had decided to leave, and with tears springing to her eyes she said, "It's this silly business with Madeleine, isn't it? I should have thought after all this time it would all be behind you." Not knowing the scope of Madeleine's resentment, she seemed to feel that their differences could be resolved as easily as some children's quarrel.

"I'm sorry, Ellen," he said. "I'm sure in time it'll all get sorted out, but right now it's not so easy."

Tess came into the room then, and Ellen turned to her. "Oh, don't leave," she said. "I know Madeleine was jealous and upset at the start but—look, let me go and talk to her. It can't be that bad, that you've got to leave. You've only been here five minutes."

"I'm sorry, but we've got to go," Tess said.

"Why?" Ellen said. "Something's happened today, hasn't it? I obviously know only half the story . . ."

Looking into her distressed face, Matt felt they had no choice but to tell her the reason for their going, and after a moment's hesitation he gave her an indication of Madeleine's resentment and the ugly scene that had taken place in the garden earlier.

"And now that she's come back," he added, "we don't really feel we've got any choice but to leave. It would be impossible for us to stay after what was said this afternoon."

As Ellen stood there Tess put her arms around her. "Look, don't worry about it," she said. "It will all be sorted out soon, I'm sure. But just right now it's all rather difficult." She kissed her on the cheek. "We'll see you soon. Very soon."

"But will your house be ready for you?" Ellen asked.

Tess nodded. "Yes. Matt phoned our neighbours, the Kinsells, from the airport this morning, and they've taken care of it all."

"But the beds . . . And what about food?"

"Dot Kinsell said she was going round to make up the beds right then, just to make sure they'd be ready for us whenever we might need them. And as for food— well, I was hoping you could let us have what we need until I can get to the shops tomorrow."

"Of course." Ellen nodded dully. "Go and ask Jane for what you need."

When Tess had gone out Ellen said to Matt, "Why should Madeleine do this? I don't understand her. I never treated them any differently. She's never had cause for her silly jealousies and envies." She shook her head. "It upsets me so. I've waited and waited for you to come home, and now she spoils it for all of us. I just don't know what goes on in her mind."

Matt went to the sitting-room doorway and called the children to him. At his words Susie frowned and said, "Where are we going this time?"

"Home."

"Aren't we at home now?" Laura said.

"No, not yet. We soon will be, though."

"Oh, Daddy, no," Susie said. "I want to stay here."

"I'm sorry, Susie, but not this time."

She went on protesting, joined after a minute by Laura, and then by Robbie who wanted to continue watching the television programme. Matt shook his head, his impatience growing. "Come along," he said, more sharply. "We've got to leave." All the while he could feel Madeleine's eyes upon him. He avoided looking at her, keeping his gaze on the children. Robbie and Laura had started to get themselves together, but Susie was still hanging back.

"Come on, Susie," he said to her. "Hurry up."

"Oh, Daddy, pleeeeeease," she said. The whine in her voice was infuriating. "Please—let's stay longer."

"Susie," he said shortly. "I've already told you—"

"No, Daddy," she broke in. "Daddy, pleeeeease."

"*Now!*" He spoke harshly, barking out the word, and as the sound rang in the room Susie jumped as if he had struck her. Quite still, mouth open, she stared at him, her expression and her protests frozen. He was aware of all the eyes upon him. A long moment of silence followed; then, his voice a little calmer, he said, "Get your things together. We're leaving now."

Her lower lip trembling slightly, Susie came towards him while Madeleine, watching, unravelled the cat's cradle in her hands.

Madeleine said, "I've only just returned and you're leaving already. I wouldn't have come back if I'd known you planned to go. Isn't there any way I can persuade you to stay?"

"I'm afraid not." He turned to the children. "Say goodbye to your aunt."

Madeleine hugged them each in turn, saying what a mean old daddy they had to take them away so soon, kissed them and sat watching as Matt ushered them before him out of the room. "Matt—" Quickly she rose from her chair, the piece of string falling from her fingers onto the carpet.

"Yes, what is it?" He stopped in the doorway, becoming aware as he did so of the children standing in the hall, waiting. He said to them, "Excuse us for a moment," and closed the door on their surprised faces. Turning back to Madeleine, he said again, "What is it?"

"Look, I—" She stopped, gave a little shake of her head and then, stumbling on, continued, "I want you to—to listen to me for a moment . . ."

"I've heard all I want to hear from you." He turned to open the door again, but her voice came more urgently, stopping him. "Matthew, please. Just one minute—that's all I ask."

He gazed at her and she went on, her voice low. "Look, don't go home. Not tonight. Stay here."

"It's too late now. Our plans are made."

"I don't want things to be this way."

"Well, that's entirely up to you."

"No, it isn't. You won't even be friends with me."

"It's not possible, is it? You've made that quite obvious."

"It *is* possible. We can be friends. Just be—be nice to me."

"What does that mean?"

"Just that. Just be nice to me, and I'll go and leave you in peace here and—"

"We've tried that," he said. "Both of us —Tess and I. We've tried being nice. It hasn't got us anywhere. No, Madeleine, you don't have to leave. *We* will. There's no point in our staying, anyway. You've ruined it all for us; our coming home, our coming to see your mother. All we want to do now is get away."

"Is that it, then? You're going, just like that."

He nodded. "Just like that."

"Well." She shrugged. "I tried. I offered you my friendship and you rejected it. Okay, if that's the way you want it, then go and take the consequences."

He frowned. "What the hell are you on about?"

"I was quite ready to leave again," she said. "I was quite prepared to go away from here and—well, anything I've done wrong I'd try to put right, but now—"

He interrupted. "What are you talking about? I don't understand you."

"Forget it," she said. "You've decided the way you want to play so that's it; there's nothing else to discuss. My offer of friendship is withdrawn."

He said with heavy, mock concern, "That's too bad, Madeleine. That's really heartbreaking. But I guess we'll just have to be brave. We'll just have to get by somehow."

She glared at him. "Yes, you be brave. You be very brave."

"And what is *that* supposed to mean?"

But she waved a hand, dismissing him. "Go on now. Don't keep your children and your precious wife waiting." She sat back in her chair and picked up a magazine. He looked at her for a moment, then stepped towards the door.

Her voice came, stopping him once more. "I shall have you one day, Matt."

He turned to face her and she added, smiling, "One day, Matt. One day you'll come to me, for some reason or other. Maybe you'll want some help, some comfort. Something. But whatever it is you'll realise I'm the only one who can give it you. And when that happens you'll come to me. And maybe when that day comes I'll be there. And maybe I'll be ready to help you, if I still care. Rest assured, though—one day you'll need me."

"I really think you believe that," he said.

"I'm sure of it."

He nodded, then opened the door and went into the hall. As he did so Tess came from the kitchen with a large plastic bag full of groceries. Jane was walking behind her. She had no idea what was going on.

Five minutes later they had made their farewells and were driving away. Their last view was of Ellen as she stood on the front steps, waving, tears in her eyes.

It took just over an hour to get to Ashford Barrow; the clock on the dashboard pointed to eight-twenty as they entered the village. The children, very much in need of sleep, had now become irritable with each other and the endless travelling.

In the soft summer light Matt stopped the car outside 22 Meadowbrook Close, the fairly large, four-bedroomed thirties house situated at the end of a *cul-de-sac* off the main street. He got out and opened the rear door for the children. For a moment they just stayed inside, too tired, it seemed, even to give up their discomfort. Then, one by one, with some gentle urging, they got out and stood on the pavement.

Matt said, "I'll come back for the cases," and picked up a yawning Laura in his arms and unlatched and pushed open the gate. Tess, walking behind Robbie and Susie, was vaguely aware through her own weariness that the children didn't have enough energy to show even the slightest curiosity about this place that was to be their home from now on.

Matt unlocked the door, opened it and stepped through into the hall. As Tess followed she was momentarily stirred from her fatigue by the sight of the strangely familiar interior. She'd forgotten the redecoration that had been done and the fresh, new colours of the walls and the woodwork took her by surprise.

She followed Matt into the sitting-room and watched as he put Laura gently down on the sofa. Susie, very silent, sat down beside her while Robbie sat on the other side.

"I'm tired, Mommy," Laura said. "I'm tired."

"Yes, baby, I know," Tess said, "but don't worry, we'll get you to bed very soon." As she spoke her eyes fell on a large bunch of pink roses set in a glass bowl on the small table by the window. "Look," she said to Matt, a note of happy surprise in her voice, "look at what the Kinsells have left . . ."

She moved to the table and bent her head to the scent of the flowers, then looked at Matt. "How thoughtful of Dottie and Dave." Straightening, she gazed around her at the room. "Oh, Matt—it's so *good* to be back!" Then, putting her mind to the practicalities she turned to the children, looked at their sleepy faces and shook her head. "Uh-uh. No baths for you tonight. Just a quick wash and straight to bed."

While Matt went for the rest of the luggage she checked that there was hot water and that the children's beds were ready for them. To her great relief she found that everything was in perfect order, just as she had hoped and just as the Kinsells had promised it would be. And even the phone had been connected. Wasn't it nice, she said to Matt as he came in carrying two heavy suitcases;—wasn't it nice and refreshing when you found you could rely, really rely, on people.

Matt finished bringing in the luggage while she washed the children, gave them each a glass of milk and a couple of biscuits, and got them ready for bed. When they were all set she and Matt took them upstairs to the room where one single bed had been prepared for Robbie, and a larger one nearby for Susie and Laura. They tucked them up, Robbie with his one-eyed, one-eared teddy bear, Susie with her Raggedy Ann, and Laura with her thumb stuck in her mouth. Tess kissed and hugged them in turn, wished them a good night and sweet dreams, and then, turning to Matt, whispered that she would go downstairs and start preparing supper.

In the soft light of the last of the sun that filtered between the slightly parted curtains Matt looked across at Robbie. He was already asleep, his face quite expressionless in its total repose. Laura, too, was sleeping, her little pink, damp thumb still half in her partly open mouth. She was nestled up to Susie whose eyelids fluttered as she fought a losing battle to stay awake. Matt leaned down closer to Susie and whispered softly into her perfectly modelled ear, "Go to sleep now."

She nodded; her eyes opened again, so wearily, and then she said softly, "Daddy, are you still mad at me?"

"With you? No, why? Why should I be?"

"You looked so angry when I wanted to stay and play with Aunt Madeleine. You yelled at me."

He put out his hand and gently brushed a wisp of hair from her cheek, and her small hand left its hold on her Raggedy Ann and grasped two of his fingers. He leaned closer and kissed her on the forehead.

"No," he whispered, "of course I'm not mad at you. Forgive me for yelling. I didn't mean to."

She closed her eyes, smiled and nodded her head on the pillow. He could feel her fingers holding tight for a few moments and then begin to relax their grip. Gently he began to ease his hand away, but just before he would have been free she stirred, briefly surfaced again and held onto him once more. "Daddy," she said without opening her eyes, "is this Ashford Barrow?"

The name sounded strange coming from her. "Yes, it is," he said.

"And is it home?" She sounded concerned. "Are we at home now?"

"Yes, we're home. This is home."

"And will it be nice? Will it be like Laurel Canyon?"

"Oh, it won't be like Laurel Canyon, but it'll be nice—though in a different way. You'll like it, believe me, I promise."

She nodded and then released her hold on him. She was drifting deeper, deeper into sleep. He kissed her once more, kissed Laura, then got up, moved to Robbie's bed and leaned down and kissed him too. Then he moved quietly to the door and went back downstairs.

In the kitchen he found Tess preparing a light supper and he left her to it and went outside and along to the Kinsells, two doors away. His knock at number 18 was answered by Dot Kinsell. She was in her late thirties, a short, stocky woman with a bright face and dark, wavy hair. Seeing Matt standing there she greeted him warmly and expressed surprise that he was back so soon. Apologising for the fact that Dave was out, she led him into the small sitting-room and asked if he'd like some coffee. He thanked her but said he couldn't stay; he'd only called to tell her that they had all arrived and to thank her for preparing the house for their return. It was a pleasure, she said and asked whether he needed any milk, bread or anything. No, he told her; they'd brought various bits and pieces with them from Tess's mother. He did ask, though, if she would leave a note for the milkman and the baker to call at number 22 in the morning. He remained talking for another couple of minutes and then, wishing her goodnight, made his way out into the hall.

As he opened the front door she said, "Well, I'm glad I got your beds ready, but if we'd known that you were coming back today for certain we could have arranged it all so much better. I could have got in whatever groceries you wanted and done a bit more to make the place look a little more welcoming. You know—a few flowers from the garden, that sort of thing . . ."

Matt faltered in his step to the gate. With her words he realised all at once that she had had nothing to do with the roses in the house.

Tess was setting the table when he entered the kitchen. When he had told her of his meeting with Dot Kinsell she asked, yawning, "And did you thank her for the flowers?"

He looked at her for a second then turned and went into the sitting-room where he moved towards the small table on which the bowl of roses stood. Tess, made curious by his expression, followed and stopped beside him as he leaned down and peered into the heart of the bouquet.

She watched as he reached in and drew out a small white envelope almost hidden among the blossoms. The envelope was blank. From inside it he took a white card which he looked at for a moment then placed in her hand. Silently she read what was written there: *Welcome home. Forgive me, please—for everything. M.*

There was a little silence, then Tess said, "So, these flowers—it was Madeleine all the time. She's been here in our house . . ."

"Yes."

"While we were at Mother's."

"Yes. She obviously came here straight from West Priors and then returned there."

"But how did she get in?"

"I don't know." He stared at her for a moment in thought, then looked at his watch. Just on nine-twenty. He moved away, lifted the telephone receiver and dialled. "Who are you calling?" Tess asked.

"Your mother." He waited a few moments and then, hearing Ellen's answering voice, said, "Ellen? It's Matt . . . I thought I'd give you a quick call just to let you know we got here safely." After another minute or two of chat he said, "Oh, by the way, you told me the house agent returned a spare set of keys to you and that you put them in the hall. Are they still there? I thought I picked them up, but maybe I didn't. Maybe I imagined it."

Ellen went off to check and came back a moment later to say he must have taken the keys as they weren't in the hall. He thanked her, made some comment about being too tired to remember what the hell he was doing, and put Tess on the line.

While Tess talked to her mother he sat staring into space. Madeleine . . . she'd taken the keys that Ellen had left in the hall. Then she had driven here—all this way—just to leave a welcoming bunch of roses and a note asking for forgiveness. Her behaviour seemed to get more inexplicable by the moment.

And what about when she'd returned to Ellen's house? Had she been genuine in her offer of friendship? If so it was not surprising that she'd been angry when he'd rejected that offer. But what else could he have done?

He turned and watched as Tess said

goodbye to Ellen and put down the phone. After a moment or two she said, "I hate the thought of Madeleine having come in here while we were away—even though her motives were all right." She stood in silence for a moment then set the card down on the table next to the bowl. "Well," she said, "I'm tired and I'm hungry. Let's eat and go to bed."

In the kitchen they ate a scratch supper of soup and scrambled eggs. Afterwards Matt began to wash the dishes while Tess, yawning, started into the hall, saying she'd go on up. She felt so weary that as she moved up the stairs she was aware of the effort of lifting her feet up, one after the other. All she wanted was to lie down and sleep.

Reaching the landing she moved quietly along it to the children's room, softly pushed the door open wider and peeped in. As she stood there she became aware of the sound of their breathing, calm, regular, reassuring. In the faint light from the landing she could just make out the shapes of their covered forms. After a moment she pulled the door almost closed again, then moved to the main bedroom and went in.

She screamed the moment after she turned on the light.

When Matt came hurrying up just seconds later he found her pressed against the wall, her eyes tight shut.

"It's all right," he said, "it's all right," and she clung to him, hardly able to believe that it was all happening. "It's all right," he said again. "Don't worry. Everything's all right."

After what seemed a long, long time she opened her eyes and turned her gaze nervously in the direction of the bed again.

The great ugly doll was propped up in bed against the pillows, Madeleine's old dressing-gown about her shoulders. The hair on the head had been roughly dressed so that it was similar to Madeleine's own style, while the strange eyes cast their sinister, dead gaze in Tess's direction. In the light from the bedside lamp the scene was like something from a nightmare.

4

"MOMMY, Mommy, what's wrong?" It was Robbie's voice. Awakened by Tess's cry, he and his sisters had left their beds and now stood in the doorway looking at Tess with fear and bewilderment in their faces. The sight of the children had an immediate effect upon her, and she broke from Matt's grasp, wiped hands over her tear-marked face and stepped towards them, urging them back onto the landing. Matt followed.

"But, Mommy, what's the matter?" Robbie said, looking wide-eyed into Tess's face. The corners of his mouth were pulled down and his eyes sparkled with tears. His safe, secure world was suddenly threatened. "Are you all right? Why did you scream?" And then Laura joined in, echoing him as she so often did: "Why did you scream, Mommy? Why?"

Matt stooped and wrapped his arms around them, gathering them close.

"There's nothing wrong," he said. "She just gave herself a little fright, that's all."

"Yes, that's right." Tess nodded in agreement. She had made a fuss about nothing, she said. After a moment she and Matt ushered the children back to their room, where, seeing them tucked up in bed once more, they sat with them in the soft, shaded light of the lamp, waiting for them to settle again.

"Mommy," Susie's voice came whispering into the stillness, "did she give it to you instead?"

"What, darling? Give me what?"

"The doll." Susie gestured in the direction of the main bedroom. "There—in your bed. Aunt Madeleine's doll. Did she give it to you?"

There was silence for a moment, then Tess said, "No, dear. She lent it to me, that's all." She paused. "It's going back tomorrow."

Susie frowned. "Why would she want to lend you a doll? You're too old for dolls." Tess didn't answer. After a second Susie added: "Anyway, I'm glad you're sending it back. I don't like it. I hate it."

When at last the children were asleep

Matt and and Tess rose and, leaving the little lamp burning, tiptoed out of the room. Downstairs Tess went into the sitting room. Matt followed, closing the door behind him. He watched as she sank down onto the sofa and sat gazing, unseeing, into space. Sitting beside her, he put an arm around her shoulders.

"I shall be all right," she said. Then, her voice breaking slightly, she added, "What's happening, Matt? I don't understand. My sister hates me so much that she takes a key and lets herself into our house so that she can ruin our homecoming. It scares me."

"Don't say that. There's no need to be scared."

"No? I wish I could believe you. What if she does anything else?"

"She won't."

"How do you know? She takes you into her confidence?"

"Tess—forget about it." He held her closer. "It's one last gesture. It's over now."

Perhaps tomorrow, he thought, when he went up to London he would go and see Madeleine. He would tell her what he thought of her, and warn her never, never do anything like it again.

Putting a hand to Tess's chin, he gently drew her face to him. "Are you okay?"

She nodded. "Yes."

"Good. I'll make us some tea, shall I?"

"Fine."

On the way out of the room he picked up the bowl of roses. Tess watched but said nothing. Outside in the yard he dropped the flowers into the trash bin. Returning to the kitchen he put on the kettle and then, taking a large, black plastic garbage bag, went upstairs to the bedroom where the grotesque doll sat up in the bed, staring in the direction of the door with her sinister, unmatching eyes.

Unceremoniously he stuffed the doll into the bag and closed the bag with a twist fastener. That done, he took it out to the garage and put it in the boot of the car. He would get rid of it tomorrow. Tess would never have to see it again.

Matt's purpose in going to London next morning was to buy a car and return the hired Cortina. He also wanted to see his agent, and when he was ready to leave he telephoned to arrange to call in for a chat. Finally he rang up a locksmith and asked him to come round and replace the locks on the front and back doors.

Now, about to leave, he stood with Tess in the hall.

"Are you going to be all right?" he asked her.

"Yes. I'm fine." She appeared calm, but the shock of the night before showed like a bruise in her eyes.

"I don't *have* to go today," he said. "I could easily put it off till tomorrow."

"No, you go. You've got things to do. I'm all right, really." She hadn't asked what he had done with the doll. She didn't want to be told, he knew.

"Are you sure you're okay?"

"Yes, really."

"Okay."

He held her to him and kissed her. A few minutes later as he drove away he looked back and saw her still standing at the door.

Later, driving through the outskirts of London, he drove past a builder's skip full of debris. Pulling the car to a halt he got out, took the plastic bag from the boot, walked back to the skip and dropped it in.

In Hammersmith he stopped at a second-hand-car showroom that he had patronised before his departure for America. He was pleased to see that they not only recognised him from the American TV series, but remembered him as a customer as well. After looking at the vehicles on offer he picked out a two-year-old dark blue Rover which he asked to take out for a test-drive. A few minutes later he was sitting behind the wheel with the salesman at his side. The vehicle came up to all his expectations, but it didn't bring the pleasure he had anticipated. Somehow the comfort of the upholstery, the smoothness of the engine and the elegant lines of the body hardly touched him beyond his acknowledgement of their presence. He felt somehow shielded from the pleasure he'd anticipated by the preoccupation that enclosed him.

He told the salesman that he would buy the car and return for it after lunch; by that time, the salesman promised, he'd have the paperwork ready and would have given the vehicle a tune-up and a final test. Matt left then and drove to Earl's Court where at an Avis office he handed over the hired Cortina and paid the bill for the rental. That done he took the Tube into the West End and made his way to Brewer Street where his agent had his offices.

Five minutes later he was sitting in a comfortable chair facing Paul Bryant across his desk and having a cup of coffee placed before him by Bryant's assistant, Joan.

For a while they discussed the state of the business and then the series that Matt was to go into at the BBC. Called *The Apprentice*, it was a six-part serial based on a spy novel that had enjoyed considerable success a couple of years earlier. In it Matt was to play a junior member of MI5. Rehearsals for the first episode were due to begin in about six weeks. The whole project would take ten weeks from start to finish.

It was almost twelve-thirty when Matt said his goodbyes and left. Outside, the June sun was very warm and the pavements were thronged with shoppers, tourists, and office-workers on their lunch breaks. He walked for a while and then found a respite from the bustle in a pub where he drank a lager and ate a steak and French fries and salad.

When he had finished he emerged again into the sun and set off for the Underground where he caught a train back to Hammersmith.

The car was all ready when he arrived at the showroom, and five minutes later he was driving away. As he moved the car along the busy street in the direction of the motorway his mind went back to the happenings of the previous night, and he saw again the doll, propped up against the pillows like some deformed, prematurely aged child.

As he turned into Meadowbrook Close at the end of his journey the incident was still on his mind. And what, he asked himself, was he going to do about Madeleine? In spite of his avowed intentions he hadn't called to see her; and here he was, home again.

But perhaps that was the best thing, he thought: do nothing; try to forget the whole episode and leave Madeleine to herself.

At the front door he found that his key would not fit the lock, and then the realisation came to him: of course, the locks had been changed.

He rang the bell and then Tess was there, smiling in welcome. Suddenly reassured, he told himself that everything was going to be all right. It would be, he was sure of it.

The time that followed was peaceful. And such a welcome peace. It stretched out, day by day, without a ripple of trouble to disturb even slightly the calm of the warm summer. It was only in Tess's and Matt's minds where, fostered by their imaginations, disquiet lay. But as the days passed even this shadow grew less.

One thing that helped Tess was the absolute necessity to hide from the children the fact that there was any cause at all for concern—and, succeeding in this, the feeling of calm that was produced became more of a reality. It was bad enough that the children had suffered fear on their first night in the house, but now that episode was behind them they must never experience anything like it again.

Silently observing her family, Tess was aware of how quickly the children were settling down. And no longer did they have only each other's company; they had other friends now. On the very first morning there Robbie made friends with the Kinsells' son Kevin, of the same age as himself, while Laura palled up with the children of other neighbours—the Randalls, who lived very nearby—and Susie found friends in two sisters, Sally and Jane Aldous, both close in age to herself, who lived on the corner of the street.

Also for the children there was the joy and excitement of discovering their new home and its surroundings. Ashford Barrow was a small village and it took only a short walk in any direction before you found yourself in the rich, unspoilt green of the Berkshire countryside. Not that the children went away from the house a great deal, anyway. The land belonging to it was adequate for most of their needs. Stretching to just over an acre and a half, it was partly laid to kitchen produce, partly to lawns and flower beds, and the rest, the farthest section, divided between orchard and uncultivated ground. It was in the latter area where the children spent most of their outdoor playing hours. Tess, when wanting any of them, would go down towards the orchard and call to them, and they would come to her, flushed with the fresh air and the sun, their patched jeans dusty from the earth and not one of them missing California.

And nor did Tess miss it, either. And while England for the children was a new experience, for her it was like coming home after a long day out; and though home was by no means perfect, still it had the comfort of the familiar and that alone, in terms of relaxation, was worth a lot.

To add to Tess's burgeoning calm Ellen came to stay for a few days in the middle of July and very soon the sadness that had marred their earlier parting was erased. There was also a visit from Matt's younger brother, Geoff, his wife Stella and their five-year-old daughter, Tamsin, from their home in Marlborough, Wiltshire, where Geoff was a maths teacher. It was a visit during which Tamsin and Susie became firm friends, so much so that Stella suggested that Susie might like to go and stay with them for a while later in the year. It was an idea which the two girls took to eagerly and it was further suggested that perhaps the mid-term school holiday in the autumn might be a good time. In the meanwhile, Geoff said, they must all come down for a day sometime soon.

Matt and Tess also got to see something of their neighbours. Apart from the Kinsells coming for dinner one evening they also got to meet the Randalls and two or three of the other couples who had come to the area while Matt and Tess were abroad. And so the time went by, and Tess found that she was relaxing more and more. And one of the main reasons for the calm, she knew, behind everything else, was the fact that there had been no further sight nor sound of Madeleine.

It was on the first day in August, just six weeks after their return to England that the growing calm came to an end.

That day, a Monday, also marked the beginning of Matt's involvement with the new TV serial. The rehearsals that first day hadn't gone on that long and he was back home just before five. Half an hour later, after he had gone upstairs to shower and change, Susie came into the kitchen where Tess had gone to start preparing dinner. There, while she chattered about her experiences of the afternoon with her friends Sally and Jane, she helped herself to a glass of cold milk. Tess, busy cutting up vegetables, only half took in what she was saying. But then all at once she was looking round and standing very still, the vegetable knife poised an inch above the cutting board.

"What did you say?" she said.

Susie, milk coating her upper lip, shook her head in exasperation. "Mommy, you don't listen when I tell you things. I *told* you: I saw Aunt Madeleine."

"Aunt Madeleine . . ."

Susie chuckled. "You know, it's really weird how much she looks like you. At first, for a second, I thought it was you driving somebody else's car."

"Where was it—her car?"

"In the street."

"In Meadowbrook Close?"

"No, no, the High Street." Susie waved a hand indicating the junction of the main street and Meadowbrook Close. "I saw it just as I came out of Sally and Jane's front garden."

Tess nodded. "Yes . . . go on."

"Nothing," Susie said. "That's all. Her car was coming along the High Street and going very slowly past our turning. And I saw her and waved." She laughed. "I don't think she knew who I was at first. But then she must have realised because she stopped the car. And then I went over to her."

"What did she say to you?"

"Nothing much. She said I confused her because I was coming out of the wrong house. That's all. She asked me how I was."

"Nothing else?"

"No, that's all. I thought perhaps she'd been here to see you."

Tess stood motionless for a few moments, staring into space, then she put down the knife and went upstairs to the bedroom where Matt had just come out of the shower. When she told him about Susie's meeting with Madeleine he frowned. "What the hell does she want? What is she doing round here?"

Tess said, "Perhaps—perhaps we're

trying to read something into it when there's nothing in it."

"Nothing in it? What are you trying to say—that her being here was pure coincidence? That just by chance she happened to be driving by within a few yards of our house? In a village of this size, miles from her home?"

Tess shrugged. "Yes. Oh, I don't know —I'm just trying to find some—some acceptable reason for it, I suppose."

Going back into the kitchen she saw that Susie had gone out again, only the empty milk glass showing that she had been there at all. She got back to her work. She must try to put thoughts of Madeleine out of her mind.

When she had finished preparing the vegetables she went to the window and looked out over the back garden. It suddenly seemed to be so still. She could hear no sound of children's voices.

Leaving the kitchen and moving into the sitting-room she looked out over the front lawn where Laura and Emma Randall had been playing house. There was no one there now; only the little tablecloth and teaset still lay on the grass next to the path.

Tess felt panic rising in her chest while at the same time she told herself that she was being totally unrealistic; there was no cause for panic. The children were bound to be somewhere nearby. And what harm could they come to? None at all. Still, she couldn't get rid of the anxiety. And it grew. All her new security had been shaken, and now all at once she was questioning the safety of everything she had previously accepted without question. Because Madeleine had been there. As the thought made the panic rise again she moved out of the house, and a moment later was hurrying through the back garden, calling out to the children as she went, "Robbie . . . Susie . . . Laura . . ."

And then, suddenly, Laura was there. With Emma Randall tagging along behind her she had emerged from the patch of currant bushes that flanked the south side of the garden and, now with a frown creasing her forehead, was saying, "What do you want, Mommy? What do you want?"—quite obviously disturbed in her play and anxious to get back to it again.

Tess felt foolish. "It's all right," she said. "It's nothing. Go on back to your game."

"But what do you want? What did you call me for?"

"It's *all right*," Tess replied, and now her voice was touched with impatience. Laura looked at her a second longer then, taking Emma's hand, ran back the way she had come. Tess watched them go, then, hearing the sound of Robbie's feet, turned in the direction of the orchard.

Her brief exchange with him was much like the one she'd had with Laura, and in just a few seconds he was moving away again, eager to get back to the den that he and Kevin Kinsell were building. No, he called back over his shoulder as he ran off, he hadn't seen anything of Susie.

Without hesitating Tess went round to the front of the house and set off along the length of the short street towards the house on the corner. The last of her fears were dispelled even before she reached it. Even as she drew near to the front garden she heard the sound of children's voices, Susie's easily recognisable among them. Just a few steps closer and she could see over the hedge and catch a glimpse of Susie and her friends; they seemed to be dressed up in somebody's old clothes. Tess turned around and went back to the house.

In the kitchen she made herself a cup of instant coffee that she didn't want and carried it into the sitting-room. There she placed it beside her and sat gazing out at the quiet little street. She felt unutterably depressed.

In bed that night she lay silent and far from sleep. Matt, aware of her wakefulness, put his arm around her and pressed himself to her. Taking his hand she held it close to her breast. She couldn't stop thinking about Madeleine. She had hoped that it was all over, but now . . .

There was silence but for the sound of her breathing and Matt's. She could feel the light touch of his breath against her hair. Then his voice came, as if he were thinking of the same thing, "I talked to Susie. I asked her about her meeting with Madeleine."

"And?"

"Nothing. That's all there was. Just what she told you. There was no more. I didn't want to question her too closely for fear of making her suspicious and afraid. But I'm certain there was nothing more to it." His hand moved to her shoulders. "You're so tense. Try to relax."

"Easy to say."

"Worrying's not going to help."

"No." She felt his arms come around her again and tighten, holding her close to him. Then with a little pressure of his hand he urged her to turn so that she was facing him. She was held close, her chin in the warmth of his neck.

"Don't be afraid for the children," he murmured. "Don't be. Nothing's going to happen to them. It's us Madeleine wants to punish; not the children."

They lay quite still for some moments and then she felt the touch of his mouth, light kisses, moving in a small area on her forehead and then lower to the bridge of her nose. And then his hand was moving down, caressing the hollow of her back. He kissed her mouth, softly at first and then with growing passion. She felt his growing hardness become insistent against her lower belly, pressing against her, and she pushed forward to meet it, acknowledging his desires and her own. Then at his silent urging she moved slightly so that she lay supine and vulnerable. His hand touched her breasts, her stomach, and then, lower still, moved to caress and discover. She trembled with the ecstasy he brought—those invading fingers—and she gasped out into the quiet room and opened herself to him, silently urging him to take her.

Moments later she lay beneath him, feeling the hard, full shape of him inside her body, moving, thrusting. And she lifted herself to meet him, as if she could never get him deep enough. *"Oh, Matt, Matt, darling, darling, darling,"* she breathed as he filled her body with his quickening movements, while at the same time deep, deep inside her head another voice, much smaller, but more insistent, called out Madeleine's name. Hearing it, and realising it had been there all the time and that it was part of the very reason for her present overpowering need, she thrust herself upward to meet him with even more urgency. It was as if she wanted to feel the violence of his assault more keenly, to be hurt by his pleasure and her own, and in so doing perhaps be able to blot out, to force into oblivion, that still small voice that called her sister's name.

On Wednesday afternoon Susie came home from playing at her friends' house and told Tess that she had seen Madeleine again. She had been playing with Jane and Sally on their front lawn, she said, when Madeleine had looked over the hedge at them.

Two days later, on Friday, when Susie didn't come home at the expected time Tess walked up the street to the Aldous's house to bring her home. There she was told that Susie had gone off in her aunt's car.

5

AS Matt parked the car in the drive he was met by the sight of Tess hurrying towards him from the house.

"What's up?" he said, "What's happened?"

"It's Susie!" Tess seemed on the verge of hysteria and panic flared in him.

"*Susie?* What's happened to her?"

Tess shook her head, the tears starting, and he gripped her shoulders more tightly. Then, the words coming out in a rush, she told him all that she knew. When she had finished he said quickly, "When was this —that the Aldous girl told you that she'd gone?"

"Over half an hour ago. At about twenty-past-five. Since then I've been waiting for you to get back. I called the rehearsal studio and they said you must have already left, so I knew you wouldn't be long."

He turned away, his face pale. "Where

are you going?" Tess said as he flung open the gate.

He said over his shoulder, "To see the two Aldous girls." Fifteen minutes later he was back. With their mother looking on, the Aldous sisters had stood before him in the front room of the little corner house, self-conscious, fidgeting and eager to get away again; two small girls in blue denim, looking like miniatures of their short, red-haired mother. Matt had questioned them gently, carefully hiding his impatience. Jane, at five years old, would hardly open her mouth in answer to his questions, but shyly hung her head and pressed back against her mother. Sally, though, at six, happily proved more communicative and it was from her that Matt eventually got what information was available. They had, all three, she told him—herself, Jane and Susie—been playing on the front lawn when Susie's aunt had got out of her car and stood looking at them over the hedge. "And that's what she did on Wednesday too," she added.

"You saw her then as well?"

"We both did. She got out of her car and stood looking over the hedge at us. At first I thought it was Susie's mother, but Susie said no, it was her Aunt Madeleine."

"And did she say anything, Susie's aunt?"

"Not much. Just asked us what we were doing, and then she just talked to Susie for a minute. She asked her if she was having fun and that sort of thing—that's all. Then she went away."

"That's all?"

"Yes."

He gave a nod. "And today?"

"Today she looked over the hedge again and talked to us for a few minutes."

"What about?"

"Nothing much. She said what a nice day it was, and how lucky we were to have it so fine."

"And," Jane said, finding her voice, "she asked us our names."

"And then what?"

"We told her."

"There was nothing else," Sally said. "Susie said she was going home and then went outside. I went to the gate just after and I saw her getting into her aunt's car. She turned and saw me and waved to me

—and then she went off." She paused. "That's all there was."

Mrs. Aldous looked at Matt helplessly for a moment, then said encouragingly, "I really wouldn't worry about her. I'm quite sure she'll be all right. After all, she *is* with her aunt, isn't she? It's not as if she's gone off with some stranger."

Matt made no comment to this. After a moment he asked her, "What time was it, do you know, when Susie went off?"

"Oh, getting on for half-past three, I should think."

He nodded and looked at the clock on the mantelpiece. "That's over two and a half hours ago now."

Long moments of silence went by. Tess sat at the kitchen table with her chin sunk into her palm. From across the hall came the sound of the television where Robbie and Laura sat watching some children's programme. Matt paced. He had dialled Madeleine's number to see if she and Susie were there, but had got no reply. After that he had called Ellen. She had seen nothing of them either, she said. When he had put down the phone after their brief conversation he knew he was leaving her bewildered and upset. It couldn't be helped. Now, coming to a halt in his pacing, he turned to Tess and said, "We'll wait for a while, and then if she's not back we'll go to the police."

Tess reached out to him and he took her hands, held them in his and said gently, "We can only wait. She'll be back soon."

After a while Tess got up and began preparations for dinner. She looked over at Matt and shrugged. "We've got to eat," she said, "and we're late as it is. Besides, it's better that I have things to do." And then all at once she was clinging to the side of the sink, the tears streaming from her eyes. Matt put an arm about her shoulders, waiting till her crying had ceased.

When at last she was quiet again he said, "She'll be home soon, Tess. Believe it. I know she will."

Robbie came into the room a minute later to see what had happened to dinner, and it was clear that he was impressed by the atmosphere he encountered. "What's the matter?" he asked, looking from one parent to the other. "What's wrong?" And being told by Matt, "Nothing!" he shrugged it off and asked "Where's Susie?"

"She'll be back soon," Matt said, trying to sound casual.

"Yes, she'll be back soon," Tess added. "Now you go on upstairs and wash before dinner." Her voice was too sharp, though, too peremptory, and as Robbie turned away to go up to the bathroom he looked back at her in some surprise.

Matt was in the car.

Since returning to England he had looked forward to driving out through the countryside around Ashford Barrow, visiting all those places he and Tess had known before going away, and showing the children that California didn't have the monopoly on interesting spots to visit. He'd never got around to it, though.

And now his rediscovery of the various places had to be in this fashion: a frantic driving around from one to another, when he saw nothing of the attractive scenery but only cars and the women who walked by with small girls at their sides. He went searching all the while, sometimes in panic, sometimes in hope, but always giving up eventually and going on elsewhere. But it was either that or stay indoors and wait—and that had proved unbearable. In the house he had not been able to settle to anything; he had spent the crawling minutes just sitting or wandering around, trying not to pace—while Robbie's and Laura's questions grated on his nerves and he'd had to prevent himself from snapping at their display of what was only a very normal curiosity. And of course they were curious. He and Tess were worried and preoccupied and it was impossible for the children not to notice it. And in the end Matt had got out. It had seemed a positive move; at least he was doing something.

Now, looking at the clock on the dashboard he saw that he had spent over an hour just driving around. There had been nothing, though, and at last, after leaving a little wooded area which was occasionally frequented for picnics he drove on till he found a phone box and dialled home.

Tess answered almost before the phone had a chance to ring. The disappointment in her voice was unmistakable when she heard Matt on the other end of the line. "Do you know anything?" she asked him breathlessly, as if afraid what the answer might be.

"No. I was just calling to see whether you'd heard anything yet—from anybody."

"No . . ." Her voice sounded unutterably weary. "Where are you?"

He told her his whereabouts and added that he'd be heading homeward right away.

He met little traffic as he drove back along the winding country roads. On either side the verges were lush in their height-of-summer growth, the nettles as tall as the hedgerow. It was all so much a part of the England he loved best and remembered so well—and a part of it that had managed to remain the same and unspoilt. It meant nothing to him now.

When he got back to the house he could hear the sound of the TV coming from behind the closed door of the den as he went into the hall. The children watched far too much television. Though whereas at some other time he might have gone in, turned the set off and urged them to do something else, now he was content for them to stay glued to it.

Opening the door, he looked in and saw the two of them: Robbie in his pyjamas on the old sofa, and Laura in her nightdress on the rug.

"Laura, baby, don't sit so close," Matt said and, without taking her eyes from the screen she moved back a few feet. Matt closed the door again and went in search of Tess.

He found her upstairs in the bedroom, lying on the bed, the telephone on the side table, only inches from her hand. She didn't look round as he entered but lay still, her dull eyes directed ahead, unfocused, unseeing. He knew it was useless to ask whether she had heard anything since he had called.

After a while she said: "Are the children okay? They've had their baths. They must go to bed soon." She raised her head and glanced at the clock. "It's getting on for half-past eight."

He nodded. "Don't worry. I'll see to them." He moved closer and touched his hand to her hair. She didn't move. After a few moments he lay down beside her, cupping her body with his, spoon-fashion, his right arm over her, enclosing her in his warmth. From below he could hear the sounds of doors opening and closing and of the children's voices. After a few moments he got up, moved silently away from the bed and left the room.

Reaching the hall he was just going past the den when he heard the unmistakable sound of Susie's voice coming from within. Quickly he threw open the door.

She sat there on the small footstool facing Robbie and Laura, the television programme continuing unheeded as she chattered away. Matt stood staring at her for long seconds. He could hardly believe it. She was back. Here she was, talking to her brother and sister as though nothing whatever had happened.

Tess and Matt waited till Susie had eaten and Robbie and Laura were in bed before asking Susie what had happened. There was not, though, it seemed, really much for her to tell. She'd been playing with her friends, the Aldous girls, she said, when Aunt Madeleine had looked over the hedge. And of course she had gone to her.

And that's when Aunt Madeleine had said she had a surprise for her . . .

At this, Tess gave the slightest nod of understanding. The promise of a surprise. That had been enough for Susie, and she had lost no time in getting into Aunt Madeleine's car.

"And where did you go?" Matt asked.

Susie sighed, then told how at first they had just driven around, but then how later they had gone to a town where Aunt Madeleine had taken her to the movies to see *Pinocchio*. Afterwards, she said, they had come back to Ashford Barrow and Aunt Madeleine had dropped her off at the corner of the close. She began then to tell them about Jiminy Cricket but more questions came instead, questions concerned with what else she and Aunt Madeleine had done together. What else? She looked at her parents uncomprehendingly. There was nothing else, she said. And then, suddenly, she looked from one to the other and mischievously rolled her eyes.

"There was something else?" Matt said.

Susie nodded. "Yes, but promise you won't be mad at me."

"No, of course not."

She paused for a moment then said to Tess who sat beside her on the sofa, "I'll whisper it to you."

As Tess bent forward, Susie whispered into her ear; just a few words, and that, it seemed, was that. After a few more minutes Tess took Susie—still wondering what all the fuss was about—upstairs where she washed her and put her to bed. Afterwards Tess came back downstairs and joined Matt in the sitting-room.

As she sat in the easy chair facing him he said, "What was it?"

"What was what?"

"Susie's secret—what she whispered to you."

Tess shook her head and gave an ironic smile. "Oh, that, yes. Popcorn and ice-cream."

"What?"

She nodded. "Her big secret—what Madeleine bought for her at the cinema. Popcorn and ice-cream."

Seeing the expression on his face she began to laugh, the sound becoming a little shrill and touched with hysteria, then she put her hands up to her mouth and fell silent. It was all too ridiculous. While Matt had been frantically, desperately scouring the countryside and while she herself had been lying on the bed, numbed, hardly knowing how to live through each minute, Susie had been in a cinema watching *Pinocchio* and eating popcorn and ice-cream.

6

"BUT why did she do it? Why did Madeleine do it?"

Matt shook his head at Tess's question. "Why does she do anything?" he said. "You must have realised by now that your sister is motivated by different things than we are."

"Anyway," Tess said with a sigh, "Susie's all right. And it hasn't left her with any bad memories. Just the opposite, in fact—she has very *pleasant* memories. I mean, from her point of view what was so terrible about it? She went off with her aunt, and her aunt took her to see *Pinocchio*. And after all, we'd encouraged the children to be nice to her." She gestured towards the children's bedroom above. "You know, Susie's really quite confused up there, I think. She can't understand what all the fuss is about. Mind you, we've got to make it quite clear from now on—to her and to the others—

that they mustn't go off with *any*one, no matter who it is."

"I don't understand you," Matt said, frowning. "You seem to be saying that we should forget the whole thing."

"No, no, of course not." Tess shook her head, then added wearily, "Oh, I don't know. I suppose I'm just so—so relieved that Susie wasn't harmed. And I can't see any further than that right now. But anyway—what can we do?"

"Well, for God's sake," Matt said, "we've got to do *something*. Susie might think it was all nothing, but you know it wasn't, and so do I. And so does Madeleine. She knows better than anyone. She did exactly what she set out to do today. She made us absolutely terrified for Susie's safety. And do you think she didn't have that in mind all the time? Of course she did. You don't really believe, do you, that she did it all for Susie's benefit? That out of the kindness of her heart she decided to take her to the movies? Of course not. She did it to get back at *us*— you and me—to hurt *us*. It was just another of her cute little tricks in this weird game she's playing." He moved away and stood looking out at the quiet street. "Well," he added, "I shall go and have a word or two with Madeleine. Nothing like this is ever going to happen again. I'll make sure of that."

Next morning, Saturday, he set off to drive to London.

Before leaving he had debated calling Madeleine and telling her that he wanted to see her. In the end he had decided against such a course; she would almost certainly not agree, or wouldn't keep the appointment. So, there was only one thing to do—go there and hope that she'd be in.

The motorway leading into the city was busy, but at last he was off it and driving along Chiswick High Road towards the area of Madeleine's flat. After parking the car he consulted his street guide then set off to walk the little distance to Madeleine's address. A few minutes later he was turning into a narrow side street where rows of terraced houses looked out over a small park. Finding the number of the house he was seeking, he went up the three steps to the front door and rang the bell with "Rayfield" on it. There was no answer. He rang again. Still nothing. He gave one more ring on the bell, waited another half-minute then turned away.

As he reached the foot of the steps the door opened and a plump, middle-aged woman emerged carrying a plastic shopping bag. "Was that you ringing?" she asked.

"Yes." He nodded. "I wanted to see Madeleine. Miss Rayfield."

The woman looked at him with suspicion in her eyes. "I'm afraid you've missed her," she said. She closed the door behind her. "She's out."

"Have you any idea where she's gone? Or how long she'll be?"

The woman ignored his question. Looking at him appraisingly from the top of the steps she said:

"I've seen you before, haven't I?"

"I don't know. Have you?"

"Yes, I have. Have you been here before?"

"No, never."

"Well, I've seen you. Somewhere." She stared at him for a second longer then said, a note of triumph in her voice: "Yes, of course. You're on the telly."

"Well . . ."

"You are, aren't you?"

"Sometimes." Matt nodded.

The woman smiled, warming to him now. "I knew it," she said. "You were in that series, weren't you? The one about the doctors." Her whole demeanor was now quite different. Then, as if the subject had never changed, she said, "Yes, Madeleine's out. Mind you, I don't think she'll be that long. She was only going to do a bit of shopping, so she said. Are you a friend of hers?"

"Well—yes, you could say that."

She came down the steps and moved past him to the gateway where she turned back to face him. "You were good in that series," she said.

"Thank you."

"Yes, really good." With a final nod and a smile she turned and moved away along the street.

Matt watched her departure, waited there for a minute or two longer then set off in the same direction. He would give Madeleine a chance to get her shopping done then come back and try again.

On King Street he dodged the pushchairs and the wheeled shopping carriers for a while then went into a pub where he ordered a scotch and soda, and carried it over to a nearby table.

It was not an easy place to relax in. For a while he tried to carry on a conversation with an elderly white-haired man who spoke of the changes he had seen in the area over the years, but the blare of the juke box wouldn't allow it. In the end Matt downed the rest of his drink, wished the man goodbye and went back out onto the street.

There was still no answer when he rang Madeleine's bell. For a moment he considered waiting for her at the door, but decided against it. If she saw him she might stay out of sight somewhere until he got sick of waiting and went away. Eventually he decided to go into the park across the street and watch for her from there.

In the park he moved to a vacant bench beside the path and sat down facing the house. He could see the front door with no difficulty. Taking off his jacket, he prepared himself to wait. All about him as he sat there children played in the sun and dogs sniffed about or ran in pursuit of balls. He was glad that his own children lived in the country. Not for them the boundaries of this irregular strip of land where the dusty grass was dotted with ice-cream wrappers and dog-turds.

He had been waiting for some fifteen minutes or so when, turning his eyes from their focus on the house, he saw Madeleine coming towards him across the park.

She was wearing culottes—surely, he thought, the most unbecoming garment ever designed for a woman—and a pale blue blouse and sandals. She was walking along one of the asphalt paths, carrying a bulging shopping bag. He wondered what to do—wait where he was, get out of sight for the moment, or go forward and meet her. A second later the decision was out of his hands; he saw her sweeping glance light upon him and her step falter slightly in the shock of seeing him there. Then as he got to his feet she was moving towards him, giving what looked like a smile of welcome and surprise.

"Matt!" she said. "What are you doing here? Don't tell me you've come to see *me*. Have you?" When he nodded and said, "Yes, I have," she gave a broad smile.

"Well, what a nice surprise. Come on—let's go and have a cup of tea."

Putting on his jacket he walked at her side to the house. She unlocked the front door and he followed her into the hall and up a flight of stairs. It all seemed very cramped and tight; the result, he thought, of the conversion into flats of an old house that hadn't been big enough in the first place—and a conversion that appeared to have left room only for the barest practicalities and nothing whatever for aesthetics.

On the first floor Madeleine stopped before a door marked *2*, unlocked it and stepped inside. Matt followed her and found himself standing in a small sitting room with a dining area off to one side.

"God, this place is a mess," she exclaimed, and putting down her shopping she began to hurry about the room, tidying and rearranging various items. Left standing there, Matt looked about him. The room was just as cramped as the stairway and hall had led him to expect. Apart from the limitation of space, though, there also looked to be a shortage of comfort. There were the obligatory sofa, chairs, table, TV and stereo, etc., but nothing of it seemed to boast any identity. Nothing had the appearance of being any kind of personal belonging or to hint at ever having been anything in the way of a personal choice.

"Well, do sit down."

Madeleine turned her warm smile on him. She seemed to have finished her bout of tidying. He sat on the sofa. As he did so she added, "This place gets pretty untidy during the week, and my cleaning time isn't till later on today."

She turned from him and went into the small adjoining kitchen and he watched as she filled the kettle and put it on the gas. He called out to her: "Don't make any tea on my account," and wondered at himself for just sitting there like someone who had dropped in for a casual chat.

She came back into the room with cups and saucers on a tray. "You can't go without having a cup of tea," she said as she set the tray on the coffee table. "I'm going to have one anyway, and I'm sure you must be thirsty on a day like this."

As she moved back to the kitchen his glance took in a little group of framed photographs that stood on a small table at the end of the sofa. One was of Madeleine herself when younger; he was sure it must be Madeleine; he couldn't see her displaying a photograph of Tess. Another was of Ellen—Tess had a copy of the same picture—and another was of Tess and Madeleine's long-dead father. Matt picked up the photograph. Tall, fair, handsome, in his late twenties, the girls' father was pictured standing beside a horse. Matt studied the photograph for a few seconds, put it down and idly picked up an old copy of *Time* from a stack of magazines. As he lifted it his movement was arrested. Lying beneath the magazine was another framed photograph, lying face down.

Glancing towards the kitchen he saw that Madeleine had her back to him. Turning the frame over he found himself looking at a photograph of himself.

The photograph had been taken some three or four years earlier; he recalled that Tess had sent it to Ellen from California along with pictures of the children. But how did it come to be here? Either Ellen had given it to Madeleine—which Matt found hard to believe—or Madeleine had simply taken it. The latter, he considered, was more likely. It was likely also, that Madeleine had hidden it away during her quick flurry of tidying when she had brought him into the room.

After staring at the picture for a moment longer he slipped it back beneath the magazine.

When Madeleine came from the kitchen a minute later she carried a teapot which she set down on the tray. "There." She gave him a bright smile. "We'll just leave it for a moment or two . . ."

Somehow, Matt felt, he was losing the initiative; she it was who seemed to be orchestrating the meeting. Abruptly he said: "You know why I'm here, don't you?"

Her smile wavered and vanished.

"You do know, don't you?" he said.

She hung her head and stood before him like a remorseful child. Giving a grave little nod she said with contrition in her voice:

"Of course I know why you're here. I knew as soon as I saw you in the park. In fact, I've been expecting you to come— or to phone." She pressed her hands together. "All I can say is that I'm sorry. What else can I say? It was a stupid, irresponsible act, and I—"

Matt broke in: "I don't think you realise the seriousness of it, Madeleine—of what you did." He got to his feet. "You took Susie away. You enticed her into your car with promises of surprises and treats and went off with her."

"Yes—I know." Her voice now sounded a little tearful.

"Why did you do it? Imagine what it was like for Tess. She went round to the neighbour's house to bring Susie home, only to be told that she'd gone off in your car. Why did you do it?"

She turned away from him. "I don't know."

"You don't know? Of course you know. Jesus Christ, you must have been aware of what you were doing."

"Susie was all right, though," she said. "She didn't come to any harm. I'd never have let anything happen to her. I know I shouldn't have given her popcorn *and* ice-cream, because it probably wasn't good for her teeth, but I'm sure it couldn't have done any harm."

Matt shook his head in disbelief. "Christ alive!" he said. "I can hardly believe I'm hearing this. Listen, I don't give a shit about the popcorn and the ice-cream. You took my daughter away! That's the issue —not what sweets you bought her!"

"I *know*. I know that. I'm just trying to point out that she didn't come to any harm."

"No, she didn't—but *we* weren't to know that, were we! What do you think it did to us—not knowing where she was? We were worried sick!"

"But she was with *me*. You knew she'd be all right."

Matt groaned. It was impossible to get through to her. Keeping his voice low, he said, "*That* was your *idea*, wasn't it? To make us suffer. You were trying to get back at us through Susie. My God, Madeleine, aren't you ever going to give up? Don't you realise what it's doing? To *all* of us?"

She made no reply.

"I don't know what your intention is," he said, "but whatever it is you've got to stop. You've got to be aware of what you're doing. To yourself as well as to us.

Oh, you might succeed in making our lives miserable, but for what purpose? What will you get out of it in the end? If you're trying to destroy our happiness you must realise that you're wielding a two-edged sword. You'll end up destroying your own happiness as well."

"Happiness," she said with quiet bitterness. "That's a joke."

He ignored her words. "You've let yourself become obsessed," he said. "This whole thing—it's consuming you. For God's sake, life's got to have more to offer you than this. What are you getting out of it? And what are you going to do? Spend all your life pursuing some vendetta? Something for which you never had a motive in the first place? Madeleine, whatever you're trying to do, you've got to realise once and for all that there's no future in it—for any of us."

She took a step towards him. "Please, Matt," she began, but he went on, overriding her:

"And anyway, whatever reason you think you've got, haven't you done enough? You made us so unhappy in the past, before we went away. And you ruined our homecoming when we returned." His voice rose again as memories of recent events came back. "Christ, can you imagine what it did to Tess, discovering that—that monstrous thing you put in the bed? And now this." He shook his head. "I'll say one more thing and then I'm going. I just want to say that whatever grievances you feel you've got with us—whatever you've dreamed up—then take the matter up with *me*. Do I make it clear? Don't do anything, ever again, that involves Tess or our children. Any of them." He paused. "And that is a warning."

There was silence in the room when he had finished. Madeleine was looking at him with tears glistening in her eyes.

"Do I make myself clear?" he said.

"Yes," she murmured; then: "I can only ask you to forgive me."

Hardening his heart in the face of her unhappiness he said, "I don't really think you're in a position to ask *anything*."

"Please." She almost sobbed the word out. "I do know what I've done. And all I can say is—give me another chance. Please. I won't do anything like it again."

He moved to the door, opened it and turned back to face her. "Your verbal assurances are good only up to a point. You must realise that. If you mean what you say, then you must *show* us—by your actions. That's the only thing you can do." He shrugged, sighed. "Well—I'm going now."

"The tea will be ready," she said. "Please—won't you stay and have a cup?"

"No, thanks." He looked at her in wonder. After such an onslaught she could still offer him tea. He started out again then stopped and turned back to her once more. "There's just one other thing . . ."

"Yes. . . ?"

Stepping past her he went to the coffee table and there stooped, lifted the magazine and picked up the framed photograph. He held it in front of her for a moment then put it in his inside jacket pocket. "You won't be needing this," he said.

Leaving her standing there he left the room, went down the narrow staircase to the front door and out into the street. He felt relieved to be out in the air again.

As he walked back to the car it occurred

to him briefly that he had had no lunch. He didn't care. All he wanted to do now was get back to Tess and the children.

Driving homeward he thought of the warning he had given Madeleine. Just what he had been warning her of, though, he didn't know. He was only sure that where Tess and the children were concerned he would stop at nothing to ensure their safety.

7

LATER that afternoon Matt took the children aside and impressed upon them that no on account must they ever go off with *anyone* in the future—their Aunt Madeleine included—and they said yes, without curiosity, impressed by the seriousness of his tone.

A little earlier, on his return from London, he had told Tess of his meeting with Madeleine, and she had sighed with relief when he had finished by saying that now it was all over and done with. That, he had said, was the end of it.

To their great relief, in the days that followed there were no further incidents to cause them distress, and as the time went by they felt the reverberation of Madeleine's actions diminishing. Gradually it was all being left behind, and each uneventful day that passed was one more positive sign that they could relax; another mark in favour of welcome humdrum normality.

And they continued in the process of settling. Matt had his TV serial to work on while Tess had her own responsibilities around the house. And apart from their work, they wove into their lives new threads, while at the same time they took up some of the threads from their earlier days in England. They forged familiarities on which to build and watched the children settle too. The lives of all five of them were, day by day, falling into comfortable, recognisable patterns. It was noticeable too how the children's references to Laurel Canyon and California had almost become things of the past. Now, one could see, their former home had become to them little more than a distant dream.

The time saw other changes too. A second car was acquired, a year-old Renault 5. Bought for Tess's benefit, it promised to help her considerably in the way of making her workload easier to cope with—which was also the reason they sought someone to come in and help around the house. After enquiries it wasn't long before they found Ruth Atkinson, a middle-aged widow who lived in the next village. She was a tall woman with mousy brown hair, a gentle face and broad, hard-worked hands. She wasn't, intellectually, the brightest person they could have found, but they took her on with references testifying to her capability, her practicality, her willingness and her honesty, and these qualities, evident in good measure, allied to her enviable way with the children, made her, in a very short time, indispensable.

It was on Monday, August 22nd that the letter arrived.

Tess stared at the envelope, addressed to Matt and herself, and seeing Madeleine's familiar, round, almost childishly careful handwriting, felt that the little time of peace had come to an end.

After a few moments' hesitation she tore open the envelope, took out the sheet of folded notepaper and read what Madeleine had written:

Dear Tess and Matt,

I've let some time go by before writing this—in the hope that the intervening days have enabled you to think of me a little less angrily.

All I can say is that I know I did wrong in doing as I did, and that I hope you will forgive me. I don't truly know why I did it. I don't really want to go into it now with post mortems. All I really want is to start over again. Is that possible? Please say that it is. I know that I have no right to ask this or anything else of you, but I must. Please. I want us to be friends. I want to make a new start. And I can only do that with your forgiveness. So please, tell me you forgive me and give me the chance to make it up to you. That's all I ask, all I want.

Madeleine

Tess read the letter through again then put it back in the envelope to await Matt's return from London. When he eventually got back to the house she handed him the letter and sat in silence, watching him as he read it.

When he had finished he shook his head. "I want, I want, I want," he said. "She wants this, she wants that. She's done everything she possibly can to upset our lives and now all she can talk about is what she wants from us . . ." He tossed the letter contemptuously aside where it fell on the sofa.

Tess picked it up. "What are we going to say to her?" she said.

"Say to her? Nothing. Say nothing to her at all."

"But we can't just leave it like that, can we?"

"What exactly do you want to do?"

She shrugged. "I don't know, Matt. I just know that—well, that we can't just ignore her." She indicated the letter. "She's written asking us to forgive her so—"

"Well, I can't," Matt interrupted sharply. "Have you forgotten what she's done? If you have, I haven't. And if she wants my forgiveness she's got to earn it. And if she ever does earn it it's not a foregone conclusion that she's going to get it. Oh, no." He waved a dismissing hand. "It's easy for her to talk as she's doing now. But talk is cheap. If she really means what she says then she can show it, not talk about it. Let her prove it. Let her show us that she wants to make it up to us. Let her show us that she intends to behave herself in the future. And the best way she can start doing that is by not bothering us." All the time his voice had been rising with his growing anger. "We don't want her coming to the house!" he said. "We don't want her phoning us up, and we don't want her writing to us!"

With his last words he got to his feet, snatched the letter from Tess's hand and tore it across again and again. Then he dropped the pieces into the wastebasket by the fireplace. "And that's that!" he said. "That's what I think of your crazy sister and her pleas for forgiveness."

Tess flinched at his words, while he seemed unaware of the stab of pain he had caused. She gazed at him, and the swift thought came to her that it was almost as if she were seeing a stranger . . .

Later, when the children were in bed Matt went up and kissed them goodnight. When he came back downstairs he found that Tess was not in the house. Looking from the kitchen window he saw that she was outside, standing at the edge of the lawn. He went out to her and moved to her side. The sound of birdsong was all around them, as also were the signs of the summer dying.

After a minute he said, "What's on your mind, Tessie? Tell me."

She sighed and said, "We can't just do that, Matt—ignore Madeleine. Disregard her letter."

"Oh, no," he said wearily, "not that again."

"Please—at least let's discuss it."

"Tess—" he shook his head, "there's nothing to discuss, and if—"

She interrupted him. "*Please!* Please, Matt . . ."

"Okay," he said, "so you don't think we should ignore her letter . . ."

"No, I don't. I don't think we can solve the problem as easily as that."

"Then what's your answer?"

She sighed. "I haven't got one. All I know is that this isn't the way. Can't we write back to her?"

"And say what?"

She shrugged. "I suppose just to say that we'll give her another chance."

"But Tess—"

"Please, Matt, let's do it. She sounds so sincere . . ."

"She's sounded sincere in the past." He shook his head. "I think sometimes you forget who you're dealing with. Tess, when you deal with Madeleine you're not dealing with any rational, normal person. She's neither of those things. I'm sorry to say it, but you know as well as I do—your sister's not right in her mind. She's just not like other people."

"Oh, God, Matt, that's a terrible thing to say."

"I know it is. But it's true."

"Stop it!" she cried out. "Stop it! Now!" She clapped her hands over her ears and sat with her eyes screwed up tight. When she took her hands away she said softly, "Oh, Matt, don't you understand? It could have been *me*. We're both from the same source. We're the same—identical. And it could—it could have been me. What you say about Madeleine, can't you imagine what that does to me? And it's not only that, though; it's more. It's not just to do with those—those ties between us. It has certain implications. Don't you realise that?"

He stared at her and suddenly her voice rose and broke on a sob. "Oh, for God's sake, Matt! How can you be so blind!" She moved quickly away across the grass. Near the back door she whirled to face him. "How can you be so bloody obtuse?" With that she wrenched open the door and went into the house.

After a minute or two Matt followed her. Finding the downstairs rooms empty he went upstairs and found her in the children's bedroom, sitting by the window. She didn't raise her head as he quietly pushed the door open wider and moved towards her. She seemed intent on the sleeping children. Laura lay on her right side, her mouth slightly open, small soft curled hands up to her chin. Matt gazed down at her for a moment then looked at Susie who lay next to her. She too was sound asleep, as was Robbie in his bed nearby. Matt moved his glance to Tess then reached out and touched her shoulder. She looked up at him and in the pale light he could see the shine of tears in her eyes. *Oh, Madeleine, you've got so much to answer for.* After a second he nodded in the direction of the door. "Come on," he whispered, and she got up and followed him from the room.

In silence downstairs he poured drinks and carried them into the sitting-room where Tess sat quietly on the sofa. He handed her a gin and tonic, took a drink from his own scotch and soda and said: "First of all, just let me say that I do appreciate how you feel about Madeleine. I know how you must be torn." He shook his head. "Perhaps I just don't understand these things that well. Twins . . . Those ties—I think they're pretty much of a mystery to outsiders." He fell silent then went on, "No, Tess, I'm not obtuse. I know what you mean. And don't you think it's occurred to me too—touched me as well?" He moved closer, put his hand to her chin and tilted back her head so that he was looking directly into her eyes. "They're my children too," he said softly.

"Yes."

"Yes. And I know them pretty well, I think."

"Oh, Matt—"

"As well I know you."

"Yes."

"And believe me, I know as surely as I know anything in this world that the only way in which you and Madeleine are alike is in the way you look."

She opened her mouth to speak at this but he went on, his voice trembling slightly, "No, listen. I know what's been on your mind. And of course I've been aware of the—the implications you speak of. And let me say now that that's it. Forget it. You are *not* Madeleine, and my children are not Madeleine's children." As the thought of Tess's torment reached deeper within him he felt tears well up in his eyes while the sudden, growing constriction in his throat made his voice hoarse. "They're our children. They're yours and they're mine. They're three beautiful, perfect children that we have made, and they owe nothing in any way to your sister or to anyone else. They're a part of you and a part of me. Madeleine —she had no part in it—no part in it at all."

Another letter arrived from Madeleine a week later.

My dear Tess and Matt,
I had hoped by now that I would have

heard from you, that you would have replied to my letter. I've been disappointed, though.

I'm sure you will appreciate that it wasn't an easy letter for me to write. When I said that I was truly sorry for any hurt and unhappiness I've caused I meant it, and I hope, most sincerely, that you believed me.

Please write. Don't ignore me. I couldn't bear that. Eating humble pie can be very indigestible; a little word from you, though, can make it easier to swallow.

Yours as ever, Madeleine

"What are we going to do?" Tess asked, looking at Matt as he studied the letter. "Do you think we should ignore this one as well?"

"Yes." Matt crumpled the letter in his hand and tossed it into the wastebasket. "Why not?"

Later, when he had gone from the room, Tess retrieved the letter, smoothed out its creases as best she could, put it back in its envelope and slipped it into a drawer of her small desk that stood near the window. In two or three days she would talk to him about it again.

The next Monday Robbie and Susie were starting school. The school was in the next village and Tess drove them there in the Renault, taking Laura along for the ride. Matt had left earlier to go up to London. On returning to the house Tess found that Ruth had arrived and was already busy in the kitchen. Calling Laura to her, Tess turned on her portable radio and took it with her into the sitting-room where she sat down at her desk. While Laura played on the carpet with her dolls Tess dealt with a few bills and the household accounts. From the radio came the sounds of Richard Harris singing "MacArthur Park": *"Birds like tender babies in your hands. And the old men playing chequers by the trees . . ."*

For a while Tess sat and listened as his light, plaintive voice filled the room, and then the song faded from her consciousness as the thought of Madeleine came to her. From the drawer of the desk she took out the letter and read again the words Madeleine had written. For several minutes afterwards she sat staring into space, then she took a sheet of notepaper and a pen and began to write.

Dear Maddie,

I'm sorry we haven't written, but what with one thing and another we've been so busy. Now, though, with Matt at the studios and Susie and Robbie at school I've got time to write a few lines.

Yes, of course, we both realise that it must have been a difficult letter for you to write—and this, now, you will appreciate, is a difficult letter to write also. Somehow this is not the time for clever words or subtle turns of phrase. Instead I must just be very direct and honest and say, Yes, yes, yes, of course I want this whole thing to be over, and I know Matt does as well. And, yes, I must tell you, I want us to be friends again. There has been so much unhappiness in the past. Can we at last believe that it is all over? I pray so.

Yes, Maddie, I do forgive you. All I want now is to put the whole business behind us. Life is so short. Surely we shouldn't be wasting it in petty hatreds and revenges.

Yours ever, Tessa.

When she had finished she wrote Madeleine's address on an envelope, sealed the letter inside, stamped it and then went out and posted it at the pillar box on the corner.

As she came back to the house she said to herself that she should have waited until Matt was back. She should have shown him the letter. She hadn't, though, and now it was too late.

8

LOCATION shooting was being done on the series the next day, Tuesday, and as Matt wasn't involved he was free for the day. He started it by driving Robbie and Susie to school, then returning and, with Laura's dubious help, getting to work on the garden. In the afternoon he planned to drive into Maidenhead to buy something for Tess's birthday next day. She would be thirty-three.

Throughout the morning Laura stayed close to Matt as he worked. She soon got bored with toting small containers of hedge clippings, though, and eventually turned instead to the tried amusement offered by her dolls.

After lunch Matt left Tess at work with Ruth in the house and took Laura in the car to Maidenhead where, impressing on her the need for a secrecy he didn't think she could possibly keep till the next morning, he bought Tess a pale blue silk blouse.

Next day, at breakfast, he gave Tess the blouse and as she opened the package he caught the expression on Laura's face which told him as clearly as words could have done that she hadn't been able to keep the secret from Tess. Inwardly he smiled. It didn't matter; he'd never expected her to.

Tess received gifts from the children, too. From Robbie there came a small wooden boat, crudely made from fortuitously shaped pieces of wood, a couple of nails and colours from his paint box. Susie gave her a little picture made from a couple of fragile honeysuckle flowers which she had picked earlier in the summer and pressed between Kleenex and books. Laura, obviously taking her ideas from Susie, had, in the absence of real flowers to press, drawn her own in bright crayon. What kind of flowers they were, though, neither Matt nor Tess were able to discern.

Matt, having a late call for rehearsal, was having a last cup of coffee just before leaving when the post came. As expected, most of it was for Tess and the children crowded round her as she opened the envelopes. When she came to the fourth one she didn't read it aloud as she had done with the others, but looked at it in silence. And then Robbie, who was looking over her shoulder, read, "From Aunt Madeleine." Tess raised her eyes to Matt and handed the card to him.

"She doesn't give up, does she?" Matt said. The design was from an English Victorian painting. Apple pickers busy in an orchard. Adults and children, all as rosy-cheeked and healthy-looking as the fruit they were gathering. Inside he saw the now familiar handwriting. *Love, Madeleine*. In the same violet ink. He returned the card to Tess, got up and pushed back his chair. It was time he went. He kissed the children and, followed by Tess, went to the front door.

"You won't forget we're going out tonight, will you?" she said, smiling, and he shook his head.

"No, of course not." He had booked a table at a restaurant they had frequented before their time in America and they were looking forward to going back there and renewing their acquaintance with the place. Now, as he opened the door he turned and said, "Did you send *her* one—Madeleine—a birthday card?"

Just a momentary pause then Tess said, "Yes."

He nodded. "I guessed as much. Why did you?"

She hesitated then said, "I answered her letter on Monday. After that I couldn't ignore her birthday."

He said wearily, "Oh, why did you do that?"

She said a little defensively, "And I sent more than a card. There was a silk scarf that I had never worn . . ."

"I suppose you sent it from both of us."

She shrugged. "I couldn't just send it from me. And I told you—I couldn't ignore her birthday."

"You did while we were away."

"That was different. We never had *any* contact then."

He shook his head again. "It's a mistake, I'm sure. She's best ignored, if it's at all possible."

Tess said nothing.

"Well," he said, "we'll talk about it later. Though I wish you hadn't done it."

161

She said with some sharpness, "Well, I *have* done it. And there's an end to it."

"I hope you're right."

He saw hostility in her eyes and felt that his own anger must be clear in his face. He was angry. So angry that his impulse was to just get the car out and drive off. He couldn't, though. It was something they had never allowed themselves to do: to give in to momentary anger to the point where they would part for even the shortest period with a quarrel unresolved. And, also, today was her birthday. "Hell," he said, "we can't go off like this, can we?"

They looked at one another for a moment longer, then Matt put his arms around her and her own arms came up around his back. They kissed.

"Happy birthday," he said. "I love you."

"I love you, too."

He returned home just after six-thirty and found Tess almost dressed for the evening. At once he went upstairs to shower and get ready, coming down a little later to find that Ruth had arrived for her evening's baby-sitting stint.

He had booked the table for eight o'clock and at seven-forty he and Tess set off, driving out of the village and through the next one, Bourne, to its border where the restaurant stood. Here Matt parked the car and together they went into the old building where they were warmly welcomed by the owner. Then with the greetings over they were shown to a table near one of the windows—the same table they had used years ago—and in the soft light they drank cocktails and ordered from the menu.

It was good to be back. Everything about it, Tess thought, was perfect, the food and the wine. They ate whitebait, after which they were served duck in orange sauce. They had just begun to eat the latter when Tess found her eyes drawn to the entrance, seeing the arrival of yet another customer. And she froze. Matt, who had been telling her about an incident that had taken place during rehearsals that day, saw the expression on her face and, turning, followed the direction of her eyes to where Madeleine, dressed in a blue blouse and darker blue slacks, stood handing her coat to a waiter and smiling in their direction.

"Jesus Christ," he muttered, "I don't believe this."

The next moment the restaurant owner was at their side, saying that Mrs. Severn's sister was there to see them. And then there was Madeleine, too, right there at his shoulder, smiling at them and then stepping foward, putting her arms around Tess and kissing her.

"Happy birthday, Tessa," she said.

"Thank you, Maddie. Happy birthday to *you*." Tess's voice sounded odd in her own ears. A little awkwardly she returned the embrace. She saw that Madeleine was wearing the silk scarf she had sent to her the day before. A deep blue, it was flecked at the edges with gold.

She watched as Madeleine turned to Matt and, bending to him, gave him a light kiss on the cheek. "Hello, Matt, and how are you?"

"Fine, thanks, Madeleine." He made only the slightest token gesture in the way of getting to his feet. "Many happy returns," he added.

"Thank you." Madeleine looked around her and Tess, seeing what was coming, quickly forestalled her, saying, "Will you join us?" and, catching the eye of the restaurateur, asked if they could have another chair. She didn't want Madeleine to stay, any more than Matt did, but there was nothing else to be done. The next moment Madeleine was sitting there with them, and the perfect evening was a thing of the past.

Madeleine gave a little laugh as she put down her bag and settled herself. "I hope I'm not disturbing you," she said, and Tess, ignoring Matt's swift dark glance across the table, said no, no, of course not. Madeleine turned and made a little sign to the waiter and he came forward, put another wine glass on the table and took her order. When he had gone away again they sat in silence while Matt, doing his best to ignore Madeleine, gave his attention to the food before him.

Tess said, too brightly, "Well, what a surprise, Maddie—seeing you walk in here," to which Matt added, covering the coldness of his words with the hint of a smile.

165

"Yes, why exactly did you come here, Madeleine?"

Madeleine gave a little laugh that had no amusement in it, only a touch of desperation. "Why—to see you both, of course. And to wish Tess a happy birthday. And I wanted to thank you both for my nice scarf." She told then how she had gone to Ashford Barrow and how Ruth had given her the address of the restaurant. "So," she added, "I decided to come along."

The waiter appeared, bringing Madeleine the turkey salad she had ordered and she began to eat. Tess watched her for a moment then went back to her own food, picking at it and wishing the time to be over so that she could go home.

When the main course was through they skipped dessert and just had coffee and then Matt paid the bill. Madeleine offered him the money for her share but almost without looking at her he waved her offer aside. Then, with thanks and goodnights to the restaurateur and the waiter, Matt led the way out into the warm September night. It seemed that Madeleine was waiting for an invitation to return with them to Ashford Barrow but he forestalled this by saying that he was tired. After wishing her goodnight he headed for the Rover. Madeleine, having come to a stop not far from her own car, called out thanks and a goodnight to him and stood looking after him as he strode away.

Tess, hesitating at her side, saw the frown on her face, the anxious, hurt look in her eyes. Then, her glance returning to Matt, she watched as, without looking back, he unlocked the car and got in. The evening that had started out so well had turned into a disaster. Was she herself in part to blame? If she hadn't answered Madeleine's letter or sent her the birthday card and the scarf Madeleine wouldn't have sought them out tonight. Anyway, it was done now. She turned back to Madeleine to say goodnight and found her holding out a small package.

"What's this. . . ?"

Madeleine shrugged as she put the package into Tess's hand. In the dim light Tess could see that the wrapping was of patterned paper and that it was tied with a ribbon. "For my birthday," she said.

"Yes, but don't open it now; wait till you get home."

"Maddie, you shouldn't have."

"Oh, nonsense. After you gave me that lovely scarf?" She looked over towards the Rover. "Anyway, you'd better go. Matt's waiting for you."

They stood there facing one another almost shyly. Then Madeleine stepped forward and kissed Tess on the cheek. "Goodnight," she said.

"Goodnight, Maddie."

Madeleine smiled at her and moved away. Tess watched her go then turned and walked off across the car park in the direction of the Rover.

Matt hardly looked at her as she got in. As soon as she had buckled her seat-belt he switched on the motor and put the car in gear. As they drove off Tess turned to glance from the rear window and caught a brief glimpse of the lights of Madeleine's car as she followed them out of the car park and set off in the opposite direction.

With a sigh, Tess said, "I'm sorry about all that. I suppose I encouraged her, didn't I?"

His hand moved and briefly touched her knee. "It's done," he said, "And anyway,

Madeleine doesn't need any encouragement."

When they reached the house Tess got out and went indoors while Matt turned the car around, waited for Ruth to come out and then drove her home. Just before he let her off at the gateway of her little cottage he asked her not to tell Madeleine anything else, should she call again at the house. Of course, Ruth said, and apologised for doing as she had that evening where Madeleine was concerned. "Forget it," Matt told her; "you weren't to know."

When Ruth had vanished into the doorway of her cottage he set off back to Meadowbrook Close. Tess was doing a few odd jobs in preparation for the morning when he got back. She had made some tea, too, and they sat drinking it together in the quiet. On the coffee table there lay, next to a small jewellery box and some wrapping paper, a little brooch. Matt had never seen it before and with a glance at Tess he picked it up.

"From Maddie," Tess said. "She gave it to me tonight."

Matt studied the brooch. It was in the form of a small jester with hinged, movable limbs. He looked up at Tess. "It's gold," he said.

"Yes. It's quite an expensive piece."

He placed the brooch back on the table.

Tess said, "It looks as though she's very anxious to make it up to us, doesn't it?"

He nodded. "Yes, it looks that way."

The next morning Robbie awoke with a slight temperature and complaining of a sore throat. No school for him, Tess decided, and went to tell Dot Kinsell— who had offered to drive the children to school that day—that he would be spending the day in bed and Susie would be going to school alone.

Later, just when Tess had begun to prepare a light lunch, the telephone rang. It was Madeleine.

She said she was just calling to say thanks for last evening. It had been so nice to see the two of them again, and to be able to sit and relax and talk—in circumstances a little more pleasant than at other times lately. "And do please thank Matt for me, won't you?" she went on, "and tell him that the next time we have dinner together, the three of us, it's on me."

"Yes, I'll tell him," Tess said, while she wondered at Madeleine's assumption of a closeness: *the next time we have dinner together, the three of us* . . . It was a closeness that didn't exist; it wasn't true.

Then, suddenly remembering the parting gift that Madeleine had put into her hand outside the restaurant, she added, "Oh, I haven't thanked you properly yet for my birthday present. Maddie, you shouldn't have done it."

"Why not? Don't you like it?"

"Oh, of course I do. I love it. It's beautiful. It's just that—well, it looks so expensive."

"Aw, so what." Madeleine laughed and added, "It's Italian, by the way. I got it when I was in Rome a few months back."

And so the conversation went on; all of it, Tess thought, totally without purpose. She wanted to end it, and several times made half-hearted attempts to do so, but each time Madeleine kept it going with trivialities. When, eventually, the talk got around to the children, Tess told her that Robbie was in bed. At this Madeleine sympathetically clicked her tongue. "Poor little boy," she said. And then at last the conversation came to an end and, saying a final goodbye, Tess replaced the receiver.

Robbie spent most of that day, Thursday, in bed. The next day there arrived a card for him—a get-well-soon card—from Madeleine. To Robbie who, like most children, was only accustomed to receiving cards on his birthday, it came as a great surprise and a great thrill. Matt looked at the card and agreed with him, yes, it was super, and realised that whatever anyone else might think of Madeleine, she was all right in the estimation of his son.

Earlier in the week Tess and Matt had talked of taking the children over to West Priors to see Ellen for the Saturday afternoon and had made tentative arrangements with her. Robbie's condition, however, had given them cause for second thoughts and they'd put off the final decision. Now, with Saturday here and Robbie appearing to have shaken off whatever was ailing him, they decided to go.

They set off after lunch and got there at about two-thirty. It started to rain while they were there, and the children, denied the open air, came indoors and sat in front of the TV. They were restless, though, and particularly Robbie who, in addition, seemed especially hard to please. At half-past five, as soon as tea was over, they got up to leave.

The rain came down again as they drove back, added to which Susie and Laura became irritable with one another. Tess, growing increasingly impatient with them, was relieved when at last the familiar landmarks came into view, showing that Ashford Barrow wasn't far away.

And at last they were turning into the main street of the village, and then, just minutes later, into Meadowbrook Close.

"God help me!" Matt muttered and Tess groaned under her breath, shaking her head in disbelief as she peered through the rain-clouded windscreen at Madeleine's light blue Golf.

9

"IS Madeleine still upstairs?" Tess asked.

Susie, sprawled on the carpet next to Laura, looked up and said, "Yes, she went up to the bathroom." She returned to the puzzle they were making: big, chunky pieces that promised to make up a colourful picture of kittens playing with somebody's knitting. A present from Madeleine.

They had arrived at the house to find Madeleine sitting in her car, and seeing them drive up she had got out, all smiles, and followed them into the house. There, for the sake of peace, Matt had forced himself to try to be pleasant and, by way of offering her a drink, to show her hospitality. It was uphill, though, all the way.

The children had taken quite a different view of Madeleine's presence. She, hardly giving them a chance to get their breath when they all entered the house, had opened the carrier bag in her hand and taken out the gifts she'd brought. For the two girls there had been the kitten puzzle; plus, for each of them, a book of paper dolls which could be cut out and dressed in a variety of little paper outfits. For Robbie there had been two packets of foreign stamps for his collection. All three children were thrilled with their gifts.

Their return had been over an hour ago now. Since then Tess had got Robbie ready for bed, to which he'd gone without the slightest demur, and made a light snack for Susie and Laura and given them their baths. Now in their nightdresses and dressing-gowns they were making the most of the time remaining before they, too, went upstairs.

Matt still didn't know the purpose of Madeleine's visit. When she had met them at the gate she had simply said that she'd wondered how they were and, on impulse, had thought maybe she'd drop in. Now Matt, sitting nursing his drink, silently repeated her words. *Drop in*. The phrase was hardly an apt one when you had to travel some sixty-odd miles in order to do it . . .

And what did she plan to do now? he

wondered. Was she hoping to stay on for dinner? Did she imagine that once Susie and Laura were up in bed the three of them—she, Tess and himself—could spend a cosily quiet evening relaxing together?

He turned and gazed out of the window. The rain was still falling; not heavily now, but at a monotonous, depressing rate. Turning from the sight and seeing Susie and Laura making their puzzle on the carpet, he felt suddenly impatient with them and wanted them upstairs and out of the way. The feeling was totally unreasonable, he knew, and he hated himself for it. But why should he wonder at it? he asked himself; Madeleine's presence always had a totally disrupting effect.

He looked towards the door. Where the hell had she got to all this time?

Robbie, lying with the covers drawn up to his chin, gazed sleepily at Madeleine in the faint light that came from the partly drawn curtains. It was strange seeing her there, sitting on the edge of his bed. As he looked at her she leaned towards him and asked, "How are you feeling now?"

"All right, thank you." It wasn't true, though. His throat felt sore, and he had a headache.

Madeleine reached out and brushed soft fingers across his forehead and asked him about the trip to West Priors. He had just begun to tell her about it when he saw the door open and his father's head appear. Robbie smiled uncertainly at him. "I was just telling Aunt Madeleine about our visit to Grandma's," he said.

"I see." Matt nodded. "I'm sure that's all very interesting," he said, "but you're not up here to hold conversations. You came up here to rest. Isn't that right?"

"Yes." Robbie was puzzled by his father's tone.

"Right. So I think we'd better leave you to sleep, don't you?"

Madeleine looked contrite. "Oh, Matt," she said, getting up from the bed, "it's my fault. I just looked in to say goodnight." She turned back to Robbie, bent low over him and lightly kissed him on the forehead. "Goodnight," she whispered.

"Goodnight, Aunt Madeleine."

She moved to the door and Matt stepped aside as she passed through. When she had gone he turned back into the room, closed the door and came over to the bed. "What did Aunt Madeleine want?" he asked.

"Oh, nothing much. She just asked me how I was feeling and then about our going to see Grandma."

"That's all? Were you asleep?"

"Asleep?"

"When she came in . . ."

"Oh, *then*." Robbie nodded. "Yes, just about."

Matt nodded then leaned down and kissed him. "Okay, now you get back to sleep, all right?"

"Yes."

"Goodnight, then . . ." Matt was moving to the door.

"Goodnight, Daddy."

Downstairs Matt went to the kitchen where Tess was busy. As he appeared in the doorway she looked up at him and said softly, "Madeleine's staying to dinner."

He frowned. "Oh, yes? When was all this arranged?"

"Just now." She indicated the clock on the wall. "Look at the time. We can't wait any longer before we eat. If we wait for her to go we might wait all night."

Three or four minutes later when Susie and Laura had completed their kitten puzzle and demanded that it stay undisturbed in the lid of the box, Matt saw them up to bed where Robbie was now sound asleep. There, with strict, whispered instructions to them not to wake him, he tucked them in and went back downstairs.

There, hearing sounds from the dining room he looked in and found Madeleine setting the table for dinner.

"Madeleine—" he began.

She turned to face him. "Yes, Matt . . ." She was smiling, her head a little on one side. The look of her was disarming and he had to remind himself of some of the things she had done.

"Madeleine," he said again, and after a breath the words came out in a rush. "Madeleine, don't go waking my children from their sleep. Especially when they're sick and have been sent to bed to rest. What do you think Robbie was there for —his amusement? He was put to bed for a purpose and that wasn't to lie there and talk to you."

She stared at him, blue eyes wide, lips slightly apart. In his brain he heard the echo of his words and realised how pathetic they sounded. But still he went on.

"After you took Susie off without our permission and practically drove us insane with worry, I told you never to bother our children again. And I *meant* that, Madeleine. I just don't want you to have anything to do with them. And whether that includes taking them off on some jaunt or disturbing their sleep, it's the same thing. I meant it *then* and I mean it *now*. Leave our children *alone*."

Throughout the brief tirade she had tried two or three times to interrupt. But now that he had finished she just stood there in silence, one hand clutching the spoons and forks and the other raised to her mouth. Matt, glaring at her, saw the tears flood her eyes and start slowly down her cheeks. Vaguely, to his right, he heard the sound of footsteps and became aware that Tess had come to stand in the doorway.

Madeleine spoke then, and with her words her tears were released in a flood. "Oh, don't, Matt—*please!* Don't say that! I've never meant any of the children any harm. You must know that. I'd never hurt them—never." Her words became lost momentarily in a spate of sobbing, then, more coherently, she added, "I *love* your children." She put the silver down on the table, then very quickly stepped forward and moved past him, past Tess in the doorway, and out into the hall.

Tess turned into the hall after her, and a second or two later Matt followed. There was no sign of Madeleine at first but then a moment later she reappeared, coming from the sitting-room where she had gone to fetch her bag. They watched as she moved to the front door. When she reached it she put her hand to the catch and turned her tearful eyes to Matt.

"I've done some pretty awful things," she said. "I know I have. And do you think it's easy living with the memory of what I've done?" She shook her head. "Believe me, it's not!" For a moment or two her speech became smothered by her sobbing. Then, her voice clear once more, and small, like that of a child, she said, "Can't you understand? All I'm trying to do now, all I *want* to do, is to make it up to you—to *all* of you. Won't you even let me try to do that? Are you going to deny me any means of gaining any self-respect?"

Then she was turning, wrenching open the door and hurrying out into the rain.

Matt, with Tess at his side, stood watching as she ran up the path, through the gate and across the pavement to her car. He watched as she fumbled in her bag for her keys, saw her drop them and stoop to pick them up from the rain-wet road. He saw her straighten and wipe the back of her arm across her eyes. Then he watched as she sagged against the side of the car, her shoulders drooping, her face distorted with her weeping, heedless of the rain that beat down, drenching her clothes so that her soaked sweater clung to her breasts and her hair was plastered to her face.

And then Tess was hurrying past him, running up the path to Madeleine and putting her arms around her, and from the doorway Matt watched as the two sisters stood together in the rain. He stood watching for several moments, then he turned away from the open door, moved into the kitchen and poured himself another drink.

"Maddie, come back into the house," Tess said. She, too, was weeping now. She clung to Madeleine, feeling the unpleasant sensation of the wet wool of Madeleine's sweater under her fingers.

"No," Madeleine said, "I'm not going back in there."

"Come in, please. We're both getting soaked."

"You go in," Madeleine said. She pulled free of Tess's arms and, turning, glanced towards the front of the house. Matt was no longer in sight.

"Oh, Tessie," she murmured, "why does he hate me so?"

"No, no, he doesn't hate you. He doesn't."

"Oh, yes. You do too."

"No, Maddie. No one does. You must believe that."

For answer Madeleine just threw her a look of disbelief then opened the car door and clambered in. Tess moved to the other side, tried the handle and found the door was locked. Madeleine leaned across and released the catch and Tess opened the door and got in beside her.

They sat there in silence for some moments then Madeleine said, "Tessie . . ."

Tessie, she had called her again: the name from the very early years of their childhood. The sound of the old name touched Tess and brought fresh tears to her eyes. "Yes, Maddie?"

"I—I know why I did what I did," Madeleine said after a moment, stumbling over the words. "What I mean is—I—I haven't been well. I can't have been. I don't know what was wrong—but—well, I can only think I must have had some kind of—of nervous breakdown—some kind of mental breakdown." She didn't look at Tess but kept her gaze fixed on the surface of the road where the rain continued to fall with unwavering monotony. There was a little silence during which Tess could hear only the sound of their breathing and the drumming of the rain. Then Madeleine went on, "It's not an easy thing to talk about, but I have to—if for no other reason than that it might help you to—to understand."

"Maddie," Tess said, "you don't have to say all this."

"Yes," Madeleine said quickly, "I do. Only then can you begin to understand—and perhaps see things a little differently."

"I think I do understand, Maddie."

"Do you?" Madeleine turned to look at her. Then she sighed and shook her head. "But Matt—he never will. He'll never forgive me for the things I've done."

"Yes," Tess said, "he will. You must just—give it time. You must just let him see—well—that you're no longer any kind of—of threat. And that can only be done with time. Don't you see? Once he sees that then everything will be okay."

"Do you really think so?"

"Oh, yes, I do. I do, Maddie." Tess reached out and touched her arm. "Come on now, let's go into the house. We can't sit here like this; we'll catch pneumonia."

As if she hadn't heard, Madeleine said, "I can't forget how Matt looked at me, the things he said." She began to cry again, but more quietly. She made no effort to brush the tears away. After a moment, she said, "And I meant what I said about the children. You know that. I would never, *never* do anything that would harm them in the slightest way. Surely you believe that, don't you?"

"Yes," Tess nodded. "Of course I do."

"Matt doesn't, though. I saw his face." Madeleine hugged herself. "Make no mistake, Tess. He hates me. He really does." And then it seemed that all her control had gone, and she gave herself up to her sobbing, her head hanging foward, hands clutching herself while she rocked back and forth in her misery, the sobs, hoarse and racking, shaking her body.

For a moment Tess just looked at her, the tears spilling from her own eyes, then she leaned over and wrapped her arms around her. "Come on," she said, "you're coming back into the house with me. This minute. All right?"

"Yes," Madeleine whispered.

"Right." Tess's voice managed to sound both soft and efficient at the same time. "Come on then . . ." She opened the door, got out into the steadily teeming rain and slammed the door. The next moment Madeleine stretched across and pressed down the locking button on the door. Then, keeping her eyes averted from Tess's gaze, she quickly inserted the key in the ignition.

"Maddie, what are you doing?" Tess cried. "Open the door and—" But the rest of her words were lost in the sound of the engine roaring to life, and she could do nothing but stand and watch as Madeleine, the tears still streaming down her cheeks, set the car in motion and accelerated away. In seconds Madeleine had reached the junction of Meadowbrook Close and the High Street and was taking the corner with the tyres protesting. She didn't look back. In moments she was out of sight.

In the house Tess found that Matt had continued preparing the dinner. He glanced up at her as she appeared then went back to this task. She stood in the kitchen doorway and watched as he tore the washed lettuce leaves and tossed them into the salad bowl. She no longer felt hungry.

"Madeleine's gone," she said. "And very upset, too."

He nodded. "Well, just so long as she's gone."

She screwed up her eyes in distaste at the callousness of his words. "Oh, Matt, please . . ."

"Please?" He raised an eyebrow in an exaggerated gesture of surprise. "All of a sudden you're her ally?"

"No!" she said. "No, it's just that—oh, Matt, she's so upset. She was in a really bad state when she left."

He nodded again. "I thought she might be." He didn't seem in the least concerned. For a few moments he appeared absorbed in his work, then, glancing back to Tess, he said, "You'd better get out of those wet clothes unless you want to catch your death."

For him it seemed as if the subject was finished. Tess started to turn away, then she stopped. "Matt," she said, "I truly believe she's different now."

"Oh, yes?" He looked at her quizzically. "What makes you think that?"

She shrugged. "Well, going by what she said . . ."

"She had something to say, obviously," he said dryly; "you were out there for several minutes. And whatever she had to say it must have been to good effect."

She began to tell him something of the disjointed conversation that had taken place, but then came to a stop. "I'm wasting my breath. You're not in the least bit interested, are you?"

He shook his head. "Not really, no."

"Oh, Matt, please, don't be like this— so cold, so distant. I mean it when I say I think she's different. I do. She's changed." She stepped towards him. "Oh, if you could have seen her out there you would believe me; you wouldn't be like this."

He shook his head. "She's really managed to get to you, hasn't she? Oh, Tess, do you forget so easily?"

"Of course not. But does that mean I can't have any feeling at all for her? She *is* my sister. And I don't mind telling you, Matt, that I'm concerned for her. The way she went away from here just now, I— well, I'm concerned. And if you'd seen her you would be, too."

"You think so? I very much doubt it."

"Matt, for God's sake!" Her voice rose higher and she put a hand on each of his forearms, gripping tightly. "Oh, I know we've got to try and cut free of her if we can, but for God's sake, Matt, we've got to leave her with something. She's got her pride, you know. We can't strip her of every shred of self-respect." She fought back her tears and added more softly, her words almost a plea, "Matt, don't you have any feelings at all for her? Don't you have any sympathy whatsoever?"

He released himself from her grasp, then put his hands on her shoulders and looked into her eyes. "Perhaps I could if I allowed myself the luxury," he said. "But I can't. No, Tess. The answer to your question is no. I don't feel any sympathy for her at all." He paused and added, "I can't afford to."

It was still raining when Madeleine arrived back at her flat. It didn't bother her, though. At the window she stood and looked out at the wet street with its reflected pools of lamplight. She realised dully that she was still holding her weekend case. What a joke that was. Her weekend case—packed for nothing. If

Matt had known about that he'd really have got a laugh.

She put the case down on the sofa and went into the bathroom where she put the plug in the bath and turned on the taps. After she'd added bath salts she went into the sitting-room, took some notepaper and a pen and sat down and began to write.

It didn't take her long. When she had finished the letter she sealed it in an envelope, wrote on the envelope's face and propped it up against a lamp, near her little array of birthday cards on the coffee table. That done she went into the bedroom and took off her clothes.

Back in the sitting-room she moved, naked, to her small stereo record player. She chose a record by Joan Baez. There was a song on the album, a setting of a poem by Byron. She put the record on, and then carefully set the automatic changer-arm above it. After that she went back to the bathroom, made a slight adjustment to the taps and got in, lowering herself slowly and lying back, her head against the small pad made by her folded flannel. The water felt good. The tears that ran down her cheeks fell onto her breast and were absorbed by the soft, lavender-scented water. The music from the record player went on, the voice of the soprano accompanied by a guitar. The volume was much higher than was customary in those small flats, but tonight Madeleine, usually so particular and careful not to disturb her neighbours, didn't give the matter a second thought.

Her tears flowed like the music.

After a while she reached out to her razor, unscrewed it and took out the blade. She made the first cut, in the left wrist, very quickly. It wasn't nearly as easy as she had thought it would be. She would have to press harder with the right one . . .

When she had finished she dropped the blade over the side of the tub onto the floor. In the water the blood flowed from her wrists in little billowing clouds. The pain was just a dull, pulsing ache. It was quite bearable.

Lying back she closed her eyes. Her tears had stopped now. Everything else, though, was still flowing: the warm water from the taps, the blood, the music from the record player. The song she had waited for came on . . .

> So, we'll go no more a roving
> So late into the night,
> Though the heart be still as
>   loving,
> And the moon be still as bright.
>
> For the sword outwears the
>   sheath,
> And the soul outwears the breast,
> And the heart must pause to
>   breathe,
> And love itself must rest.
>
> Though the night was made for
>   loving,
> And the day return too soon,
> Yet we'll go no more a roving
> By the light of the moon.

The changer had been set so that when the record came to an end the pick-up lifted off and swung back to the start. The music began all over again.

10

ON Sunday morning Matt took breakfast on a tray upstairs to Robbie and found him sitting up in bed arranging the stamps that Madeleine had given him in his album. Matt waited till he'd put his things to one side then placed the tray over his knees and sat on the edge of the bed. Watching Robbie eat it was clear that his appetite was back and that he was feeling better.

A little later as Matt stood up to go Robbie said, "Daddy, would you say we were halfway settled yet?"

"Halfway settled? What are you talking about?"

"You said that when we were halfway settled we could have a dog . . ."

"Did I say that?"

"Yes, you did."

"I see. Well, then, I suppose we'd better give it some thought. What kind of dog did you have in mind?"

"We've talked about it," Robbie said,

"Susie, Laura and I. And we'd like a big dog. Like a St. Bernard."

Matt laughed and said unfortunately St. Bernards were a bit *too much* on the big side. "I think you'd better think again," he said.

Downstairs Matt rejoined the others at the table where he helped himself to orange juice and cereal, followed by scrambled eggs, crispy bacon, toast and marmalade. Outside the sky was bright; the only sign of yesterday's rain being the ease with which the blackbird on the lawn found the worms he was after.

Across the table Matt caught Tess's eyes, held her gaze for a moment and smiled; a smile which she only returned in token before looking away to give her attention to Susie and Laura who were asking to leave the table.

"Yes," she told them, and added that they were not to leave the garden without permission. When the girls had gone out of the room she began to clear away the breakfast things. A few moments later when she came near and reached for Matt's empty cup he put out a hand and lightly grasped her wrist.

"Come on, Tess," he said.

She said nothing, only stood still, avoiding his eyes and waiting for him to release her. He sighed, let go of her and said, "How long are we going to go on like this?"

Ever since the evening before she had been quiet and uncommunicative with him —because of Madeleine, of course—and even their physical closeness in bed hadn't eased the situation. Then, he had put his arms around her, only to find her still cool and unresponsive, while the goodnight kiss she had given him in return for his own had been an empty gesture.

And now, well into the morning, the coolness was still here, and threatening to spoil the rest of the day.

"Come on, Tess," he said again. "I can't remember the last time we were like this."

She shrugged. "And I can't remember a time when you were so cold and so heartless."

He shook his head. "Not cold, not heartless. Just anxious to protect what's mine."

"Don't you think sometimes you can

pursue that protection with a little too much zeal?"

"Perhaps. Not at the moment, though. Not where your sister's concerned."

"I see." She gazed at him for a second then nodded, turned away and went from the room.

Upstairs Tess told Robbie that he could get up when he wanted to and, leaving him busy with his stamps, brought his breakfast tray downstairs. In the hall she stopped at the door of the playroom and looked in on Susie and Laura. They were engrossed in the paper dolls that Madeleine had brought and Tess stood watching for a few moments as Susie, tongue working in the corner of her mouth, juggled with the scissors, cutting out one of the little paper costumes. Laura looked up at Tess, smiled at her and said, "Look! Look—what we're doing."

Tess smiled approvingly at their efforts and backed out into the hall. At the breakfast table Matt sat reading the morning papers. She put the tray down, took up a basket, dropped in her little vegetable knife and went outside.

Following the centre path she walked

between the lawns with their central rose-beds and on towards the vegetable garden where the path was fringed with bushes of redcurrant and blackcurrant and gooseberry; the latter still bearing some fruit, now golden-yellow and overripe.

After she had picked runner beans, a cabbage and a lettuce she moved back onto the path, turned right, and headed on down to the orchard where she opened the gate and walked beneath the trees where the apples, pears and plums were heavy on the boughs. After she had picked a number of apples she moved on across the grass to an old, rough wooden bench near the hedge. She sat on the bench, placed the full basket beside her and looked around her. It was so peaceful here in the very last of the summer sun. She breathed deeply. The air was filled with the scent of the fruit and the sound of birds. She thought, looking around her, We could get some chickens and a couple of goats, as we had before we went away . . .

"Tess. . . ? Tess. . . ?"

It was Matt's voice, calling from the direction of the house, and she got up and took a step forward. Then she came to a halt, hovered for a moment and stepped back and sat down again. His voice went on calling several more times and then fell silent.

She leaned forward, elbows on her knees, chin cupped in her hand. She was confused. Where Madeleine was concerned she didn't know what to think any more. Granted, in the past Madeleine had done some extraordinary things, and not only extraordinary, but also horrible, frightening things. But they were in the past. And besides, it must count for something when Madeleine herself could only look back on her past actions with horror and shame. Did Madeleine, then, have to go on paying for her actions? Hadn't she found enough punishment through her conscience? There must come a time when one had to forgive and forget.

Thinking back to the past hours with Matt, Tess reflected on her own behaviour. She hated the way she'd been since Madeleine's departure yesterday. She saw herself in her manner towards him: cold and unresponsive. It was unlike her to be this way, but she couldn't get over his treatment of Madeleine. How could he be so unforgiving? Keeping Madeleine out in the cold wasn't going to do anything for anybody's happiness, she was sure of that.

She sat there for several minutes more. From the far end of the village came the pealing of the church bell. It took her out of her reverie and she sighed, picked up the basket, got to her feet and started back over the grass.

She had just reached the orchard gate when she heard Matt's voice again, calling to her. It sounded closer than before. And there was something in his tone . . . She stood still, her free hand on the gate, waiting, then saw him come into view, rounding the bend in the path, his head visible beyond the leaves of the greengage tree.

"I've been calling you," he said. "You didn't answer."

"What is it?" she said. "What's up?"

"Ellen—" he said.

Tess cut in quickly, "Mother? What's wrong? Is she all right?"

"She's fine. She was on the phone just now. She wanted to talk to you, but I didn't know where you were."

"What's up?" she said again. "Tell me."

"It's—it's Madeleine." He raised his hands in a pacifying gesture. "Now, don't get upset. She's going to be all right."

"What's happened to her? For God's sake, *tell* me."

"Apparently she was taken to hospital last night. She—tried to kill herself."

"Oh, God, no . . ." Tess leaned back against the gatepost, vaguely aware of the basket slipping from her fingers and spilling its contents on the grass. Matt stepped forward, reaching out to her, but she flapped a hand, warding him off. She shook her head. "Oh, God! I was afraid something was going to happen. I could see it." Sudden tears ran down her cheeks.

He told her what Ellen had told him on the phone; the story that she had learned only that morning, that Madeleine was in the Charing Cross Hospital where she had spent the night after being found in her bath with slashes in both wrists.

"How was she found? How did they get to her?"

"Madeleine's neighbour found her, apparently, and called an ambulance. She's been on the phone to Ellen this morning as well, the neighbour, apart from the hospital. Anyway, Madeleine's going to be all right. She's lost some blood but she's okay. They've stitched her up and she'll be going home today."

"So soon?"

"Well, if they can't do anything more for her . . ."

"I guess so."

There was silence between them, then Matt said, "I wasn't to know, Tess. How was I to know?"

"No." She could see the hurt in his eyes.

"Your mother wants you to call her," he said.

She nodded. "Yes, I will." She stooped, and Matt bent beside her and together they gathered the spilled fruit and vegetables into the basket. As they straightened, Tess said, "I'll go and call her now. Then we must go and see Madeleine." She paused then corrected herself. "Or *I* must go and see her."

"No," Matt said. "We'll *both* go and see her."

Tess called her mother when she got

into the house and arranged that she and Matt would drive over after lunch, pick her up and take her to see Madeleine and collect her from the hospital. Then, when Tess asked whether Madeleine had any clothes in which to leave the hospital, Ellen replied that she had made arrangements with Madeleine's neighbour, Mrs. Norris, to let them into Madeleine's flat. The neighbour had a key, she said. When the conversation was over, Tess called Ruth and asked her if she could come and look after the children while they were gone. She would be glad to, Ruth said.

"Where are you going?" asked Robbie, who had just come downstairs. Tess looked at him closely. She didn't like leaving him but he would be all right with Ruth, she knew; and anyway, he seemed to be recovering well from his minor setback. His question as to where they were going was echoed by Susie and Laura.

"We're going to see your Aunt Madeleine," Tess said. "She's sick. We're going to take her to Grandma's to stay for a few days until she's better."

Robbie, who had been discussing with

Susie and Laura his forthcoming birthday and the party he had been promised, asked whether Aunt Madeleine and Grandma could come to it. Matt and Tess looked at one another, then Matt said, "Well, I expect they're busy but—I tell you what —why don't you write them each a note to invite them. Then we can give it to them when we see them . . ."

Lunch was over fairly quickly and immediately afterwards Matt went to pick up Ruth and bring her back to the house. He and Tess were all set to leave then and they kissed the children and made their way out to the car. They had just got in when Robbie came running after them. They were going without his letters, he said; the invitations to his party. Matt took the two letters from him, carefully folded them and put them in his pocket while Tess silently reassured herself again that Robbie would be okay. Then, a few seconds later they set off.

Ellen, hearing the car pull up, came out to meet them. She put her arms around Tess and wept. Matt looked on.

In the house Jane brought them tea and

some cakes she had just baked and left them alone again. They talked about what had happened. Ellen was at a loss. Why would Madeleine do such a thing? What had happened to make her so desperate? After some hesitation Matt told her what had happened the previous evening.

"I realise now," he added, "that I was very wrong to speak as I did. I misunderstood her. I know that now."

They drove first to Madeleine's flat where Mrs. Norris, Madeleine's downstairs neighbour, had said she would be waiting. Matt parked the car nearby and, leaving Ellen sitting inside, walked with Tess to the house. There, after ringing the bell marked "Norris", they found the front door opened to them by the same middle-aged woman whom Matt had met on his first visit to the house. She recognised him at once, and after being introduced to Tess, whom she greeted with obvious fascination, she invited them in and led the way up the stairs to Madeleine's flat. Here she opened the door, which was unlocked, and ushered them in.

She stood beside them as they looked around. "It's a mess, isn't it?" she said.

Matt nodded his agreement as he took in the soaked towels that lay to one side, some of them bloodstained, and the general look of disarray about the small room. He was aware, too, that the carpet beneath his feet was wet.

The woman, noticing his glance, nodded. "Yes, that's one of the things that got me up here. The water coming through my ceiling. And of course there was the noise from her record player—and the same record playing over and over. It wasn't like her at all. So I came up here and knocked on her door. She had to be in—all that noise, and with the lights on. But she didn't answer. I knocked and knocked—and very loudly—but still nothing at all. Then I went back downstairs and got the key."

"It's so lucky you had one," Tess said.

"Oh, I'd had it for some while. Since the spring when she was away and the decorators were coming in . . ." She moved to the window and looked down the street. "A terrible shock that gave me," she said, "coming in here, and finding her like that."

"How did the hospital know to call my mother?" Tess said. "Did you tell them?"

"Yes. I found Madeleine's address book and gave them her mother's number. Then later I phoned her myself. I told her I had a key to the flat if she needed it." She frowned. "Oh, listen to me talking so much. You'll want to get on and go to the hospital." She took a bunch of keys from the shelf and handed them to Matt. "These are Madeleine's own keys. You'd better take them to her." As he put them in his pocket she added, "Will you be bringing Madeleine back here from the hospital?"

He shook his head. "I don't think so. We're going to suggest that she stays with her mother for a few days."

She nodded. "Yes, that'll be the best thing." She moved to the door, stopped and gazed around her at the room. "It is a mess, isn't it?" she said. "Still, if she's going to be away for a few days it'll give me a chance to get it cleaned up."

"It sounds as if Madeleine has a good friend in you," Tess said.

"Oh, well . . ." She shrugged, awkward, a little embarrassed. Then, as Matt looked into her plain, kind face he saw her eyes fill with tears. "Madeleine's been a good friend to me," she said. She turned away and rubbed a hand across her eyes. "I can't imagine why she did such a thing. I never guessed she had anything on her mind that could be so—so . . ." Her words tailed off, then she added, "It just goes to show, doesn't it? You think you know a person, and you really don't." She stepped across the landing towards the stairs, gave a final little nod and started down.

When she had gone Tess went into the bedroom and a moment later Matt could hear the sounds of drawers opening and closing. He picked up the towels, took them into the bathroom and dropped them in the bath. There he could see further signs of Madeleine's desperation of the night before. There was a bloodstain on the wall, and though the bath itself had obviously been cleaned (Mrs. Norris's handiwork, he thought), the once white rug that lay in it was a mottled pink. He saw, too, on the floor, a razor blade. There were bloodstains on it. He wiped it clean on some toilet tissue, laid the blade beside the hand basin and flushed the paper away.

Returning to the sitting-room he looked around again. Several birthday cards stood on the coffee table. They looked so pathetic there. Some of them had fallen down and he went to stand them up again. Among them he saw the one that had been sent by Tess. As he replaced them he realised that one was not a card at all but a sealed envelope, on which Madeleine had written in the familiar violet ink: *Mr. Matthew Severn.*

Matt stared at it then put it in his pocket. A moment later Tess emerged from the bedroom carrying a small over-night case. "I've just packed a few things," she said. "It's probably all wrong, but it'll do till she gets herself sorted out."

They got to the hospital just before five-thirty and went at once to the ward where Madeleine lay in bed.

As they came through the door she looked up and gave a smile. It was a smile that, to Matt, seemed to be a mixture of happiness, relief and shame. She was pale and there were bandages on her wrists, and she wore a drab hospital nightdress.

Ellen went to Madeleine and kissed her and as they embraced Madeleine looked as if she might start to cry. She recovered her composure, though, and Ellen stood aside while Tess came forward. And then it was Matt's turn. He had wondered what he would do in this moment but now there was no time to wonder any longer. Stepping to her bedside he leaned forward and lightly kissed her cheek.

After the greetings there was an awkward silence, but then the three women, keeping to safe subjects, began to talk. Matt glanced around him. The hospital was relatively new and the wards were small. Madeleine's bed was one of four there, all of them occupied. One of the others was taken by a young woman who lay with her head and arms in plaster and bandages; another by a woman whose appearance gave no clue as to her injuries or illness, and the third by an old woman. The two younger women had visitors at their bedsides; the old woman was alone. Her partly bandaged face pitiably bruised and swollen, she lay with her eyes closed. Matt turned away from the sight and gave his attention again to Madeleine.

"When will they let you go home?" Ellen was saying.

"Anytime I want to," Madeleine replied. "There's nothing else they can do for me now. I only take up valuable bed space. I'm sure they'll be glad to see the back of me."

It was arranged that Madeleine would return to West Priors with Ellen, and a moment later the Sister came by and seeing the case by Madeleine's bed asked if she was ready to change into her street clothes. Matt, Tess and Ellen moved out of the ward while the screens were put around the bed, and while Tess and Ellen went to sit in a nearby waiting-room Matt waited for the Sister to come back out into the corridor. Seeing him there she smiled at him as she approached, a tall, dark-haired attractive woman in her thirties. She said, "I understand that Miss Rayfield will be going back to stay with her mother tonight. That's good. So often patients go through traumatic experiences and then have to be left alone as soon as they leave here."

"Is she all right now?"

"You mean is she fit again? Oh, yes. She's been sewn up and given some blood. She's perfectly all right now—physically."

"Was she in danger?" he asked.

"Of losing her life?"

"Yes."

She nodded after a moment, then went on, "She had cut one of the arteries, but not as deeply as she might have done."

"What sort of state was she in?"

"Well," she said, "I wasn't on duty when she was brought in, but I understand she was conscious—but only just. She'd lost about a litre of blood. Quite a lot, when you've only got five to start with."

Matt had wondered earlier whether Madeleine's suicide attempt was anything more than a gesture. The nurse's words shocked him. "So she would have died," he said.

"Oh, yes, if she hadn't been found. Anyway, as I say, she's perfectly well now, physically, and the psychiatrist has given her the all-clear, so that's it as far as we're concerned."

"The psychiatrist?"

She nodded. "Everyone who comes in here after attempting suicide has to see the psychiatrist before they go. Obviously we want to be sure they're not going to try the same thing again as soon as they get outside." She paused, then said, "Well, if you'll excuse me, I must get on." Matt thanked her and with a little parting smile she stepped away. He watched her for a moment as she walked along the corridor, then turned and made his way to the waiting-room where Tess and Ellen sat side by side. After three or four minutes Madeleine came in. She was dressed in the clothes that Tess had brought, and carried the overnight case.

They drove first to the house in Chiswick where Matt parked the car. Madeleine and Tess got out and, leaving him and Ellen sitting there, went up the narrow stairs to Madeleine's small flat. There Madeleine went into her bedroom to change again into more suitable clothes and to pack a case to take with her to West

Priors. She emerged from the bedroom a few minutes later carrying her newly packed case and with her Burberry over her arm. All she had to do now, she said, was to have a word with Mrs. Norris, and she put down her case and went out onto the landing and down the stairs. When she returned after a short while she announced that she was ready to leave. She was just about to pick up her case again when she stopped and went towards the coffee table where the birthday cards stood. She stood there for a moment looking down at them.

"Is anything wrong, Maddie?" Tess asked.

"No." Madeleine shook her head. Then, with a bright smile she added, "Okay, let's go."

Downstairs, just before she got into the car, Madeleine suggested that she drive her own car to West Priors. That would make it easier for everyone, she said. Ellen could ride with her, and then Matt and Tess would be free to drive directly home. But Matt quickly vetoed the idea. It was no trouble, he said, and besides, he didn't think she was really fit to drive; not with her wrists injured as they were. She made no further protest. Five minutes later they were in the car and heading towards the motorway.

11

WHEN at last the car arrived at Ellen's house Matt and the women got out and went inside. There, while Madeleine took her case up to her room, the others went into the sitting-room where Matt poured drinks for them. Ellen asked if he and Tess could stay for dinner but he said no, they'd better get back to the children. He gave her Robbie's party invitation, and she read it and said yes, she'd love to be there.

A few moments later Madeleine came into the room and Tess put down her sherry glass, went over to her and put her arms around her. They had to be going, she said. "Are you going to be all right now?" she added.

"Oh, yes . . ."

"You're sure?"

"Quite sure, thank you . . ."

Matt turned to Ellen and began to make his farewells, and then Tess was standing beside them also, putting her arms around

216

Ellen, kissing her and saying goodbye. Matt, looking around for Madeleine, saw that she was no longer in the room and going into the hall he called to her up the stairs. There was no answer. After a moment's hesitation he turned and, by the rear door, went outside.

The sun had set and there was the scent of autumn in the evening air. He could hear nothing but the song of a solitary blackbird. And then, from his right came the sound as of a shoe on the pathway and he looked over and made out the figure of Madeleine. He moved towards her.

She was standing by a tall yew tree on the edge of the wide lawn, facing away from the house. She gave a little laugh as he drew near and he heard the ring of desperation in the sound.

As he stopped before her she said, "I just thought I'd come and get a little fresh air. Get rid of the smell of that hospital." As if to endorse her words she closed her eyes and took a deep breath.

Matt said, "I looked around to say goodnight to you but you'd vanished." She said nothing and he looked about him at the shadowed garden. He could smell the roses now. He sighed. "It's so beautiful out here."

"Yes, it is. I've always loved this place."

"How could you not."

She gave a shy, sad half smile, and began to walk slowly across the grass. Matt waited a second and then set off to walk at her side.

After a moment she said, not looking at him, "Thank you so much for bringing Mother and Tessa to see me, and for bringing me back here."

"Oh, it was nothing. I was glad to help."

"I appreciate it very much."

They reached the path and slowly set off along it. She said into the silence that had fallen between them, "It's good to get away from my little flat, too." She shook her head. "God, I shall have to get busy once I get back."

With her words he thought of Mrs. Norris as she had stood in Madeleine's little flat and looked around her. He thought of what she had said: *Madeleine's been a good friend to me . . .*

"I felt so ashamed," she was saying in a low voice, "today—at the hospital."

"Ashamed?"

"That you should all have to come and see me there. That I had done what I did . . . And I felt ashamed and guilty, too, for other reasons. And, in a way, an impostor."

"What do you mean?"

She paused then said, "Did you see the old lady with all those awful bruises in the bed opposite mine?"

"Yes."

She nodded. "She was brought in this morning. She'd been mugged and raped, in her home. She was eighty-one. And the other two women? One was in for surgery and the other, the younger one, had been in a car accident. That's why I felt ashamed and guilty. Those other women were there through no fault of their own. I, though—I inflicted my own wounds."

"It's over now. Forget about it."

"It's easy to say that."

She came to a stop on the path and he halted beside her. "You must try," he said. "Think about the future."

"The future . . . huh . . ." Her voice had a mocking note, as if the future was something that didn't exist. "I'd like to forget this whole thing," she said. "I'd like to."

"You will, in time."

"Perhaps." She turned away and he suddenly saw that her shoulders were shaking, and then the sound of her sobbing burst out and she put her hands up and covered her face. He didn't know what to do. After a little while the sound of her crying became quieter and then ceased.

"I've made such a mess of everything," she said. "Every single thing."

"No, don't say that."

"It's true." She shook her head. "And I don't know why you've been so kind to me. I don't deserve it. Why have you done all this?"

"Oh—let's not go into that."

She took a tissue from her pocket and dried her eyes. "Anyway, I've learned my lesson. Don't worry, Matt, I shan't bother you again. You can rest assured of that."

Silence. He was aware of the singing of the blackbird again, then she went on, "I wrote you a letter. I left it on the coffee table in my flat."

He nodded. "Yes. I found it there when I went up with your neighbour."

Before he could say any more she said, "I'm so sorry about it. About what I wrote. Believe me, I wasn't thinking straight. But that must have been obvious. Please—take no notice of what I said. Tear it up." Then she added, a brisk note in her voice, "Hey, it's time we went in; and you'd better go on home to your nice children."

She turned back along the path. He stood there for a moment, watching her. Then he called out her name, softly, into the quiet, "Madeleine . . ."

She stopped and waited as he moved towards her. Frowning, she looked at the piece of paper he held out. "What's this?" She made no attempt to take it.

"It's from Robbie."

She took it and said, "I can't read it in this light. What's he writing to me for?"

"It's an invitation to his birthday party —this coming Saturday."

Later, back at home, Matt waited till he

was alone then tore open the envelope and read Madeleine's letter.

Matt,
You leave me no choice but to do what I have to do. Being left with no self-respect, and no future at all where you are concerned I've got no reason now to go on living.

I would have given you everything—while you have given me nothing—nothing but unhappiness and, now, the determination to end it all. Which I am about to do.

Remember me. Madeleine

Remember me. If she had died he would have been saddled with those words forever. That she had wished to leave him with so much guilt . . . But no, it was all right. She had not died. She was alive. She was safe. And now he would be all right, too.

He put the letter in his briefcase. He wouldn't mention it to Tess.

Robbie, quite fit again, had been to school all week, during which he had waited impatiently for Saturday to arrive, the day of his eighth birthday and his birthday party.

Matt and Tess had ordered a new bicycle for him which, due to some inefficiency on the part of the Maidenhead store, wasn't delivered until Saturday afternoon, just before the party guests were due to arrive. With Tess keeping the children out of the way, Matt put the bicycle in the garage. Later on he and Tess would dress it up a bit.

Ellen arrived soon after the bicycle's delivery, while Madeleine was the last one of all to turn up, arriving to find Tess and Ellen busy in the kitchen. Having expected her much earlier they had begun to wonder whether she had decided not to come. But then there she was, smiling and looking wonderfully fresh with her fair hair shining and wearing cream slacks and a tangerine-coloured blouse with long sleeves and cream trimmings on the collar and cuffs. She seemed to have quite recovered from the traumatic experience of the weekend before.

She had stayed five days in West Priors with Ellen, after which time Ellen had driven her back to her London flat. Next week she would be returning to work—her boss, apparently, not being any the wiser as to the true reason for her week's absence. While Madeleine had been staying with Ellen, Matt, on the way home from the Television Centre, had called at Madeleine's address in Chiswick to check on the state of her flat and do what he could to ensure that it was ready for her return. He need not have been concerned. Mrs. Norris had already taken care of everything. With the spare key she showed him into Madeleine's flat and he looked around at the results of her labours. There remained no signs of Madeleine's desperate hours.

Now, with the party preparations finished, Tess, followed by Madeleine and Ellen, moved from the house down towards the orchard. In Tess's pocket lay the first clue of the treasure trail that would lead Robbie to the bicycle, which now stood in the garage, festooned with ribbons. As they drew nearer to the orchard the sound of the children's voices grew louder. Above, the sky was cloudless and silently Tess gave thanks that the weather had turned out so well.

She turned and smiled as Madeleine caught up with her and walked at her side and then watched as Madeleine lifted a hand to brush back a lock of hair that blew across her cheek. The bandages were gone now, and the cuffs of her long-sleeved blouse hid the scars on her wrists. That very morning she had been back to the hospital and had the stitches removed.

When they reached the orchard gate Tess opened it and led the way through. The children, under Matt's overseeing, seemed to be playing some kind of game of charades. It was hard to be certain, though, as with all the yelling, running back and forth, the falling over and the frequent collapsing into fits of giggles, the pattern of it all became a bit obscured.

Robbie, seeing Tess and the others approach, ran forward and after saying a breathless hello to Ellen and Madeleine, asked Tess, "Did you bring my present with you?"

Tess laughed. "Yes—in a way . . ." and took out a folded envelope from the pocket of her jeans. "There you are." She handed it to him and at once the other children, the game forgotten, drew closer. Robbie tore open the envelope and took out a small sheet of notepaper. He studied it for a moment then read aloud:

> If a clue you need
> To where your gift might be,
> Hurry, go with speed,
> To the greengage tree.

Robbie frowned for a moment; and then realising the note's significance, whooped and ran off in the direction of the gate. While the rest of the children followed Matt turned to shoot a look at Tess who shook her head and said, laughing, "Well, I don't pretend to be a poet."

With Ellen and Madeleine close at hand, they set off after the children, catching up with them a minute later by the greengage tree. Robbie, in the centre of the group, was saying, "It's got to be here somewhere!" his words immediately being followed by Kevin Kinsell yelling and pointing to a small flash of white on one of the lower branches of the tree. As Robbie reached up and pulled the spill of paper free the children pressed closer. They watched, fascinated, as he unrolled it and read aloud Tess's neatly printed little piece of doggerel:

Now you've got the second clue,
Leave the greengage tree.
Perhaps a place for feathered
  friends,
Will give you number three.

"A place for feathered friends," Robbie repeated, at which Kevin Kinsell said loudly, "A bird's nest. See if we can find a bird's nest."

This was added to by a chorus of voices, topped by Robbie yelling, "No, no, the old chicken coop!" and he darted off again.

Madeleine, watching the excited children, said to Matt, "It's a lovely idea. When did you think of such a thing?"

"Oh," he said, "Tess and I have been setting each other these little treasure trails for years now. Though this is the first time we've done it for any of the children." He chuckled. "It's a lot of fun, it really is."

They walked on and caught up with the

children just as one of them found the clue that Matt had placed at the entrance to the chicken coop. The verse that Tess had written on it led Robbie to the smaller of the two greenhouses where, hidden among some flower-pots, he found clue number four. And so he was led on from clue to clue, his excitement mounting all the while, until he was led at last to the garage and, there inside, to the bright, gleaming, ribbon-bedecked bicycle.

After Robbie had had a chance to try out his new bike for a while everyone went inside to eat. There Madeleine and Ellen helped Tess with the food and, afterwards, with the washing-up. While this was being done Matt set up the projector and screen and ran a film show of a couple of clips from Disney cartoon features and some shorts of Mickey Mouse, Tom and Jerry, and Sylvester and Tweetie Pie. The show ran for an hour, and when it was over the children said their goodbyes and went home, some to walk just along the street, others collected by parents in cars.

When the last of them had gone, Robbie, Susie and Laura had their baths and went up to bed. Afterwards Matt and

Tess sighed with relief at the chance to relax. It had been a long day.

Ellen wasn't going back to West Priors that night but was staying on for two or three days. Madeleine, though, had to get back, and eventually she got to her feet, kissed her mother goodbye and then went out to the kitchen where Tess was doing a couple of final chores. She put her arms around her and hugged her. "Thank you," she said. "I've had a lovely time."

Then, accompanied by Matt, she went out to her car, and there said goodnight and thanked him. "You've been so kind to me," she said.

"Oh, no, please . . ." He waved her words away, but she persisted. "It's true. You have—both of you. And you won't regret it. Really, you can't imagine what this has meant to me: to be here today. I've loved it—being an aunt to the children—helping with the preparations. It's been very special." Her smile seemed to glow as she looked up at him. "It's like I've come through the worst and now I'm safe."

"You *have* come through the worst.

From now on it's upwards all the way for you."

"Yes." She was silent for a moment, then she said. "There's something I'd like to do—if you wouldn't be offended." Her expression was a little anxious. "It's just this," she added. As she spoke she took a ring from one of her fingers, and he saw that it was the ring she had found in the little cottage at West Priors. She gave a little twist and the two sections of the ring came apart. She held one of them out to him. "I'd like you to have this."

"But—why?"

"As a token. Of my gratitude—and my friendship." She held the ring a little closer to him. "Please. Take it. And take it in the spirit in which I offer it."

A little pause, and then he took the ring from her hand. He felt foolish and a little embarrassed. She smiled at him. "Don't misread it," she said, "—the gesture. I'd just like you to have it, as I said, as a little token of friendship."

He nodded. "Fine. If I ever find I'm in danger of being guillotined I'll send it to you."

She gave a little laugh. "Okay, don't

forget." Then her expression was serious again. "You don't think I'm being silly, do you?"

He found himself shaking his head. "No, of course not. Not at all."

"Good. Don't lose it."

"I won't." He put the ring in his pocket.

Later, when he was alone with Tess he showed her the ring. Just for a moment she frowned and her eyes darkened. But then the look was gone and she smiled. "That's a nice gesture," she said, "don't you think?"

"Yes," he said, "it is."

There were two letters from Madeleine on Thursday morning: one for Robbie thanking him for inviting her to his party and the other for Tess and Matt, also with thanks for their kindness and hospitality.

That same day Ellen was leaving Ashford Barrow to drive back to West Priors. It was obvious she had enjoyed her brief stay; and it was also obvious how much she had enjoyed being with the children again, and they with her. When she left them it was with many promises: yes, she would find her father's old album of foreign stamps for Robbie. For Susie she would try to find the little typewriter that Tess had had as a child, and for Laura she would look out for a really nice doll. There was so much stuff in the little cottage, she told them, and she and Jane would have a good rummage and see what they could find.

The day after she left, Friday, Matt brought home a copy of *Exchange and Mart*, and while he sat down for a little relaxation and a much needed drink the children gathered round him as he read out some of the advertisements for puppies available. It became generally agreed then that they would get a Dalmatian and, furthermore, that they'd drive out the next afternoon and try to find one.

They left immediately after lunch on Saturday. With Matt at the wheel of the Rover, Tess beside him and Robbie, Susie and Laura on the back seat, they set off for some kennels in the Wiltshire village of Purton, near Swindon. The children's conversation was all to do with the puppy they were going to buy. They had already decided what to call him: Pongo—after the

Dalmatian hero in the Disney film of *101 Dalmatians*.

When they reached the village and arrived at the entrance to the kennels Matt was surprised to see how many other cars were parked in the vicinity. Robbie looked around in consternation and waved his arms, beckoning.

"Come on, hurry up, or we shall be too late."

The kennels offered many breeds of dog, they discovered, and they joined the group of other visitors wandering around the enclosure holding the separate kennels, exclaiming over the appealing puppies. They saw cocker spaniels, German shepherds, whippets, Yorkshire terriers, labradors and retrievers, but there were no Dalmatians apart from one adult bitch who lay forlornly on a bed of straw in her pen, head on her paws, looking out at the passing people with sad, dark eyes.

"She's not a puppy," Laura said and, putting her head on one side, added, "and she looks so sad."

"Well, maybe that's the answer," Tess said. "Maybe she's the mother of the puppies we've come to see." The children stared through the chicken wire at the dog. "Her babies," Susie moaned, "—you mean they've been taken away?"

Finding one of the attendants, a young woman with a pink, weathered face and a white overall, Matt learned that there had been two Dalmatian pups left that morning and that the last one had been sold just before noon. The children, standing listening to the conversation, groaned at the news, even though by this time they were expecting the worst. They'd held on to a little hope up till now, but the words of the young woman dispelled whatever shred remained.

"We should have phoned first," Matt said to Tess on the way back in the car. "I should have made sure the puppies were available before we set out." He shrugged. "Still, there's nothing to be done now. We'll just have to be patient."

In the back seat Susie clicked her tongue and sighed. "I hate it when I have to be patient."

Not long after they returned Madeleine phoned, for no other reason than to say hello, she said to Tess, adding that she had called several times during the afternoon but had got no answer. They had been out, Tess said, and told her of their visit to the Wiltshire kennels.

A week later, on the following Saturday, not long after lunch, Madeleine phoned again. Tess took the call.

"I'm phoning to see whether you're going to be in a little later on," Madeleine said, "and if so whether it's okay for me to come over . . ." Tess said yes, they had no plans to go anywhere, and suggested that she came for dinner if she cared to. Madeleine gratefully accepted and said she'd be there early, at around five-thirty, if that was all right. "I want to see the children," she said.

After Tess had cleared away the dishes she went down to the orchard where Matt, helped by the children, was gathering fallen apples. One sack, already full, stood by the orchard gate. When more had been gathered they would be collected for a small cider-making company near Windsor. It was a good year for the apple harvest and the fruit lay thickly on the grass around the trees. As Tess went over to Matt he straightened, wiped a hand on the thigh of his stained jeans and grinned at her. "You come to help?"

"No. Sorry to disappoint you."

He smiled at her and Tess stood watching as he put apples into a sack. Then she told him about Madeleine's call. "It is okay if she comes round, isn't it?" she said. "I mean, I can phone and put her off if you'd rather . . ."

He shook his head. "No. We said we'd let bygones be bygones—so we've got to make it possible, haven't we?"

Madeleine got there just after half-past-five and Tess took her down to the orchard where Matt was still working—alone now, though, as his erstwhile helpers, long since bored with apple-gathering, had turned to more enjoyable pursuits. After Madeleine had greeted Matt she and Tess went off in search of the children.

They found Robbie, along with Kevin Kinsell, playing in the shrubbery behind the old shed, while Susie and Laura were close by playing house. The two girls had just finished washing several items of dolls' clothes and were hanging them out on a makeshift clothesline to dry.

When Madeleine called their names they

236

came to her and she kissed them each in turn and, with eyes wide, told them she had brought them a little present. "Something for all of you," she added, as their faces lit up in anticipation.

"Oh, you shouldn't have, Maddie," Tess said. "You brought them presents just the other day."

"Oh, *those* things," Madeleine said, "they were nothing. Besides, it's nice to be able to get them something they really want." She turned back to the children. "Well," she said, "are we going to stand here all day or shall we go and fetch it?"

The children didn't need asking twice and with Kevin tagging along behind they followed her up the path to the front of the house to where her car stood at the kerb. Tess and Kevin stood side by side at the gate and watched as Madeleine unlocked the hatchback of the car, swung it up and lifted out a wooden crate. She put it down at the feet of the children and lifted the lid. The cries of the children took Tess hurrying across the pavement and a moment later she found herself staring down at a small Dalmatian puppy.

12

"WHAT'S the matter?" Tess said. She was sitting in bed, leaning back against the pillows. Matt, wearing his dressing-gown, was sitting on the edge. The clock nearby said eleven-twenty. Madeleine had left to return to London just after half-past-ten. "Could it be," Tess said, "that you're upset because she stole your thunder?"

"Oh, don't be so bloody ridiculous!" He could feel his anger growing swiftly. "It's not that, and you know it."

"Then I don't understand. We said the children could have a puppy—and now they've got one. *And* it's a Dalmatian. I don't see what the problem is."

"For one thing," he said, "when we got a dog for the children I'd prefer to have chosen it ourselves."

"What do you mean?"

"I mean have you looked at it—the quality of the animal?"

"You mean maybe the pedigree isn't

that brilliant? So what; we're not going to enter her for shows, are we?"

"Oh, for God's sake, Tess." He shook his head. "Are you determined to be difficult. Of course we're not going to show her, and it doesn't matter at all if her pedigree isn't that great. That's not the point. The point is that it's one of the most pathetic-looking puppies I've ever seen."

He thought back to the moment in the orchard when they had come to him, the puppy, to save arguments among the children, held in Tess's arms. A present from Aunt Madeleine, the children had told him excitedly and he'd forced a smile and said how kind Aunt Madeleine was. And then he had taken the puppy from Tess, stroked it and put it down in the grass, and there he had noted its passivity, the way it just sat there, showing no curiosity, no energy. He'd been filled with anger. When he'd envisioned a dog for the children he'd seen a specimen with some life in it; not this creature with its lack-lustre eyes and dull coat.

Now, shaking his head as Tess gazed disapprovingly at him, he said, "Why the hell did she have to go and do that? Suppose we'd already bought a dog?"

She made no answer, and after a moment he took off his dressing-gown, got into bed and switched off the light. The house was silent. The puppy was downstairs in the kitchen, in a box with newspapers spread on the floor around it. Madeleine had said she had got it from a pet shop, and that it was eight weeks old. As it was a female, the children had sought another name, soon settling on Perdita, the name of Pongo's mate in the Disney film. Now it came to Matt that *perdita* was the Italian word for sorrow, and as he pictured the sad-looking creature he thought that perhaps the name was an apt one.

As he lay there other images came to his mind, and he saw again the look in the children's eyes and realised that the light shining out had been an expression of pure happiness. They had a puppy; something which, with the temporary nature of their residence in America, had been denied them. And he knew that whatever his feelings might be right now, the puppy was here to stay. It might not be good enough for him, but it was more than good enough for them. In their eyes, blinded to its faults by their adoration, they had got exactly what they wanted . . .

Out of the silence Tess's voice came to him.

"Matt. . . ?"

"Yes?"

"Please—I know Madeleine makes mistakes, but she's bound to. She's so anxious. Don't you see? She wants so much to be accepted again."

"Yes . . ."

"So, please, can't you give her the benefit of the doubt?"

He nodded in the dark. "Yes, I guess you're right."

After a while he slept.

When, later, he lay with his eyes open again and staring out, he realised that he had been awakened by a sound from downstairs. He sat up and switched on the bedside lamp. Tess was sleeping soundly. He slipped out of bed and crept onto the landing. There was a light coming up the stairs and as he started down he heard the faint sound of movement from the kitchen. Robbie must be there. He reached the hall, moved to the kitchen door and opened it. Standing in the doorway he looked at Robbie kneeling beside the dog's box.

"I heard her crying," Robbie said. As he spoke, the puppy, paws on the side of the box, stretched up and licked his face.

Robbie grinned but Matt frowned. "Don't let her do that."

"Can I take her upstairs with me?" Robbie said. "She's lonely down here."

"No, I'm sorry."

"Oh, please. Just for tonight."

"No, I'm sorry. You take her upstairs tonight and she'll be there every night. No, I'm afraid she'll just have to whine. She'll soon get used to it." He ran a hand over Robbie's untidy hair. "Come on, it's after two. Go back to bed now." An arm around his shoulders he moved with him to the door. "And don't wake your sisters," he added.

Sitting behind the wheel of the car, Matt took a glance at his watch. They couldn't go on much longer. Outside in the Chiswick side street the girl and the man waited, arm in arm, near the entrance to a small factory. Several yards further on stood a child, a boy of about ten years old in ragged jeans. There was only time for one more shot, Matt was sure.

And then, when everybody was ready in place there came the shout, "Turn over," followed by the identification of the scene and then, seconds later, by the demand for "Action!"

At the word the couple began to move along the pavement while at the same time the boy, calling out, "Mummy! Mummy!" ran towards them.

The woman, letting go of the man's hand, cried out, "Billy!" and stooped to the oncoming child, catching him in her arms. The little group stopped close to the car. Matt got out and closed the door and leaned back against it.

"Cut. Print it," rapped out the director, and the actors relaxed. "Check the gate!" The instructions carried on. Swift, efficient activity went on around the camera for a few brief moments and then the assistant came over to Matt and the others.

"Okay," he told them, "it's a wrap."

Matt said his goodnights to the cast and crew and started away, the small crowd that had gathered to watch eyeing him curiously as he passed by. He walked briskly, anxious to return to the Centre to change and go home. His car was parked in the next street. He reached the corner then came to a sudden halt as Madeleine stepped towards him, smiling.

"Madeleine—what are you doing here?"

"You forget," she said, "I happen to live just up the road." Then she shook her head. "But no, I didn't just stumble on you by accident. I phoned Tess earlier on and she mentioned that you were filming here, so I came along." She half raised her carrier bag. "I've just been doing a bit of shopping."

He nodded. She had walked beside him as he had set off along the street and now they had reached his car. "Did you watch any of the scene?" he asked.

"A little. Have you finished now?"

"Yes," he said and went on to say that this particular location shooting schedule was now completed and that he'd be back at the rehearsal rooms in West Acton the next day. "We finish the sixth episode at the end of the week. And that's it." When she asked him what he would be doing next he said he didn't know. He was up for a part in a new serial, he said, a period drama set on the Devonshire coast, but hadn't heard anything further about it since the interview with the director.

They chatted for another minute or so then Madeleine asked, "Could I talk to you for a minute?"

"Sure . . ." He nodded, then added quickly, "but I've got to get back to the Centre and change out of my costume." He indicated the grey suit he was wearing.

"It won't take long—just a minute or two." She gestured towards the car. "Could we sit inside for a second?"

He got in, opened the passenger door and she got in beside him. Then, turning to him she said, "I wanted to apologise."

"For what?"

"For giving the children the puppy."

"Oh?"

"Yes. I realised straightaway that I'd done wrong. I knew that you'd tried to get one for the children and had had no luck, and I knew how disappointed they were, how much they wanted one. But even so I should have talked to you about it first."

With her words he felt his resentment towards her draining away. "Forget it," he said. "Yes, you should have consulted us first, but—well, it's done now. And anyway, the children are mad about her, so everything's working out all right."

"I'm so glad you say that. Sometimes it's hard to know what to do for the best." She smiled. "Well, I feel better now. I had to see you, though. It was so much on my mind."

"Don't worry about it any more."

"No, I won't." She gave a sigh. "Well, I'd better let you go . . ." She pushed down the handle and opened the door. "Goodbye, and give my love to Tess and the children. I'll see you all soon."

"Fine. Okay . . ."

She left then, and he watched her as she moved along the street and turned the corner. She didn't look back.

He was getting out of the car at the TV Centre when he saw that she'd gone off without her carrier bag. He looked inside and saw a lettuce, a carton of milk and a smaller bag containing some frozen items —peas, beans, two small lamb chops. He shook his head in annoyance. He'd have to drop the bag off at her flat on his way to the motorway.

In his dressing room he washed and changed and handed in his key. Then, back in the car a few minutes later he rejoined the hectic rush-hour traffic and set off in the direction from which he had come. Twenty minutes later he stood at Madeleine's front door ringing her bell.

"Matt. . . ?"

Her voice had come from above and he looked up and saw her gazing down at him from the window of her sitting-room. She called out with a little shake of her head, "I know, don't say it—I'm a terrible pain in the neck. Hang on a minute." Her head disappeared from view for a few seconds, then she was there at the window again.

"Matt?" She was holding out something in her hand. "Catch."

He reached out and caught a white object that turned out to be a handkerchief wrapped around a key.

"Come on up," she said and, without waiting for an answer, she withdrew her head and pulled the window down.

With the key he let himself in and went upstairs. When he knocked on her door she opened it at once.

"Matt, come in." As he entered she

247

closed the door behind him and said, "I'm sorry I couldn't come down, but I was just finishing dressing after my bath." She was wearing a long cotton housecoat of dark blue, with white trimming on the sleeves. Her fair hair was casually tied back with a blue ribbon. He could detect the faint smell of perfumed soap and cologne. From the kitchen came the smell of coffee.

He held out the bag of groceries to her and she thanked him profusely. As she took them to the kitchen she said over her shoulder, "I've held you up so badly. Please forgive me. It was so careless of me."

"Not to worry," he said. "It's just a pity I didn't notice it when you first got out of the car."

She came back into the sitting-room and urged him to sit down. "I've just made some coffee," she said. "Have you got time for a cup? Oh, please say yes."

"Well, okay." He grinned. "It smells so good . . ."

He sat down on the sofa and she brought in cups and saucers and set them on the small table. When she had poured the coffee she handed him a cup, saying, "No milk or sugar for you, right?"

He nodded. "Right."

He sipped from the cup, leaning back on the sofa and stretching out his long legs. When he had finished she poured him another. They talked of everyday things; he told her a little about the TV series and of his time in America, and in turn she told him something of her own work. As they talked he realised that he was feeling much more comfortable in her presence and that she, too, seemed to be more relaxed and at ease. When he remarked on this latter she looked thoughtful for a moment and said:

"What I did—the other week—" She broke off and looked down at her wrists, and Matt caught a brief glimpse of the scars there. After a moment she went on, "I think in a way—well, that it was good for me."

He shook his head. "I don't understand."

She smiled. "No, of course you don't." She glanced again at her scarred wrists. "What I did was a terrible thing. Terrible.

And I'm so thankful now that I didn't succeed."

He said quickly, "Madeleine, you don't need to talk about all that," but she nodded vehemently. "I do. I want to. If you can bear it. I haven't talked about it to anyone—and I've needed to." She was silent for a moment, then she went on, "When I found out what had happened; realised that I wasn't somewhere in heaven or—or in hell, but just in some rather ordinary hospital, I was disappointed. Only for a second or two, though. And then, my God, I was glad, so glad. And I realised how stupid I'd been. How insane it was—the whole thing." She paused. "It's taught me a lot, you know. It's changed me. Completely."

She stayed silent for a moment then she continued, "Maybe it was what I needed. A real shock to get me to see reason. And it was that, believe me." She smiled at him. "Anyway, here I am; a bit scarred and a bit bruised, but in one piece and, all told, better off."

Neither spoke for some moments, and when they did it was of more mundane matters. The conversation got round to the children after a while and Matt went out to his car and brought in his briefcase in which he had a batch of snaps of the children, taken just before they had left California. Over a small scotch he proudly showed the pictures to Madeleine. By the time she had slowly looked through them he saw that it was after eight o'clock. He rose to his feet. It was getting late, he said; he must get off. Madeleine put down her empty cup, got up from her chair and stood before him.

"Thank you," she said.

"For what?" He put his open briefcase on the arm of the sofa while he put the little wad of snaps back into their envelope.

"For everything. For being so kind, so understanding. For listening to me."

"Oh, please . . ."

"No, really. And when I think back I'm amazed that you were as patient with me as you were."

"Don't," he said. "Don't go into it all."

"It's all right," she said. "Don't worry." She shook her head. "Dear God, what a mess I was. And what an awful, terrible mess I made of everything." She turned away from him, and almost involuntarily he reached out and took a step towards her. As he did so he caught the edge of his open briefcase and tipped it, bottom up, onto the sofa. As he lifted it, its contents poured out and he cursed and began to pick them up again. Madeleine helped him to gather up the various items and passed them to him in silence. One of the things she handed him was the ring she had given him that evening in West Priors after he had taken her from the hospital. He took it from her and put it back into the case. Then, turning back to her he saw tears spill onto her cheek. "Madeleine, don't," he said, "please."

"Will you forgive me?" she said. "Can you forgive me for all I've done?"

"Don't even talk about forgiveness. It's finished with. It's over."

"Oh, Matt!" She cried his name brokenly, and then suddenly she had swayed towards him and he was holding her in his arms. Her face was against his shoulder. She was sobbing.

"Don't," he murmured, "Don't—please don't." She felt very frail in his arms.

"Oh, Matt," she cried. "Say it. Tell me you forgive me—for everything."

"Madeleine—"

"Please! Tell me!"

"Yes," he said, "yes, of course I forgive you."

At his words she sobbed out, gasping at the air, all her control gone. He held her closer to him, and, at last she was quiet once more. It seemed to him that they stood together for a long time, like two statues, not moving. He couldn't see her face. And then she stirred in his arms, leaned back a little and raised her head. "I shall be all right now," she said.

"Will you?"

"Yes. And you'd better go. You're going to be very late." She paused for a moment. "Just one thing before you leave."

"What's that?"

"Kiss me. Just once." Her eyes gazed into his, pleading. "Please, just once . . ."

He stood there, not moving. She spoke again.

"Please. Just once. All I need is a little blessing."

On the way home he thought about the

kiss. He had bent his head and kissed her lightly on the mouth. It had been a gentle kiss, chaste and without passion, and she had made no attempt to return it. Now, though, he told himself, it had been a mistake. But then the next moment he admonished himself: no, he was just being over-cautious.

Next day. Wednesday. Afternoon. He had not long returned to the rehearsal room after lunch in the canteen when he saw the red telephone lamp winking on and off. Meredith, the tall, striking blonde assistant to the director, answered it and then came over to where Matt sat reading his newspaper. There was a package for him downstairs at reception, she told him.

"For me?—a package?" He was puzzled. He looked up at the clock; there was just time to go down and see what it was all about.

"A young woman handed it in," the man on the reception desk told him. He handed Matt a small package wrapped in brown paper and Matt asked whether she had given any name or left any message.

"No, she didn't."

"What did she look like?"

"As I say, she was young, and very attractive; blonde and wearing a tan raincoat."

Madeleine. Back in the rehearsal room Matt put the package into his briefcase. He would open it later on.

It was just after five o'clock when, in the car and ready to start for home, he took out the package and tore off the wrapping. Inside was a small, slim box and a little wrapping of brown paper containing his spare set of car keys, a cheap, beaten-up ball-point pen and a single cufflink—things that must have fallen from his case when he had been with Madeleine in her flat on Monday. Opening the box he found inside a gold Sheaffer pen. There was a note with it. He took it out and read:

Dear Matt,

When you upset your briefcase you did a very poor job of picking every-thing up. Mind you, I admit that there were distractions—not least a rather tearful female. Anyway, I found the keys, the cufflink and the pen down behind the sofa cushion. I hope you didn't leave anything else; if you did I don't know where it might be as I've looked very carefully where these were found.

Yours, M.

PS The pen I'm sending for the simple reason that you obviously need one.

He stared at the pen for a moment, then took off the cap and tried the nib on his left thumb. She had filled the pen with violet ink.

He put the pen, its wrappings, and the other items back into his case. He was aware of a feeling of resentment against her; everything had been going so well— and now she had spoiled it all.

He didn't mention the gift of the pen to Tess when he got back. Life, he felt, would somehow be simpler if he didn't.

The next afternoon when he left the studios at the end of rehearsals he found Madeleine waiting there.

13

REHEARSALS had gone well that Thursday. In addition, during the morning Matt had heard from his agent that he had got the part he was after in the period serial, *Cousin Lily*. Rehearsals would begin on the 17th October, after which, a week later, there would be location shooting on the Devonshire coast.

At the end of the afternoon when rehearsals were over he got into his car and drove towards the exit where the barrier lifted to let him out. He had just eased the car out onto the road when he saw her. Madeleine. She was walking by on the other side of the street, near the entrance to West Acton underground station. Then, just in the moment after his eyes had fallen on her she turned her head, saw him and waved. His spirits sank. What was she doing here?

When she waved to him a second time he smiled back in acknowledgement, pulled the car into the opposite kerb and put on the brake. Almost at once she was there at the passenger window and he leaned across and wound it down. She was wearing her tan Burberry and a neat little yellow hat with a brim. She carried an umbrella. "Well, hello!" she said, beaming, and then, with an arch widening of her eyes, she added, "You know, we're going to have to stop meeting like this."

Matt could feel his own smile had all the plasticity of cardboard. "What are you doing here?" he asked.

"I was just going into the station."

A sudden flurry of rain spattered against the windscreen and she looked up and frowned. Then before Matt could say anything she had reached in and was releasing the door lock. "May I get in for a second," she said, "before I get soaked?"

"Yes, of course," he said and she opened the door and got in. "What are you doing out this way?" he asked.

She said quickly, "Now don't you go jumping to conclusions; I didn't come here to see you."

He gave a hollow chuckle. "I didn't say you had."

She laughed, the sound artificially bright, then said, "I've had to go to a company nearby, on an errand for my boss," and began to go into details of the address and nature of the errand, and with each word Matt became increasingly sure she was lying. When she had finished she asked, "Are you going home now?"

"Yes. Are you?"

"Yes. Could you give me a lift?"

"Sure." He felt he could do nothing but agree. A moment later, with the rain beating down, he was setting the car back on the road and joining the throng of traffic.

After a while Madeleine said, "Did you get it—the pen?"

He kept his eyes on the road. "You shouldn't have done that, Madeleine," he said. "It's a lovely pen, but you shouldn't have done it."

"Why not? If I want to give somebody a little present, then where's the harm in it?"

"It's not as simple as that."

"It's not? Why not?" When he didn't answer she said, "But you do like it."

"Yes, of course. How could I not?"

She shrugged. "Then that's all that matters."

He persisted, "But you shouldn't have done it."

She nodded. "All right, so I shouldn't have done it." With her right hand she lightly rapped the back of her left. "Smack, smack, naughty Maddie. Smack, smack, naughty Maddie's done it again."

He said nothing. "Did you show Tess the pen?" she asked.

He paused briefly. "Yes, of course."

"Did she like it?"

"Very much. Of course she did."

At last, after what seemed an age, he reached the little side street in which Madeleine's flat was situated and pulled up in a vacant spot near her front door. He didn't turn off the engine.

"Have you got time for a drink or a cup of coffee?" she asked.

"No, not tonight, thanks all the same. I must get back."

"Oh, well . . ." She shrugged, but made no move to get out. "My God, look at that rain." Matt had turned off the wipers and the rain washed unhampered down the windscreen. "Are you sure you won't come in for a drink?"

He shook his head. "No, really, thanks."

Still she sat there. After a few moments she said, "I won't mention this, by the way."

He turned to her, frowning. "You won't mention what?"

"This. Your driving me home."

"Why not?"

She shrugged. "I just think it would be best not to. You know, just in case somebody jumps to the wrong conclusions."

He stared at her. "Madeleine, I don't understand what you're saying."

"I'm not saying anything." She paused. "What did you say to Tess on Monday, when you got home late?"

"Nothing—why?"

"Did you tell her why you were late?"

"Yes, of course."

"Really? Was that wise?"

"Wise?"

"I mean, wasn't she bothered by it?"

"Why should she be bothered?"

She shrugged. "Well—your being with me."

He sat quite still for a moment, his mouth grimly set, then, trying to make light of it all, said, "You know, I don't think we're seeing things in quite the same way, somehow. Why should she be concerned about it?" He laughed. "I'm afraid you've lost me, Madeleine."

"Oh, Matthew . . ." She shook her head. "Don't be deliberately dense. It's not necessary."

He glanced at his watch. "I've got to get home," he said.

"Oh, listen," she said, as if suddenly remembering something. "I've got to go by West Acton again tomorrow, just after midday. Would you like to meet for lunch? I'm sure we could find some decent little restaurant around there somewhere." Her tone was casual.

"I'm sorry. I can't. I shan't be there tomorrow. We shall be at the studios for the taping."

"Well, I could meet you at Shepherd's Bush, if you like."

"No, no." He put a more positive note into his voice. "I'm sorry. I shall be much too busy."

"Oh, shame. Anyway, perhaps we can arrange it for another day, soon."

"Maybe." His tone was non-committal. Above the noise of the idling motor there was only the sound of their breathing and the rain. She made no move to go. He looked at his watch again.

"You *didn't* tell Tess, did you?" she said.

"Tell Tess? About what?"

"About us. Our meeting the other evening."

He forced a laugh. "My God, you make it sound like some clandestine arrangement between us."

"Not at all." She gave a little smile. "But perhaps that's how you feel about it. Do you?"

"Of course not. I don't have any feelings about it at all. We met by chance. It's no big deal to make a song and dance about."

"No, I know it isn't." She smiled again. "But why didn't you tell Tess about us? And about your pen?" She paused, then added, "Because you didn't. I know you didn't. I talked to Tess today and it was quite obvious that she had no idea at all, either about the pen or that you came in for coffee."

"I don't want to go on with this conversation," Matt said. "It's not leading anywhere. Anyway, I must go home," and he added, consciously choosing his words, "to my wife and children."

Silence again. He was vaguely aware that the rain had eased and was now just spotting on the windscreen.

Madeleine said: "You know, I thought for a while that you'd changed."

He frowned, not understanding. "I—changed?"

"Yes. That you were more like yourself, somehow. Your old self. More—I don't know—warm, I suppose; a little more sensitive, caring. Perhaps I was wrong."

So everything had gone for nothing. He knew now that no matter how many times she apologised for past mistakes it would make no difference. She seemed to have no real awareness of her actions and he felt now that she would never change.

He glanced at his watch. "You'll have to excuse me, Madeleine," he said, "But I've really got to be going." He looked at her without smiling. "Okay?"

"Okay." Her own expression was serious. She opened the door. "Thanks for the lift."

"Don't mention it."

She got out and stood on the wet surface of the road in the last pattering of the rain, holding the door. "Goodnight, Matt," she said.

"Goodnight." He didn't return her smile but simply nodded. She stood there, looking in at him. When she spoke again there was no trace of humour in her tone.

"I love you, Matt," she said.

Then she slammed the door and he put the car in gear and drove away. He didn't look back.

When he got home he mentioned nothing to Tess about this latest incident. Perhaps there would come a time when he would have to, he thought, but not yet.

The meeting with Madeleine left him with a strange feeling of tension that remained with him throughout the evening, and he found it hard to get the thoughts of her out of his mind. Time and again he kept thinking of the last words she had spoken. *I love you, Matt.* The words went on, repeating over and over in his mind.

To mark the end of the series next evening a late dinner had been arranged at a restaurant near the Centre and when at last the long working day was over Matt made his way towards his car which he had left in a quiet side street near the studio entrance. As he went through the gates the time was just coming up to nine o'clock. He waited for a break in the traffic, crossed over and walked to his car. As he reached it he came to an abrupt halt. In the dimness he could make out somebody sitting inside it. After a moment he strode forward and opened the door. As he did so the interior light lit up Madeleine's face as she turned to smile at him.

"Surprise, surprise," she said. She was wearing her tan Burberry and the yellow hat he remembered from the last meeting. He could hardly believe it: she was there in his car, sitting in the front passenger seat.

"What are you doing here, Madeleine?" he asked.

She shrugged and smiled. "Waiting for

you, of course. What do you think I'm doing?" She patted the driver's seat beside her. "Aren't you going to get in?"

He ignored the question. "How did you get into my car?"

"Who's a naughty boy then?" She wagged a finger at him. "Who left his car unlocked?"

This was a lie. He never, never left his car unlocked and surely she didn't expect him to believe such a thing. He didn't contradict her, though. He stood there for another second and when she made no move to get out, he got in beside her and sat behind the wheel. When he shut the door the interior was once again in darkness. "Why were you waiting for me?"

She shrugged. "I thought it would be nice to see you."

"Well," he said, "You've seen me now."

"Oh, Matt, don't. Please. Don't say that." She put her head a little on one side and asked, "Could you drop me off on your way home, please?"

He shook his head. "I'm sorry, but I'm not going straight home tonight."

"No? Are you going somewhere nice?"

"I'm going to a restaurant with the company; a little celebration to wind up the series."

"How nice. I suppose you wouldn't care to extend the invitation?"

"I can't. It's not my party. I told you, it's just the company."

"Ah, well." She shrugged. "I'll wait for you if you like," she said. "I could sit in the car. I wouldn't mind waiting."

"No." He shook his head. "I don't want you to wait for me." He could feel himself beginning to tremble slightly. Hatred for her was welling up in him like a spring. Steadying his voice he said, "I want you gone. I know that's likely to hurt you— but I don't care any more. I realise that all along I've been trying to protect you from hurt. And it's ridiculous. From now on it doesn't matter to me whether you're hurt or not. I don't care about your feelings."

He came to a stop. She had put her hands over her ears and begun to shake her head, and now she began to hum; an odd, tuneless little combination of notes that had the sole purpose of preventing her hearing the words he spoke. Then, seeing that he had stopped speaking, she put her hands in her lap.

"I didn't leave my car unlocked," he said. "*You* unlocked it. How?" He was silent for a second as she gazed at him, then he slowly nodded. "Of course—the spare set of keys I dropped when I was in your flat . . . What did you do—get them copied before you let me have them back? You must have done. And how come you're in this area again? More errands for the boss?" He shook his head. "No, I don't want answers, Madeleine. I don't care. I just want you to go."

"But Matt—" Her expression was pleading as she stared at him. "I told you —I love you."

"You don't know what love is."

"Don't say that. I do. I *do*. That's why I've done all these things. Hasn't that ever occurred to you?"

He turned his head away. "I'd like you to go, Madeleine," he said. "I can't drive you home."

And then, after what seemed an age, he heard the sound of movement, the rustle of her coat; she was going at last.

The next moment he felt the touch of

her and then she was on top of him. He couldn't believe it. In a claustrophobic, smothering swamping of tan Burberry she put her left leg over him, between his right leg and the door, straddling him. She was unable to sit on his lap because of the steering wheel, but she was not deterred and pressing up against him she reached for his left hand, grabbed it and thrust it up under the folds of her raincoat. With a shock he realised that she was wearing nothing underneath it. He was briefly aware of the smoothness of the inside of her spread thighs and then, higher up, of her wetness and the coarse brush of her pubic hair. As he went to move his hand away she in turn tried to hold it there, pressing herself down upon it. Violently, roughly, he snatched his hand free and, grabbing at her arms, thrust her from him into the passenger seat.

"Get away from me!" He spat the words at her. "You make me sick!"

He got out of the car, moved round to the passenger side and yanked open the door. She didn't move, but shrank from him into the seat. He leaned down closer.

"Madeleine," his face was pale, "please, get out."

"I love you," she said, without looking at him. "I love you, Matt. I love you. I love you. I love you."

He shrugged. "I don't care. I don't care whether you love me or whether you don't. I don't care whether you hate me either. I just want you out of my car—and out of my life."

She swung round to him at this. "Oh, Matt, please, please be kind to me."

"No. I'm sorry. Being kind to you is a luxury I can't afford. It only brings more unhappiness for everyone else." When she still made no move he reached down and grabbed her arm.

She yanked it angrily from his grasp and glared up at him. "Don't you touch me. Keep your hands off me."

"Then get out of the car."

"When I'm ready. And not before."

It was like a familiar play, he thought. The two of them had acted out the same scene before. The only difference was the setting.

"Either you get out voluntarily or I'm going to drag you out," he said. "And don't make any mistake about crediting me with too much gallantry or any crap like that."

She said nothing but turned and began to fiddle with the radio. The next moment a deafening blast of rock music blared out. He leaned in and snapped the noise off. As he straightened again she switched the radio back on. Again he switched it off and then again she switched it on. He switched it off once more and then when she reached for it again he grabbed her. She gave a little cry of pain as his hand fiercely closed around her wrist, and the next moment she was bending her head and trying to sink her teeth into the back of his hand.

Just in time he yanked his hand free and, in a continuation of the same movement, swung his hand back and struck out, hitting her in the face.

He stood back, horrified at what he had done, watching as she put a hand up to her face and touched at the blood that had sprung to her lip. She looked at the touch of red on her fingertip for a long moment then raised her eyes to him.

"I shan't forget that," she said. She

wiped her finger on a tissue that she took from her pocket and with an air of casualness swung her feet onto the pavement. "You're hoping now that I'll go away from here and it will all be over, aren't you?" she said. "No. I'm afraid not." She gave him the semblance of a smile. "Don't worry, I can be patient. Just remember what I said, and see whether I'm right. I *will* have you in the end. You wait and see. One day you'll want me, in some way. And I shall wait for that to happen."

Then, without another word, she was turning and walking away.

He got behind the wheel, turned the car and drove to the corner where the main street crossed. He was waiting for an opportunity to move out into the traffic when Madeleine came running back towards him along the pavement. She tapped on the window.

He ignored her. He wouldn't even look at her. She tapped again, then a third time, and then moved directly in front of the car. He wound down the window.

"What do you want now?" he said coldly.

"Please," she said, "forgive me. You

make me do crazy things. I'm so sorry. Really I am."

He sighed. "Okay, Madeleine, okay." There was no point in arguing with her. "Okay. Now just let me go by."

"Are you going to tell Tess about this?"

"Why should I? She's got enough to cope with without my bothering her with such nonsense." He paused. "Please— stand aside."

He looked into her eyes for a moment, watching as she stepped back, then he eased the car out onto the road and drove away.

14

MATT and Tess had been invited out to dinner the next day, Saturday. Their hosts were James and Alice Palmer, a playwright and his wife who lived in the next village.

Before then, Matt was planning to help Dave Kinsell and repay him for some of the kindness he'd shown them. Dave's mother in Aylesbury was moving house and Matt was going to give a hand. At the same time Tess would be driving to West Priors to spend the afternoon with Ellen and help her choose some curtain fabrics. Leaving right after lunch, she would also be taking the children who, in turn, would be taking the puppy. Better that, Tess had thought, agreeing to their pleas, than to leave her to create havoc alone at home. Though, she told them, they had to look after her, and look after her properly, which meant not allowing her to become a nuisance—and that included any chewing on Grandma's furniture and messing on Grandma's carpets.

As Tess listened to the children chattering away while they got ready it came to her that they were losing their American accents. So soon. How adaptable children were.

Soon after lunch Tess said goodbye to Matt, kissed him, told him she'd be back by six, then got the Rover out of the garage. When the children had piled into the back seat she handed Perdie in along with an old piece of blanket and they set off.

When they got to West Priors Ellen exclaimed delightedly over the puppy, much to the children's delight, and said that Madeleine had told her about it. Then, turning to Tess she added, "By the way, you just missed her."

"She was here today?" Tess said.

"Yes. She came down late yesterday after work, and stayed overnight. She left just before you arrived. You might well have passed her on the road."

"No. I didn't see any sign of her car. Did you tell her we were coming today?"

"Yes."

"I wonder why she didn't wait."

Ellen shrugged. "Who knows?" She frowned. "Actually, when she arrived yesterday evening she seemed to be in a bit of a state. I don't know why, though. She didn't say."

The two women had come indoors into the sitting-room, and from the window Tess could see the children playing with the puppy on the lawn. Perdie wore a little green collar and Susie had attached the lead to it and was trying to make her walk to heel. It looked like a pretty hopeless task. Jane came in with some coffee after a while which they drank as they went over the fabric samples. The selection didn't take long, and then Tess called to the children who, leaving Perdie in the conservatory, came into the kitchen where Jane gave them cold drinks and slices of sponge cake she had baked that morning. Afterwards they all sat talking around the kitchen table.

Half an hour later Robbie got up and made for the conservatory. He was gone only seconds before he was back, saying excitedly, "Perdie—she's gone!"

Tess said, getting up and waving a hand

impatiently, "Of course she's not gone. She can't be. How can she be gone? You haven't looked." With Susie and Laura behind her she followed Robbie outside. Then, standing on the edge of the lawn she watched as the children ran off in different directions, calling to the puppy.

By five-fifteen Perdie had still not been found. Tess didn't know what to do. If she and Matt weren't going to be late for their dinner engagement she and the children would have to set off in the next few minutes. But how could they leave without the dog? All of them: she, the children and Ellen and Jane, had diligently searched the garden area surrounding the house, but there had been no sign whatever of the puppy.

Now Tess shook her head and said, "I'm sorry, but we've just got to leave. We'll have to get Grandma and Jane to keep looking." The children protested at this, and Tess added, "Grandma will phone us when they've found her. And Perdie will be found, of course she will. So don't worry about her."

"But Perdie doesn't know Grandma and Jane," Robbie said. "She only knows us."

He grasped at Tess's hand. "Let me stay and find her. Can I? Please, let me stay."

There were tears in his eyes, and after a moment Tess moved to Ellen, briefly whispered to her and then, turning back to Robbie said, "Okay, Grandma says you can stay, if you really want to. Do you?"

He gave a positive nod. "Yes."

"Okay." Tess addressed Susie and Laura. "Just Robbie, though. You two girls will come on with me. Then tomorrow we'll all come back and fetch Robbie and Perdie home. Okay?" They nodded, and Tess went on, turning back to Robbie, "You'll be all right when we've gone? No tears in the night, or anything like that?"

"No," he answered readily, "I shall be okay."

Ellen put a hand on his shoulder, adding, "Of course. We shall be fine. You three get on home and we'll get on with looking for Perdie. Then when we find her we'll give you a ring."

Five minutes later Tess and the girls were in the car and heading for Ashford Barrow.

When they got there Tess called Matt's

name as they entered the rear door of the house, but he hadn't returned. She looked at her watch. It was already after six-fifteen. As she moved towards the hall Susie and Laura went ahead of her, Susie returning to meet her almost immediately with an envelope in her hand. "It's for Daddy," she said.

"Where did you get it from?" Tess asked.

Susie gestured back into the hall. "By the front door. On the mat."

Tess looked at the envelope. In the top left-hand corner was written *Urgent*, and then, in the centre, *Mr. Matthew Severn*. The writing was in violet ink. From Madeleine. It had obviously been delivered by hand.

Tess went into the sitting-room and placed it by the telephone. "We'll give it to Daddy when he gets in," she said.

When Matt arrived just before seven Tess was upstairs getting ready. The two girls lost no time in telling him about Perdie being lost at West Priors and of Robbie staying behind to look for her. Then Susie, remembering the letter, brought it to him. He could see at once who it was from.

Why was Madeleine writing to him? he asked himself as he looked at the envelope. And what message was so important that she'd driven over to deliver it by hand? His mind went back to the last time they had met and his imagination filled the pages, picturing insults and vitriolic phrases. He didn't want to know. The evening with the Palmers was something he was looking forward to and he wasn't going to have it spoiled by Madeleine.

As he stood there with the letter in his hand he heard the sound of Tess's step as she came into the room. As he turned to her she said, nodding to the letter, "Well, aren't you going to open it?"

He shook his head. "Later." He put the envelope back behind the telephone and moved to the door. "I must hurry and get ready," he said.

Next morning Ellen phoned to say that she and Robbie, with help from Jane and the gardener, had resumed the search for Perdie but without any luck. She then said that after lunch she would drive over to Ashford Barrow and bring Robbie home.

She and Robbie turned up just before four-thirty, their arrival coinciding with a heavy downpour that showed every sign of lasting. Confined to the house, the children were unusually irritable and quarrelsome and Tess was relieved when at last it was time for them to go to bed. Later, when she went up to check on them she found Robbie still awake. She leaned down and gently smoothed back a lock of hair from his forehead. "It's time you were asleep," she said softly.

"I keep thinking about Perdie," he whispered. "What if she doesn't come back? What if we don't find her?"

"You mustn't give up yet," she said. "I'm sure she'll turn up."

"Are you?" There was a surprising hint of cynicism in his words. "I don't think she will," he said. "I think she's gone for ever."

The rain was still falling and when Tess came downstairs she suggested to Ellen that she stayed overnight. Ellen agreed after a little persuasion and phoned Jane to tell her she wouldn't be back till the morning. Tess, standing at Ellen's side while she spoke into the receiver, saw, next to the telephone, the envelope addressed to Matt. She picked it up and turned to him as he stood pouring sherry. "You haven't read Madeleine's letter yet," she said, "and it's marked urgent." Then to Ellen she added, "Madeleine must have dropped it in while we were out yesterday afternoon, and he hasn't even opened it."

"I'll get around to it," Matt said. He handed Ellen a glass of sherry and then gave one to Tess.

She took a sip, then said, "Why has she written to you?"

He shrugged. "I don't know. How should I know?"

She held the envelope out and he took it, turned it over in his hands and then placed it on top of the stereo. She frowned. "Are you still not going to open it?"

He shook his head. "Not yet. It'll keep."

"Why aren't you going to open it?" she said. "Don't you want to know what she's got to say?"

"Not particularly." He knew the instant

he had spoken that it was the wrong answer. And if he had to defend such an answer he'd end up telling her everything that had happened over the past week. "Leave it, Tess," he said. "I'll open it later," and turning away he went from the room and into the kitchen.

Tess followed him a moment later, putting on the light as she entered. She had the letter in her hand. "Matt," she said, "this is marked urgent, can't you read?" She stood there looking at him and when he didn't answer she tore open the envelope and took out the letter inside. He made no attempt to stop her but studied her face as she read the letter, trying to read from her expression what Madeleine had written. To his relief he could see no sign of any distress. Tess looked at him. "What's Maddie apologising for?"

He shrugged, held his hand out for the letter and she gave it to him. As he looked at it his eyes were drawn to a little four-line verse, then he read what she had written above it:

Dear Matt,
Please forgive me for everything. I

really am so sorry. I know I was a pain
—but I promise I won't make any more
trouble for you.

Madeleine

"What's she talking about?" Tess asked.
"Is there something you haven't told me?"

He shook his head. "It's not important." He couldn't tell her the truth.
"I saw Madeleine in the street last week,"
he said, "and we had a little disagreement."

"A disagreement? About what?"

He thought frantically, then said,
"About the dog."

Tess groaned. "Oh, God, no. You don't
mean to say you tore her off over the
puppy? I thought you'd got over all that."

He shrugged. "It's done now, and it was
nothing too heavy. Anyway, it's all right.
You can see that by what she's written
here."

"Yes, I suppose so."

He looked at the letter again and read
the little verse that Madeleine had written:

A little treat's in store for you,
So follow carefully each clue.

First to water, cool and clear,
Not high, butt low; not far,
    butt near.

"What's the 'little treat' she's planned for you?" Tess asked, frowning, and when Matt only shrugged she went on, "The clue, in the letter. It's not too difficult, surely." Then she added with a touch of exasperation, "Oh, come on, Matt, don't be like this. Enter into the spirit of it, can't you? If Madeleine feels she wants to make it up to you then at least give her the chance." She waited for him to speak then said, prompting, "Come on, 'butt' spelt with two Ts. Doesn't that tell you anything? She's telling you to go and look by the rainwater butt in the yard." She paused. "Aren't you going to?"

He didn't move. She looked at him for a few seconds, a look that became a glare. "Then *I* will," she said, and turned away, opened the door and went outside. Standing at the window Matt peered out, watching in the fading light as she moved across the yard and turned out of sight in the direction of the water butt. He heard a step behind him as Ellen came into the room.

"What's happening?" she asked, joining him at the window.

He told her then asked, "Will you be all right here for a minute? I don't want to leave the children alone in the house." He went outside and got to Tess's side just as she reached down to the base of the water butt and pulled out a folded piece of paper that had been stuck in one of its props.

"Aha!" She waved it in front of him and then unfolded it. Squinting in the pale light, she read:

> Do you like this little game?
> Do you still want to play?
> Then a one-wheeled means of
>   transport
> Will help you on your way.

She shook her head and smiled. "Metre's a bit shaky, isn't it?" She pursed her lips. "A one-wheeled means of transport . . . Of course; she means the wheelbarrow." Turning, she hurried off.

"This is nonsense," Matt said as he

followed after her along the garden path, but she laughed and shook her head.

"Not nonsense. It's just that you've got no imagination, and right now you're also pretty low on humour."

He followed her off to the left where an old wheelbarrow stood next to the compost heap. She walked around it, and then pulled out a piece of paper from one of its hollow handles. She looked closely at what Madeleine had written there, then read aloud:

> You're doing well, but do not
> wait;
> Hurry to the orchard gate.
> There you'll find another clue
> To lead to something just for
> you.

"Aw, come on," Matt said wearily. "Enough's enough. Leave it. We'll do it tomorrow."

"Aren't you curious?" Tess said. "Besides, she's gone to all this trouble, so the least you can do is go along with it for five minutes." She turned away and headed in the direction of the orchard, and

Matt hesitated for a moment then, with a sigh, followed in her footsteps.

He caught up with her as she stood by the orchard gate peering at a slip of paper in her hand. "I can only just make this out," she said, holding the paper higher to catch the last of the light. Then she read aloud:

> Now with one more little step
> The trail is at an end.
> The final clue I give to you
> Is held by Edgar Shend.

She shook her head. "Did I read that right?" and peered again at the paper. "Edgar Shend—whoever the hell Edgar Shend might be." Matt looked at her for a moment then turned and started off up the path towards the house. Tess called after him, "Where are you going?"

"Indoors," he answered. "I'd rather sit and finish my drink than carry on with this."

He found Ellen in the sitting-room and he sat down and took up his drink again. He'd hardly got settled when Tess entered.

"Have you ever heard of anyone called

Edgar Shend?" she asked Ellen, adding, "though it's probably an anagram, I should think."

Ellen wrote down the name on a page of the telephone pad while Tess said to Matt, "When did Maddie get a chance to do all this?"

"She had plenty of time," he said. "It wouldn't have taken her more than an hour to get from West Priors. And we didn't get back till after six."

Tess nodded, and then Ellen said, a note of triumph in her voice, "It's the garden shed! Edgar Shend. It's an anagram of 'garden shed'."

"Of course!" Tess said. "Of course!" Then she turned to Matt. "Well, we've done all the work for you, so now you can go and get your present!"

"Oh, not tonight," he said. "It's getting dark. Leave it till tomorrow."

Tess looked at him, then said with a note of false brightness in her voice; "Okay, I'll go and get your present *for* you, seeing that you can't be bothered to go and fetch it for yourself." Without another word she rose from her seat and went from the room.

Matt watched her go, then finished his sherry and poured himself another. He had no interest in Madeleine's gift to him, no matter how clever a trail she had set and whatever the gift turned out to be. He wanted nothing more from her, ever again.

In the quiet of the room he leaned back in his chair. And then, suddenly, the silence was shattered by a scream. Tess's voice. Catching his breath he leapt to his feet, while almost in the same moment Ellen was rising up, a hand to her mouth. Seconds later he was moving to the door and hurrying out into the night.

Above his head a bat wheeled and dipped, while higher still the moon came and went in the cloudy sky. Standing on the path Matt called Tess's name. There was no answer. He spun, dashing away into the garden. Then, just as he reached the junction of the paths, he heard Tess cry out again and all at once she was coming towards him out of the near-dark, a lighted torch in her hand throwing a dancing beam over the shrubbery. Throwing herself into his arms she clutched at him, sobbing hysterically.

He took the torch from her and held her

close. "What happened? What is it?" But she just clung to him, her breath rasping as she sobbed, her face buried in his shoulder. Glancing up he saw Ellen standing beside them, reaching out to her daughter in fear. "What's wrong, darling? Tell us what it is."

In response to the questions Tess simply clutched at Matt, and he soothed her, murmuring, "It's all right. It's all right." Turning to Ellen, he said softly: "Take her into the house, will you?" Then to Tess: "Go on into the house with your mother. I'll be there in a minute."

Putting an arm around Tess's shoulder Ellen gently drew her away, and the two women moved off towards the house. Matt stood watching them go for a few moments then turned and started for the shed.

As he drew near he saw that the open door was hanging askew, cutting off his view of the dark interior. The power of the torch was fading, and as he stepped forward its light flickered and went out. In the pale glow of the fitful moon he stepped into the shed. He shook the torch and the light came on again, the feeble beam picking out the shelves, an old tool chest, a chest of drawers, and various garden implements that stood against the walls.

He turned, sweeping the torch's beam. And then he saw it, suddenly right there in front of him, so close that he had almost touched it with his shoulder.

Palely illuminated in the dying light, the dead puppy hung suspended from the neck, its green collar hooked up over a large, rusting nail. The head and legs dangled limp, the dull, dead eyes looking at nothing. Matt could see a wound in the throat; there was blood there.

He stood, gazing at the thing in horror, until the torch flickered again and finally died.

15

MATT was up before anyone else and as soon as he was dressed he went out into the garden. The air was chill, with the scent of autumn in the air. From the shed he got a spade which he took to an uncultivated patch not far from the remains of the old compost heap and there dug a hole. Then he went back to the shed, wrapped the body of the puppy in an old sack, carried it to the hole and laid it in.

Once the hole had been filled he replanted a couple of small shrubs he had uprooted, then stamped the earth down to disguise the fact that it had been disturbed. The children would never guess there was anything there.

After replacing the tools in the shed he headed back towards the house. Just before he got there he saw Ellen coming towards him. She met him just where the two paths converged by the lawn. "I came to look for you," she said, "to say goodbye."

"You don't have to leave yet, surely," he said. "Stay and relax for a while."

"Relax? You choose your words well, Matt." She shook her head. "No, I must get back . . ."

"Aren't you even staying for breakfast?"

"No, I don't think so. Jane's got to go off for the day, and I want to get back before she leaves." She shrugged. "I'm sorry."

"Tess'll be disappointed."

"I've already told her. I think she understands."

He nodded. "I'm glad somebody does. Tell *me*, Ellen. Help *me* to understand, will you?"

She sighed. "Madeleine . . ." Her voice was low and weary. "I thought I understood her. I realise now I never did, and I never will." She knew what had been at the end of Madeleine's treasure trail. Matt had told her last night. Now she was silent for a moment, then suddenly she bent her head and the tears were streaming down her face. Matt stepped towards her and held her. She felt very frail in his arms.

She had always appeared so much in command of her little world, and now her world had fallen apart and she had no idea what to do.

He held her until her weeping had stopped, then she said, "I must go and say goodbye to the children. They're just getting up." She shook her head. "I don't know how I can face them. And when I think of how Robbie searched for the puppy yesterday." She looked away. "I can hardly believe it happened. I barely slept last night. I just kept going over it all in my mind. It's like some terrible dream; the only trouble is you wake up and it's still there . . ." She looked up at him. "What are you going to do? Have you decided yet?"

"About Madeleine?"

She nodded.

"I don't know. I must do something. Otherwise she'll just go on and on." He gazed at her. "Oh, God, Ellen, I don't know. I just don't know any-more. All I'm really concerned about is seeing that Tess and my children are safe. Beyond that, I don't really care what happens to her."

A little later he watched as Ellen took

her leave of the children. Robbie asked her again to keep on looking for Perdie and she promised she would. When they went out to her car with her she embraced them one by one and, remembering an earlier promise, told them she hadn't forgotten the items she'd said she'd find for them. Matt, listening, silently congratulated her on the front she managed to put up in front of the children.

The traffic was heavy on the roads as Ellen drove back to West Priors and the journey took her longer than she had expected. She wasn't perturbed by it, though; she had more pressing things on her mind.

When she eventually got to the house Jane said, "I was beginning to get concerned. I phoned Tess to ask what time you planned on leaving and she said you'd already left." She added that she herself would be leaving in the next five minutes. She was going on a visit to her widowed sister in Bath, a trip she made three or four times a year. In the kitchen she had filled a couple of plastic carrier bags with fruit and vegetables from the garden and

Ellen helped her carry them out to Jane's immaculately kept Mini.

"Take some flowers as well," Ellen said, and quickly went out and cut a dozen or so cream and yellow roses.

At last Jane was all set. She would be back sometime between six and seven, she said as she got in behind the wheel, then she turned to Ellen who stood beside the car. "And what will you be doing while I'm gone?"

Ellen told her that she planned to look out for some things she'd promised the children. "A few odd things that belonged to the girls and my father," she added.

"In the cottage?" Jane said. "Amongst all that dusty old junk? Must you?"

"I promised."

"Oh, well . . ." Jane shrugged. "Anyway, take it easy."

"I will."

"And don't go lifting anything."

"Don't worry."

"And keep warm there."

"Jane, stop fussing. I'm not senile or incapable yet."

"No, but I know you, once you get involved." Jane started the motor, then, frowning up at Ellen, said, "Are you all right?"

"All right?"

"There's something not—" Jane shrugged. "I don't know. *Is* everything all right?"

"Yes, I'm fine. Go on now or you'll be late."

When Jane had driven away Ellen went back into the quiet of the house. She made herself some coffee and sat in the large, bright kitchen, gazing out at the garden and seeing nothing. After a while she picked up her cup and found that the coffee was almost cold. How long had she been sitting there? She must stir herself. It did no good to keep thinking of Madeleine, and the puppy. She tried not to think of what had happened to the puppy. Although she hadn't seen it in the shed she had pictured it in her mind a thousand times, and the imagined, terrifying image was still there now in her head.

She drank the cold coffee and then, rising from her chair, went up to her room and changed into some old clothes. She had come back downstairs and was just moving to the rear door of the house when the telephone rang. Going back into the hall she lifted the receiver.

"Hello?"

"Mummy?" There was a note of pathos in Madeleine's voice, a sound that had been there over the years whenever she was hurt or upset in some way. "Mummy?" It was almost like the voice of a child.

"Madeleine, hello." Ellen fought to keep the emotion out of her voice.

There was a pause, then Madeleine's voice came again. "You sound different somehow. Is—is anything wrong?" Obviously, Ellen thought, her daughter wanted to know how much she knew about the puppy. "What could be wrong?" Ellen said.

"Good," Madeleine said, then, "Will you be at home for a while? I thought I'd drive over and see you."

"Haven't you got any work to go to?"

"Oh, that!" Madeleine laughed; a false, brittle sound without joy in it. "No, I've taken the day off."

"Well, I'm going to be pretty busy . . ." Ellen had never before made an excuse to avoid seeing either of the girls. Now she could do nothing else.

"What are you up to that's so vital?"

"Oh, nothing much, just that I promised the children I'd look out a few things for them. Things that belonged to your grandfather and you two girls and were put away in the cottage."

"Well, can't Jane help you?"

"Jane's not here. She's gone for the day."

A little silence, then, "Well, I'll come and help you."

"No, no . . ." Ellen protested, "that's okay. I'll manage." She tried to force a note of lightness into her voice but it didn't come out right. Another silence. She could hear only the sound of Madeleine's breathing. With an effort to break the little thread of awkwardness that was holding them she sighed and said, "Well, I must get on . . ." And then she was forcing herself to say goodbye, forcing the answering goodbye from Madeleine, replacing the receiver and moving away. As she emerged from the house she leaned back momentarily against the closed door. She became aware of the beating of her heart and realised that she was trembling slightly.

After a moment or two she left the house and made her way towards the cottage. As she walked up behind the garage she felt the chill in the October air and pulled the collar of her old blouse more closely about her neck.

When she reached the cottage she took the key from beneath the stone frog, let herself in and stood in the open doorway looking around her at all the cardboard boxes and tea chests. The place seemed to have become the repository for all kinds of discarded things from the house. Once, though, it had been the girls' own adopted place and used only to store their own belongings. They had regarded it then as theirs, their own private house. It had been a perfect place for the games they had played.

With a sigh for the past Ellen closed the door behind her, and wondered where to start.

In order to get into the centre of the room she had to negotiate several boxes and odd bits of old furniture. When she had done this she began to make her search. The place was so full of memories. It contained so many things she'd forgotten existed. To her surprise she found several items that had once belonged to her husband; somehow they had found their way here from the house. There were his old golf clubs, his tennis racquet. There, too, were his ciné equipment and three or four boxes of old 8mm film.

Twenty minutes later she had found a doll for Laura, the little sewing machine for Susie and was in the process of trying to find for Robbie the stamp album that had belonged to her father.

She was still searching when she heard a sound at the door and, looking around, she saw Madeleine standing there.

Madeleine entered and closed the door behind her. "Well," she said, "you certainly picked a job for yourself." Ellen could detect a faint ring of desperation in her voice.

Madeleine came towards her and took up the doll that Ellen had put to one side. She wistfully held it to her breast. "I called her Sandra," Madeleine said. She looked down into the doll's face, at the pink, dimpled cheeks framed by blonde curls. The doll wore a white-lace-trimmed dress of pale blue with small sprigs of spring flowers on it. "She was my favourite," Madeleine added.

"Once she's dusted off and her clothes have been washed and pressed she'll be fine," Ellen said. "Laura will love her, and you've got no use for her any more, have you? And it's nice for something to be used, don't you think?" She was making conversation.

Madeleine looked at the doll again and said, "But she's mine."

"Don't you want Laura to have it?"

"Well," Madeleine said, "I mean, I thought I would hang on to my things— my dolls and things—and then hand them on to my own children." She paused. "When I have them . . ."

Ellen stared at her for a moment, her emotions torn. Then she said, nodding and forcing a smile, "Yes, of course. Then you must keep her. I'll find something else for Laura. Maybe one of Tessa's dolls . . ."

Madeleine continued to look at the doll. Then she reached out and handed it to Ellen. "Take her. Give her to Laura. I shan't ever need her."

While Ellen thanked her, Madeleine turned away. Ellen couldn't see her face. "It's cold in here," Madeleine said after a moment. Her voice was low and surly. "It needs a fire. Cheer the place up a bit."

"There hasn't been a fire in here for years."

"Then it's about time there was." Madeleine indicated the cut logs stacked beside the fireplace. "It won't take a minute to get one going."

Ellen started to protest, saying there was no point, but Madeleine wouldn't be dissuaded and at once she went back outside and gathered up kindling and returned and placed it, together with some twists of old newspaper, in the fireplace. She took a book of matches from her handbag, struck one and set the paper alight. When the kindling was burning she placed a couple of logs on top. The flames crackled and snapped. Smiling, she turned to Ellen. "There, that's better, don't you think?"

Ellen forced a smile. All she wanted to do was finish up and get back to the house, to be on her own again.

Madeleine crouched before the fire for a

minute, then, when it was burning steadily she straightened and said, "Tell me what you're looking for and I'll give you a hand."

"Your grandfather's stamp album. You remember it, don't you?"

"Of course I remember it. You gave it to me once."

Ellen nodded. "Yes, not that you used it, though, more than a few weeks. It was a very short-lived phase where you were concerned, stamp-collecting." She paused. "I promised to look it out for Robbie. I'm sure it's here somewhere."

Madeleine nodded, turned to a tea chest packed with children's books and began to look through them. After a moment or two she said, without looking at Ellen, "Have you seen the children since their visit on Saturday?"

When Ellen didn't answer, Madeleine repeated her question. There was a little silence then Ellen said yes, she had driven to Ashford Barrow yesterday and stayed overnight. "I left just this morning," she added. With the words Madeleine stopped her searching, turned and looked at her. It was as if Madeleine was trying to read what was going on in her mind. Under the intent stare Ellen's nerve quickly failed her and she looked away again.

"You know, don't you," Madeleine said at last.

"About the puppy? Yes." Ellen nodded. Still she couldn't meet Madeleine's eyes. "I was there when—when it was found."

"Mummy—*no!*" The words sounded as if they had been wrenched from Madeleine's throat. Bursting into sobs she dropped the book she was holding and moved to Ellen who held out her arms to receive her. She wept while Ellen, weeping also, rocked her as if she were a child. The two of them remained there, standing together, holding on to one another while their tears fell and the fire crackled in the long disused fireplace.

After a while Ellen wiped a hand across her cheeks and straightened, pulling back slightly out of the embrace.

"Why did you do it?" she asked. "Oh, Madeleine, why did you do such a thing?"

Madeleine didn't answer.

"Why?" Ellen said again.

"I don't know. Forgive me, please."

"It's not for me to forgive."

"Tess and Matt—they'll never want to see me again, ever." The tears welled again in Madeleine's eyes.

"I don't imagine they would," Ellen said. Then there was a little silence, broken only by the sound of Madeleine's weeping and the occasional crackle of the burning wood in the fireplace. "*How* did you do it?" Ellen asked. "I thought you had gone from here on Saturday before they came. When I told you that Tess and the children were due you said you couldn't stop."

Madeleine nodded. "I went off before they got here, but then I saw Tess driving the car. She didn't see me. And I came back, just a couple of minutes after they got here. I left my car down at the bottom of the drive and walked up to the house."

"Why?"

"I didn't want anyone to know I'd come back."

"Why did you come back?"

A pause. "I don't know."

"What happened?"

Madeleine turned away at this and gave a little shrug. "From a distance I watched and I saw the children playing with the

308

puppy. Then when they went indoors I came round the back to the door of the conservatory and I saw the puppy again where the children had left her." She came to a stop.

"And you took her away."

"Yes. At first I didn't mean any harm. I don't know what I was thinking of at first. All I could think of was how mean Matt had been to me, and how he'd been angry with me for buying the puppy in the first place. So, seeing it there with nobody around, I—I decided to take it back again." She shrugged. "I just picked it up and carried it to my car. Then once it was there I didn't know what to do with it. In the end I drove over to Ashford Barrow. I thought I'd see Matt and talk to him. But when I got there he wasn't in. So then . . . I did what I did . . ." She hung her head and looked away. "Oh, Mummy, forgive me. Tell me you forgive me."

"I told you—it's not for me to forgive."

"Will *they* ever forgive me. I would forgive *them*."

"For what? What have they done to you?"

"Are you serious?" Madeleine raised her

head and looked into Ellen's bewildered eyes. "What have they done to me? Oh, you know what they've done to me. You know very well. Tess, Matt—between them they've just about ruined my life."

"Oh, Madeleine, no . . ." Ellen stepped back and stood looking at her in disbelief.

"Don't pull away from me like that!" Madeleine said. "You know very well what they did to me. Why else would I do the things I've done?"

"Madeleine, don't . . ." Ellen shook her head. "Don't talk like that. They never wanted to hurt you, *never*."

Madeleine's eyes grew cold as she looked Ellen up and down. "I should have realised," she said at last. "I should have realised they'd get you on their side. I should have guessed—if it's anything to do with Tess then I should have known you'd take her part. As you always have done."

"No, Madeleine, that's not true, and you know it. It's not true. It never was."

But Madeleine went on as if Ellen hadn't spoken. "I shouldn't have come here today. It was a waste of time. I wanted to be with you, though. I was so unhappy. And my one thought was to come here, to be with you." She shook her head and her mouth curled in the touch of a sneer. "I should have known."

Still shaking her head she turned away, leaning over the tea chest in which she had been searching. "And here am I, even now, helping you look for things for *their* children. *My* things." She looked back at Ellen. "You said to me just now that I'd have no more use for them. Right! I won't need them now. And why? Tell me why! I'll tell you why. Because I shan't be having my own children. No. I shan't be getting married. Not now. I shan't get any more chances. And I don't want any more chances. Not after Matt. Not after she took him away."

"Tess didn't take him away," Ellen said. "It wasn't like that at all. You know that. It was—"

But Madeleine broke in, "Please! Spare me. I don't want to hear your defences of your dear daughter." Then, glancing down, she reached in among the books and took out a large, leather-bound album. "Here!" She held it aloft. "What you were looking for, isn't it?"

Ellen nodded and reached out for it and

Madeleine lowered the album as if to hand it to her. But then she drew it back again, opened it and looked at the pages of neatly arranged postage stamps. "This was mine, too. I know it had been Grandfather's but you gave it to me."

"Yes, I know I did . . ."

"And now you want to give it away. First the doll and now this."

Ellen shook her head. "It doesn't matter, Madeleine. You keep it. Keep it if you want it. The doll, too . . ."

"*Their* children. They should have been mine. They should have been *my* children —not hers."

With the ending of her words her eyes blazed and she began to tear at the pages, violently ripping them out and scattering them around her. Ellen briefly put out a hand in protest, but then let her hand fall back to her side and just stood watching as Madeleine completed her mutilation of the album. Soon there was nothing left of it but its cover, which Madeleine tossed aside.

Then she stepped forward and took up the doll. "Mine!" she cried out, and holding the doll by its legs she swung it against the chimney breast. "Mine!"— smashing its head savagely against the bricks. "Mine! Mine!"

As Ellen watched, flinching and screwing up her eyes, she saw the doll's head disintegrate into an exploding shower of pink fragments, saw the blonde wig fly up and land on the floor nearby, saw, again and again, the doll's body, like a weapon, repeatedly brought down— *"Mine! Mine! Mine!"*—striking against the bricks, long after there was any trace of a head left to smash.

And at last Madeleine stopped and, looking at the remains of the doll in her hand, contemptuously tossed it on the floor in front of Ellen. "There—" her breath came harshly, "see how Laura likes the doll now!"

The floor was littered with fragments of the doll and bits of paper from the stamp album. Madeleine looked at Ellen and then around her at the results of her actions, and now there was an expression of bewilderment in her eyes; as if she couldn't quite understand how it had happened. There was a small coal shovel in the hearth and she took it up and ineffectually began to scrape up some of the bits of the doll's shattered head. Ellen gazed at her for a moment longer then wrenched her eyes away and stepped towards the door.

She had just reached it when she felt her wrist seized and she was spun around to face Madeleine who stood glaring at her. "Where are you going?" Madeleine asked.

Ellen shook her head. "Please, let go of my wrist."

"Tell me," Madeleine insisted.

"I'm going back to the house, that's all."

"Why?"

"Why? To get away from you, that's why."

Madeleine nodded. "Yes, I can imagine it. And you'll be straight on the phone to dear Tess, isn't that right?"

"Of course not. Why should I?"

"Oh, you think I don't know. I can imagine what you're like, the two of you." Her hand gripped Ellen's wrist more tightly and Ellen winced in pain. "Please," she said, "Madeleine, you're hurting me."

"Awwww." Madeleine shook her head in mock sympathy. "What a shame."

Then as she released her she added, "And what about me?"

Ellen had never known her like this before. "Madeleine, please," she said and took a step backwards. Madeleine followed. "What about me?" she said again. "What about the way I've been hurt? You never think about that, do you? No. But there, you've never cared, have you?"

Ellen looked at the fury in Madeleine's eyes then turned and moved towards the stairs. "What's the matter," Madeleine said as she followed after her, "are you afraid of me?" Ellen didn't answer until she got to the top of the open stairs, then without looking down she called back, her voice tearful and trembling slightly, "Go home, Madeleine, please. Go home and leave me alone."

Next moment, there came the sound of Madeleine's feet on the stairs and Ellen moved quickly away and began to busy herself with the dusty contents of a box of old framed pictures. In a few seconds Madeleine had climbed the stairs and now came to stand at her side.

Ellen, trying to be calm, said, "These

old pictures, some of them are lovely. Perhaps you could use two or three of them in your flat . . ."

"Why do you walk away from me?" Madeleine said.

Ellen put down the picture she was holding and picked up a large crystal vase. "This is beautiful," she said. "Once it's cleaned up it'll be lovely. It's a shame to leave it here, unused . . ."

"Answer me," Madeleine said.

"Please, I don't want to talk to you." Ellen wouldn't look at her as she spoke. "Not right now. Go away and leave me alone. Please."

"Don't you send me away!" Madeleine cried, and she reached out to take Ellen's wrist again. Ellen stepped back, and moved away towards the stairs. Madeleine watched her for a moment then walked quickly towards her. As she approached, Ellen turned and they stood facing one another, a few yards apart.

"Don't look at me like that," Madeleine said, her voice shaking, "as if I'm some sort of monster; someone you've never seen before."

"You *are* someone I've never seen

before." Ellen took a step back towards the top of the stairs.

"Well, you made me what I am."

"No." Ellen shook her head vehemently. "Not I. I refuse to take responsibility for what you are."

"Oh, yes? And what am I? Tell me. What is it you're thinking? That I'm mad? Is that it?"

Ellen stared at her for a moment, then said softly, her voice breaking, "Yes. God help me, I do."

There was a moment of hushed silence, and then Madeleine gave a cry of rage and rushed forward. As she did so Ellen, fear draining the colour from her face, raised the heavy vase as if she would use it as a weapon.

Madeleine came to a sudden stop before her, gazed at her for a moment and then said quietly, "You think you could stop me with that?"

Ellen's voice trembled. "Please, keep away from me."

"Why?" Madeleine asked. "What will you do?" She paused then added bitingly, "You haven't hurt me enough?"

"Oh, Madeleine—"

"You haven't hurt me enough?" In blind fury Madeleine spat out the words in Ellen's face and lunged forward. A moment later with all her strength she was reaching out and hurling Ellen down the stairs.

Ellen's cry was cut off as she struck the stairs halfway down, then tumbled over and over the remaining steps to the bottom. For a few moments she lay there, all the breath gone from her body, not aware of what had happened. Then as her breath and her consciousness returned she realised. She had fallen. No, Madeleine had pushed her. She leaned forward, gasping for breath, trying to pull herself up into a sitting position. Her hands felt wet with a warm stickiness, and when she tried to stand she found she couldn't make her right leg obey her will. Turning her head she caught a glimpse of a figure standing at the top of the stairs. Tess? No, Madeleine. Of course, Madeleine.

"Help me," she said. "Please, help me." The figure didn't move, and after a moment Ellen turned away and tried once more to struggle to her feet. But still her right leg would not obey. Stretching out her hand she grasped her leg as if she would force strength and movement into it, and as she did so she felt the hard shape of sharp bone beneath her flesh and realised that the thigh bone was broken.

"Help me! Oh, God, help me!"

Still the figure at the head of the stairs didn't move and Ellen raised herself and stretched out her hand towards her. As she did so she saw her fingers were covered with blood. Blood. Where was it coming from? Then, looking down around her she saw the fragments of the shattered crystal vase. As she looked at one of the razor-sharp pieces near her hand she saw blood fall on to it and she lifted the hand and discovered that a shard of crystal was embedded in her chin and another in her neck. God, no, it couldn't be true. Yet there was so little pain . . . She put her trembling fingers to the piece of crystal in her chin and with a fingernail managed to hook it out. The one embedded in her neck, though, wouldn't move for all her prodding, while all around it she could feel the blood oozing out and running down.

She screamed again, "Madeleine! Madeleine! come quickly!" and saw that she just stood there, unmoving.

Tears streamed down Ellen's face as, steeling herself, she put her hand up to her throat again, located the piece of glass and tried once more to pull it out. It was hard to hold on, though; her fingers, slick with blood, kept losing their grip. She began to whimper in her frustration and called out again for Madeleine to come and help her, but still Madeleine didn't move. And then, at last, Ellen managed to grasp the little nub of crystal and with an effort she drew it out of the flesh. And as she did so she saw blood spurt out onto her hand. Eyes wide with terror she pressed her hand to her throat and felt the blood pulsing out between her fingers.

"Madeleine, what have you done?" she cried out. "Oh, dear God, Madeleine, what have you done to me?" She turned her head towards the stairs again and before her eyes the figure of Madeleine shifted and wavered, as if seen through water. The wall, too, moved before Ellen's eyes, the fire, the door, and she felt as if she were spinning, spinning. Pulling herself up she reached out for Madeleine but her weakening hand grasped only the air. Then, suddenly, she felt a heavy blow on the back of her head and she became aware that she must have fallen. Half stunned she lay for some moments on her back and then tried to sit up again. But she couldn't; even if her leg would allow her to she no longer seemed to have the strength. She tried to call out to Madeleine again but this time no sound came and now when she looked towards her she was only very dimly visible behind the curtain of fog that had come down.

Madeleine knelt beside the still body for some minutes after Ellen had stopped breathing. She didn't look at her face, though. She couldn't. She knew what she would see: the blood, the dead eyes looking unseeing at the ceiling. After a while she moved away, then sat down on an old chest and wept.

Later when she was a little calmer she stood and looked around her. She must not leave behind any sign that she had been there.

When she was satisfied she left the

cottage and got into her car and drove away.

She didn't drive through the village on the way back to London, but instead took a roundabout route where there was very little chance that she would be noticed. As she sat behind the wheel she wept bitterly, from time to time crying out, "Mummy . . . Mummy . . ." Her tears for Ellen were mixed with bitterness against Tess and Matt. It was *their* fault that Ellen was dead. They were to blame for it all.

The inquest brought a verdict of misadventure. Ellen, it was clear, had fallen and injured herself and bled to death.

At the funeral Matt stood at the graveside with Tess and felt her shudder through the touch on her shoulder. Her face was ashen. On the other side of the grave Madeleine stood, her face as pale as Tess's. When the service was over they drove back to the house in West Priors where Jane, looking utterly bereft, had prepared sandwiches and coffee and where Tess and Madeleine passed one another without speaking. The reading of the will brought no surprises. Apart from a generous bequest to Jane the bulk of Ellen's estate was to be divided between her two daughters. The house, of course, would have to be sold. In the meantime Jane would stay on for a while; later she would go to stay with her sister in Bath.

When it was all over Matt and Tess drove back to Ashford Barrow where the children waited for them in the care of Ruth. The sight of their eager faces and the sound of their voices as they clamoured for attention made Matt realise that life had to go on; some things might change but for the rest it was business as usual.

16

JUST over a week after Ellen's funeral Matt would be going away for shooting on *Cousin Lily*. The location was just outside the little town of Bridcombe on the Devonshire coast. Set high on the cliffs there, it was a spot that actually figured in the story to be televised. The script of *Cousin Lily* had been adapted from a best-selling novel of the same name, a romantic rags-to-riches tale set in eighteenth century England, the first part of the saga being set against a backdrop of shipwrecks and smuggling. Matt was to play a young American surgeon caught up in the drama. It was a lot of romantic nonsense, he felt, and sure to be a big success.

The location shooting was scheduled to start on Monday, 24th of October, and continue for the rest of the week, the time coinciding exactly with Robbie and Susie's week-long half-term holiday from school. At any other time Matt would have gone off quite resigned but this time it was different. He didn't want to leave Tess right now. She needed him, and to leave her with nothing to do but look after the children wasn't going to make her lot any easier. She should get away from her usual environment for a while, he thought; have a change of scene. The answer, therefore, seemed obvious: he would take her to Devonshire with him.

The idea was aided by the Kinsells who invited Robbie to stay with Kevin over the holiday. And when Susie was invited by Matt's brother and sister-in-law Geoff and Stella, to go and stay with them and Tamsin in Marlborough for the week it all seemed to be working out for the best.

On the coast, most of the television company would be staying at The Five Elms, one of Bridcombe's largest hotels, a situation preferred by the producers as it ensured that everyone would be geographically close. However, when Matt said that he would prefer to stay somewhere privately the production manager made no objection. On making enquiries Matt found a small cottage available to rent just outside the town; it promised to be ideal for the week's stay.

In the days leading up to the week of location filming there was a great deal to be done and it was a busy time for both himself and Tess. He had his role in the serial to think about and, apart from a read-through and rehearsals of the first episode, there were costume- and wig-fitting sessions to attend. For Tess, meanwhile, it was a matter of getting everybody's clothes and other gear ready for their time away.

Matt, aware of her doing a hundred and one various jobs in connection with the coming week, realised he was glad of the many chores that kept her so occupied. While he regretted that they took up so much of her time, by the same token she didn't have much opportunity to dwell on the loss of her mother. Although it was clear how much she grieved for Ellen's passing, still, somehow, her busyness seemed to make it easier for her to bear. The holiday, Matt was sure, would do so much for all of them.

Ironically, though, it was in the matter of the holiday itself that Matt could foresee some slight problem arising. Susie had talked so much about going to stay with her cousin Tamsin that Laura now said she wanted to join her. It didn't matter how much Matt and Tess talked to her of the cottage in Bridcombe, she insisted that she be allowed to go with Susie. And it looked as if she was going to get her way, for when Tess mentioned it to Stella during a phone call, Stella at once said, "Well, why not? If you think she'll be okay then of course she'll be very welcome." So that was that. Laura was told that she could stay with Susie and Tamsin in Marlborough for the week and everything seemed settled.

When Saturday came Robbie was the first to go. Not long after breakfast Kevin Kinsell was knocking at the back door and five minutes later Robbie, tightly holding the small suitcase of which he was so proud, kissed Matt and Tess and went off with him. It was almost noon by the time the others were ready. Then, with Susie and Laura in the car, along with all the luggage, Matt and Tess went to the Kinsells to check that everything was okay. Satisfied, they said their final goodbyes to Robbie then got into the car and drove away.

When they reached Geoff and Stella's house in Marlborough it was mid-afternoon, and somewhat later than they had planned, so not long after their arrival Matt and Tess prepared to get on their way again. It was at this point that Laura infuriatingly said she wanted to go with them. There was nothing for it then but to put her little case back in the car. Susie, fortunately, was as keen as ever to stay with her cousin and turned a scornful glance on her sister. A couple of minutes later Matt and Tess, now with Laura beside them, set out once more.

Leaving Marlborough behind, Matt headed the car back on to the M4 and continued west to the M5. Here they drove south, heading for the coast. Tess, turning, saw that Laura had fallen asleep, and she leaned over the seat, took up the rug and gently laid it over her. She was glad that Laura was with them, Matt knew. As she faced the road again and leaned back in her seat he turned to her.

"You all right?" he asked.

"Yes, thanks."

He nodded. "Good. We'll be there soon."

Bridcombe, situated midway between Seaton and Lyme Regis, was a small town, with a percentage of its inhabitants retired city-dwellers, many of them running small hotels or offering bed-and-breakfast accommodation. Like so many similar coastal towns, it came alive only during the holiday seasons, so that Matt, Tess and Laura, arriving there in late October, found it quiet and looking somewhat forgotten.

Following the directions sent by the cottage's owner, Mrs. Salmon, Matt left the town and after driving west for some three or four miles, came at last to the narrow little road that led to the cottage. And as soon as he saw the cottage a few moments later he knew he'd made the right choice.

Named Middle Cottage, it was placed well back from the road, one of only three houses set in what looked like a large area of woodland. Like the dwelling on either side, the right one of which was inhabited

M22

by the Salmons, it was screened all around by trees and shrubs.

On entering the little house Matt and Tess found that it was all ready for them. Near the ready-laid fireplace was a stack of firewood. In the kitchen there was milk and bread, while upstairs they found the beds neatly made up; a double bed in the larger bedroom and two single beds in the smaller one.

"Laura can sleep in with us for tonight," Matt said, "and tomorrow I'll bring one of the single beds in here." He knew she would never sleep alone in a room in a strange house.

Downstairs again Matt brought in the luggage and then lit the fire while Tess unpacked the provisions they had brought and began to prepare a light supper for Laura. A while later, when Laura had eaten and bathed, Tess took her on her lap before the crackling fire and dried her in a large pink towel. There came a knock at the door and Matt answered it to find Mrs. Salmon standing there. She was a tall woman with greying hair and a round, motherly face. When he asked her in she said she couldn't stay; she had only dropped by to see that everything was all right and to urge him to call her if there was anything they needed. With that she went away again.

That night Matt and Tess lay on either side of Laura. She slept peacefully. Tess, lying with her head close to Laura's, could feel the child's breath on her cheek. After a while Matt's hand came over and rested gently on her shoulder. She felt the insistent pressure there for a moment or two and then eased back in the bed and gently shifted Laura over into the space she had occupied. Then, climbing over Laura's still figure, she lay down next to Matt. She needed his nearness. With his arm around her she lay wrapped close while on her other side Laura snuggled against her. She felt safe again.

In the morning, with Laura in the back seat, Matt sat beside Tess as she drove him to the Five Elms Hotel where the bus was waiting to leave for the location. Some of the other members of the company were taking their cars but he couldn't leave Tess at the cottage without means of transport. Outside the hotel's main door Matt got out of the car, kissed Tess and Laura goodbye and boarded the bus. Half an hour later he had arrived at the location. As he got out into the lane he saw rising above the trees the old stone tower that stood on the cliff-top. Known as the Bridcombe Needle, the landmark dated back to the times when that section of the coast had been notorious for the number of sailing ships that had foundered there. Matt gazed at the tower for a moment or two then followed the rest of the company and crew along a footpath which was a shortcut to the area where the filming was to be done. The path led them high along the edge of the cliff-top in the direction of the tower and on the way he stopped and stood with his back to the shrubbery and the fields and looked out over the wild sea. Here, where the path led very close to the edge there stood an old, low stone wall. It was falling apart now, and in some sections only a few of the stones remained. The rest had long since fallen down onto the rocky shore below. After a few moments he turned away and followed the others to the large, rambling old farmhouse in which a wide room had been adopted by the company's wardrobe and make-up departments. There, after he had changed into his costume, he sat while the make-up girl worked on his face and fitted his wig.

When work on his appearance was finished he went outside, got himself a cup of coffee from the urn and stood watching as the lighting, sound and camera technicians set up their equipment. Then, turning, he wandered away. On the other side of the field was a small cluster of old houses, the outskirts of the tiny village that was to form the basic setting for the early part of the story. He could see a small church there, too, surrounded by a tiny churchyard and, nearer, close to the edge of the clifftop, the Needle.

Standing there while the members of the company went about their work and while the gulls wheeled and cried up above, he thought of Tess and Laura at the cottage. He thought, too, of Robbie and Susie. The change would be good for them all, he said to himself. And once this week was over and they were all together again they could get back into a more normal routine.

Into his thoughts, suddenly, he heard the sound of his name being called and looking around he saw Edie, the producer's assistant, coming towards him, waving. Time to get to work.

Just after half-past three Madeleine was ringing the bell at 22 Meadowbrook Close.

The decision to go there had developed slowly during the morning, and telling her boss that she wasn't feeling well she had returned home from the office and at once set out for Berkshire. Her reasons for making the journey and the call were not that clear even to herself. All she knew was that she wanted to see Tess or Matt —or both of them. She hadn't seen them since the day of her mother's funeral, two weeks ago, and since that time they had been on her mind, a constant background to her grieving.

On reaching Ashford Barrow she had sat in her car for a while at the side of the main street. Then, at last, she had plucked up the courage to drive round to the house. Pulling up outside it she had been surprised to see no signs of life there: no windows open, no children's toys left lying around. She went up the path to the front door. Perhaps Tess would be at home alone. It was Tess who was the cause of all her misery.

When she got no answer to her ring, she turned and followed the path round to the rear of the house, and found the back door and windows closed as well. Everyone must be away. Feeling cheated and frustrated, she walked round to the front again. It was then that she saw Robbie. He was standing with another boy at the front gate.

"Hi, Aunt Madeleine!" Robbie waved to her and she smiled at him warmly. She'd come to see his mother and father, she said as she went towards him, to which he replied that they'd gone away, along with Susie and Laura, and wouldn't be back till the end of the week. Daddy had to do some filming, he added.

"Why aren't you with them?" Madeleine asked.

"I'm staying here with my friend Kevin, Kevin Kinsell." He indicated Kevin who shyly smiled at her. Madeleine returned the smile then said to Robbie, "Where are they, do you know, your mummy and daddy?"

"In Devon."

"Whereabouts in Devon? Do you know that?"

"Yes." He nodded. "I've got the address in my notebook. Do you want it?"

"Oh, yes, please."

"I'll go and fetch it."

He turned and ran off, with Kevin at his side, and Madeleine watched as they turned in at the gate of a house a few yards along. Three or four minutes later they were back, Robbie carrying a small notebook which he opened and held out to Madeleine.

"There, you can copy it out."

She looked at the address written in his round, child's hand, then took a pen from her bag and copied it on to another page of the notebook. She tore the page out neatly, handed the notebook back to him and thanked him. He seemed so pleased that he'd been able to help. "I haven't got the phone number," he told her, "but Mrs. Kinsell's got it if you want it."

"No, no . . ." She shook her head. "It doesn't matter."

"Are you going to write to them?"

"Perhaps. I don't know. We'll see." She

paused. "You say they took your sisters with them."

"Yes, but only as far as Uncle Geoff's. They didn't take them to the seaside in Devon. Susie and Laura are staying with Uncle Geoff and Auntie Stella in Marlborough."

A couple of minutes later Madeleine was driving back towards London. Maybe tomorrow she would go to Bridcombe and pay Matt and Tess a little visit.

Just on half-past four, while Madeleine was driving back on the motorway to London, Matt was coming to an end of the day's work. The director had just called a halt, and Matt, like the rest of the cast, changed back into his own clothes and got back into the bus, glad of the chance to relax. It had been a long day and his feet ached from the constant standing and walking about in unfamiliar shoes.

When he got back to the hotel he got a taxi to the cottage, arriving just after six-thirty. He kissed Laura and Tess, then poured himself a drink and sat down before the fire. On the radio a disc-jockey, smitten by nostalgia, was playing some golden oldies and Matt drank slowly and contentedly from his glass while a very youthful Dinah Shore, her voice mellow and as smooth as honey, sang "Smoke Gets in Your Eyes". On the sofa nearby, Laura, in her nightdress and ready for bed, played contentedly with one of her dolls while, from the kitchen, there came the sounds of Tess making preparations for dinner.

A little later when Laura was safely in bed they got on the coin-operated telephone and called the Kinsells. Robbie wasn't in, and Tess chatted to Dot for a minute or so and afterwards called Geoff and Stella. A few minutes later, after a short conversation with Susie, they sat down to eat, secure in the knowledge that the children were happy and content.

Several hours' night shooting was to be done the next day and Matt wasn't required on the set until eight o'clock, so for most of the day he would be free. In the morning he and Tess, with Laura walking between them, did a little tour of the town and afterwards drove out into the countryside where they had lunch at an old inn. When they arrived back at the cottage in the afternoon Matt went upstairs to rest for a couple of hours before getting ready to go off to the location.

He managed to sleep for a while before Tess awakened him, then he got up, took a shower and dressed. By the time he was all set to leave, Laura was ready for bed. He carried her upstairs, gently laid her down and pulled the covers up over her.

"Will you be all right?" he asked her, nuzzling into her neck.

"Yes," she said, and giggled.

"There's my girl." He kissed her then straightened and stood there for a little while looking down at her in the soft, dim glow of the small lamp beside the bed. He watched as she drifted off to sleep, her thumb in her mouth. Moving to the window he drew back the curtains and looked out. A storm was coming up, the darkness of the evening deepened by the low, heavy clouds that were gathering. In the gloom he could just make out the shadowed front garden with its little lawn, now somewhat overgrown and untidy, and the remains of flowerbeds. Beyond it was the narrow road and, beyond that, the dark massed shadow of the woodland.

Within his vision nothing stirred except for the dark shapes of the treetops against the sky. Closing the curtains he turned back towards the bed. Laura hadn't stirred. He moved quietly to the door and, leaving it ajar, went downstairs.

A few minutes later with Tess behind him he left the house. There at the gate he put his arms around her and kissed her. He would probably be back around two or three in the morning, he said. He got into the car and drove away. Tess waited till the car's rear lights had vanished from her sight, then turned and went back indoors.

Madeleine watched as Tess stepped into the hall and closed the door behind her. The only light visible was in the window of one of the downstairs rooms.

She was standing in the shadow of the trees, facing the house. Earlier Matt had drawn back the curtains of the bedroom window and peered out, and for a moment it seemed as if he had been looking right at her. But of course he had seen nothing. She had been quite safe.

She had left her office at lunch time, giving an excuse to her boss which he had accepted with a sigh and unsuccessfully hidden ill grace. He was getting tired of all her requests for time off lately, she knew, and was only as co-operative as he was because of her mother's recent death. She didn't care. His glances up under his eyebrows and his expressions of martyrdom went straight over her head these days. Whatever he thought of her was of no importance whatsoever. Not now. She had more important things on her mind.

On her arrival in Bridcombe she had made her way to within half a mile of the house and parked in a secluded spot among the trees, fairly sure that her car would not be seen. And now here she was, within yards of the cottage.

She sighed, shifted her weight on the dead leaves and pulled the collar of her Burberry closer around her throat. The wind was getting stronger now and when she heard the sound of rain pattering on the leaves above her head she dipped into her pocket, took out her rainhat and pulled it on.

All the time she stood there she didn't take her eyes off the cottage. Tess was alone in there. And going by the way she and Matt had parted it was likely that she was going to be alone for some time yet. Madeleine thought back to the kiss at the gate; people didn't kiss goodbye when they were just going off for five minutes.

She moved forward until she was standing on the fringe of the trees. It was so isolated out here. Only those other two houses anywhere near. Just about anything could happen. As she gazed at the cottage she thought of that other one at the rear of her mother's house, and where her mother had died. As the memory came back she closed her eyes as if she would shut out the pictures that flickered through her brain. *Mummy*. She would never forgive them for what had happened. *Mummy . . . Mummy . . .* She saw her mother as she had stood facing her at the top of the stairs in the little cottage. She saw herself raising her hands and . . . She shuddered and cast the image from her mind. *Tess*. It was Tess who was to blame for everything.

Finding a dry patch on a fallen tree she sat down in the shelter of a yew and settled herself to wait. She didn't care how long it took. She could be patient.

After a long time the light in the downstairs room went off and a light appeared at the upstairs window where Matt had appeared earlier. When that light went off the house was quite dark. Madeleine got to her feet and stretched. She felt stiff from sitting so long on the hard seat. Stepping forward she moved closer to the fringe of the woodland and the road that ran between her and the cottage. Suddenly the whole scene before her was lit up by a flash of lightning, followed by a growl of thunder, and for a moment she shrank back. Then she started forward again and in a few seconds stood at the very rim of the trees, just two or three yards from the road. Standing there, hovering on the edge of the relative openness she felt exposed and vulnerable; all Tess had to do was look out of the bedroom window and she would surely see her. Drawing back she reached up, grasping her yellow rainhat. It was like a flag, a beacon. She pulled it off and stuffed it into her pocket, then, taking the silk scarf from around her neck she covered her hair with it and tied it under her chin. She felt safer then.

After another moment she left the shelter of the trees and moved swiftly and silently across the road through the lashing rain. Reaching the front gate of the cottage she hurried through. She still had no plan formed in her mind. All she knew was that she had to get in. Quietly she tried the doors, front and back. Locked. And then she tried the windows, and she smiled in satisfaction as the rear sitting-room window moved under the pressure of her hand and opened smoothly.

When she had climbed in she stood in the middle of the room listening. There was no sound from above; she could hear nothing at all but the sounds of the storm, the pounding of the rain and the cracking of the thunder. As she gazed around her in the shadows the darkness was brightened by lightning flashes that lit up the sky and penetrated the curtains, and by the remains of the fire that burned behind the Victorian fireguard.

Turning, she moved out into the hall and into the kitchen where she switched on the light and looked about her. Over the sink there was a mirror and for a moment she stood and gazed at her reflection. There was nothing in her eyes to show the strength of her purpose or what was in her mind. Before her on the table she saw a breadboard and a long, sharp knife. She picked up the knife, then raised her head and looked upwards, as if seeing through the ceiling to where Tess lay in her bed upstairs. Then she turned, switched off the light and left the room. In the hall she moved towards the stairs. She gave no thought whatever to the effects of what she was about to do.

As she drew level with the sitting-room doorway she glanced in and saw again the glow of the fire through the mesh of the fireguard, and in the same instant a brilliant flash of lightning lit up the room, bleaching it of colour and casting great shadows that moved briefly, grotesquely on the walls. A clap of thunder followed, so loud that she cowered against the wall. She stayed there for some moments, and then it was, as she started forward again, that she realised the knife was a mistake. For one thing, if she used the knife she would forfeit her own freedom, for surely they would find her. And why should she herself suffer any more than she already had? And after all, she had succeeded once in escaping detection.

Silently she moved from the hall into the sitting-room and drew closer to the fire. As she saw the coals glowing there she thought again of the fire she had lit in the little cottage at West Priors. She gazed at the glowing coals for another few seconds, then put down the knife and got swiftly to work.

Tess had gone up to bed earlier than she would usually have done. She had no wish to stay downstairs alone in the strange house.

Upstairs, finding Laura just waking, she had brought her from the single bed into the larger one. On this wild night they would be comfort for one another. Soon they lay side by side, curled together, Laura sound asleep again. In spite of the thunder Tess was soon asleep as well.

Madeleine, her work finished, was easing her way back out of the window into the rain. Behind her the flames were already licking at the front curtains. On the back lawn she stood for some moments watching the glow of the fire grow brighter. The knot of her scarf had come loose and she took the scarf off and wiped it across her brow. Her face was wet with perspiration as well as from the rain. She gazed for a moment at the brightening glow of the fire and then hurried away, round to the front of the house, across the road to the woods, and so back to her car. There she got into the dry, and sat panting and recovering her breath. When she was calmer she lit a cigarette. The rain seemed to be growing weaker now, and the thunder and lightning had stopped. After a while she switched on the ignition, put the car into gear and set off. Very soon she would be miles away, on her way back to London.

In Tess's dream there was something burning, and when she awoke she found the dream was based in reality.

Putting on the bedside light she could see smoke clouding the room, while tears sprang to her smarting eyes. Beside her in the bed Laura stirred and awoke, coughing. "Mummy, what's happening?"

"Get up, darling," Tess said, trying to keep the panic out of her voice. "We must get up at once."

Laura needed no second bidding and anxiously jumped out of bed and stood still while Tess got her into her dressing-gown. Tess pulled on her own dressing-gown and, taking Laura's hand, moved with her to the door. On the landing they could hardly see for the choking, blinding smoke, but they could feel the heat coming up the stairs like a wave. Glancing down, Tess caught a glimpse of the flickering flames as they were reflected in the door facing the sitting-room. She turned away; they couldn't go that way.

"Mummy," Laura said, "how are we going to get down? I'm afraid."

"No, no, don't be." Tess, at a loss, spun distractedly on the small rectangle of landing at the top of the stairs. She had never known such fear. Sparks winged their way up the stairs to the accompaniment of the crackling of the flames and with each moment the way down became even more impassable.

Firmly holding Laura by the hand, Tess made for the rear bedroom and opened the door. As she did so a draught of air brought the flames and the smoke blasting into the hall and curling up the stairs in a great *whoosh*. Laura screamed and Tess pushed her forward into the bedroom, dashed in behind her and slammed the door.

Without wasting a second Tess stepped to the window and opened it. The rain had stopped. Below the window was the slightly sloping roof of the bathroom. Tess lifted Laura up onto the sill, and Laura screamed out, her shrieks piercing as she struggled against being lowered onto the roof.

"It's all right," Tess said hoarsely. "It's all right."

But Laura, terrified, clung to the window frame and refused to let go. Tess almost cried out in frustration and, setting Laura down on a chair, got out of the window and lowered herself onto the roof. Now Laura, afraid of being left alone, was more ready to follow and after a little coaxing climbed from the chair and through the window. The next moment

Tess was holding her in her arms and setting her down at her side.

As Tess crawled to the edge of the roof Laura cried out again and pulled back, dragging at Tess's dressing-gown so that Tess felt she could have struck her. Sitting on the roof, Tess pulled Laura down beside her then moved to the edge and looked down where the yard below was lit by the flames from within. The drop wasn't great; about eight feet or so, she reckoned. She inched forward so that her legs hung over the edge. Then she turned onto her front and, while Laura screamed not to be left alone, let herself down, hung by her hands for a moment and let go, dropping onto the cement path below.

As she straightened she glimpsed the interior of the sitting-room and saw the flames inside. Quickly she held out her arms to Laura. "Come on, darling, jump. I'll catch you. Jump." And Laura came closer, crawling forward until she sat on the very edge.

"Now jump . . . *jump* . . ." Tess pleaded with her, but Laura just sat there in the wet, cowering from the drop before her. Up on tiptoe, Tess stretched out to her. She couldn't reach her, though, and neither could she persuade her to lower her feet over the edge. Laura's fear of the void before her was more powerful than all Tess's pleas and remonstrations and Tess could do nothing but weep in frustration and panic.

Then, turning away, Tess saw an old wooden seat on the edge of the lawn. She ran towards it, grasped it by its back and began to drag it over the grass. It was heavy and very old and had obviously not been disturbed for many years, and as she pulled it along she was dimly aware of the soft feel of the wood and of the looseness of the joints. Dragging it onto the pathway, she placed it near the bathroom wall and climbed up on it, feeling as she did so the way it moved and shook under her weight. She stretched up and reached out her arms to Laura, urging her again to come to her. And at last Laura inched closer and closer to the edge and, after much coaxing, let herself down into Tess's waiting arms. It was at that moment that the old bench gave way. One moment Laura was safe, and then the next moment they were both being pitched backwards into the dark.

For a second Tess lay stunned by the fall, all the breath knocked out of her body, then, catching at the air again, she sat up. Laura lay sprawled some three or four feet away. She lay quite still.

Tess stared at her for a moment, then called her name. When there was no answer she moved over the wet path to her side, knelt beside her and lifted her into her arms. Laura's eyes were closed and she didn't stir. Tess said to herself, wildly, *She's dead! she's dead!* but then, touching her hand to Laura's chest she felt the beating of her heart. "Oh, dear God," she cried out, "let her be all right. Please let her be all right."

Struggling to her feet and holding Laura close in her arms, she stumbled away, around the house and out into the road.

17

DUE to the storm, filming on the location was delayed and the company was forced to sit around in the farmhouse waiting for the weather to clear.

Half an hour after they eventually got started again Matt came off the set to be told that a police sergeant had arrived to see him and was waiting in the farmhouse. Following Edie, he was shown into a room where the officer, grave-faced, told him that Laura was in the local hospital. He then told him of the fire at the cottage and that Laura had been hurt in a fall. As far as he understood, he added, she had not been seriously injured. He ended by telling Matt that he would drive him to the hospital, or guide him there, whichever he chose.

"I'll follow you," Matt said, then hurried off, heart thudding, to tell the director of the emergency. Two minutes later he was sitting in the Rover and following the police car along the narrow roads in the direction of Bridcombe.

He got out the car outside the hospital, thanked the officer and went inside to find Tess, pale and grim, sitting in one of the waiting-rooms. She was wearing clothes that he had never seen before. He held her to him and she told him that Laura was still being examined. Then he sat beside her while she gave him an account of what had happened. After getting out of the cottage she had carried Laura to the Salmons' house, she said, where they had phoned for an ambulance and the fire brigade. She put her head in her hands. She didn't know how it had happened; she had left a small fire burning in the grate, but she was sure she'd left the fire-guard in front of it when she'd gone upstairs.

A doctor appeared; a young man, tall, dark and wearing a white tunic. He said that X-rays had been taken and that Laura was suffering from concussion. She was still unconscious but there was nothing anyone could do, except wait.

"For how long?" Tess asked.

The doctor shook his head. "That's something no one knows, I'm afraid."

"May we see her?" Matt asked.

"Yes. Just for a moment." The doctor turned and led the way to the room where Laura lay. The sight of her, looking lost in the white-sheeted hospital bed, brought tears to Matt's eyes and he blinked them back and swallowed over the lump in his throat.

Later, in the corridor, Tess asked if she or Matt could stay and after a moment of hesitation the doctor said, "But there's nothing you can do. Why don't you go on home, and we'll phone you at once if there's any change."

"Home," Tess said, with rueful irony, and added, "Oh, let me stay. Please. May I?"

The doctor finally agreed. Matt said to Tess:

"Are you sure you'll be okay?"

"Yes," she said, "I shall be fine." She was silent a moment, then she asked him, "And what will you do?"

He shrugged. "I'll get us a room at the hotel and then go on back to work. Everybody'll be held up if I'm not there."

He shook his head. "It's no good my hanging around, just waiting. It's better that I have something to do."

The doctor nodded his agreement to this, adding, "She's going to be all right, I'm sure. It's just a matter of time." He turned to Tess and told her he'd get one of the porters to put a spare bed in Laura's room. When he had gone away Matt wrapped his arms around Tess and held her close. Everything would be all right, he said. It *would*. Then, after giving her a telephone number at the location where he could be reached, he left her and set off for the hotel.

Shortly after Matt had gone from the hospital a police sergeant arrived to see Tess. Interviewing her briefly in a small office not far from Laura's room he told her he had been asked to attend by the local Fire Department in order to help establish the cause of the fire. It was common procedure, he said. In reply to his questions Tess told him that she had no idea what had caused it, unless it had something to do with the storm. He left after just a few minutes, seemingly quite satisfied, and Tess went back to sit beside Laura.

Arriving at The Five Elms, Matt booked a room, with an additional bed for Laura when she was discharged, and then drove back to the location. There, although the storm and his absence had thrown the schedule out somewhat, there seemed to be a concerted effort made (and possibly for his benefit too) to make up for lost time, and everyone worked hard until the director called a halt at five o'clock.

As soon as he could, Matt made for his car and returned to the hotel. Once there in the hotel room, though, he felt like a prisoner, and wanted only to go to the hospital to see how Laura was. He didn't, however, but forced himself to remain where he was. There was nothing he'd be able to do, and Tess was already there, waiting and watching . . .

After a while he undressed and got into bed. When he did manage to sleep, though, his sleep was fitful, and after a time he found himself wide awake again and knowing that for that night sleep was over. After lying restless in the strange bed for some minutes longer he got up, made himself some instant coffee with the facilities supplied and sat waiting for the time to go by. He had never felt so lost.

He forced himself to have breakfast the next morning before going to the hospital, and it took an effort for him to sit there at the breakfast table and not hurry. There were no other members of the film crew in the dining room; they would all still be sleeping after last night's work. He looked at his watch. Not yet half-past nine. He'd have to sit there a while longer yet. They wouldn't want to see him at the hospital before ten at the earliest.

After a second cup of coffee he got up and drove to the hospital. Tess was waiting for him when he entered the reception area and he could tell by her expression that there was no change in Laura. Taking her arm he led her to the waiting-room where, finding it empty, they went in and sat side by side.

Tess began to cry. "She's still unconscious," she said. "She just lies there."

There was nothing he could say. When she was calmer she told him of the officer's questions about the fire, and Matt said he would be going to the cottage that morning. First, though, he wanted to see Laura. They got up and walked to the room where Laura lay. Even in the daytime the room was kept in shadow. Matt stood beside the bed and looked down at the small, pale face. She looked just the same as she had last night.

They left Laura's bedside after a while; Matt to go to the cottage, and Tess to go to the shops to buy something for herself and Laura to wear. Fortunately Matt had had his money, cheque book and credit cards with him at the time of the fire, for everything in the cottage had been destroyed. The clothes Tess was wearing had been lent to her by Mrs. Salmon.

After Matt had dropped Tess off at the hotel he drove to the scene of the fire and stood looking at the blackened shell that had once been Middle Cottage. Then he turned and walked along to the Salmon's house and rang the doorbell. After a minute Mrs. Salmon opened the door and invited him in, and a few minutes later they sat opposite one another, grave-faced, and drinking the coffee she had poured. She told him how Tess had come to the house last night with Laura in her arms, and how they had called the ambulance and the fire brigade. Then she went on to tell how, while Tess and Laura had been taken away, she and her husband had watched the cottage burn. The fire brigade, manned by retainers, had taken some time to get there, by which time the building had been almost gutted. Later, after the Chief Fire Officer's investigations were complete, they had learned from him that the probable cause of the fire was the storm in conjunction with the cottage's electricity.

Matt left her, saying he would keep her informed as to Laura's progress, and then walked back along the lane to where the remains of the cottage stood in the patch of ground that had once been the garden. Now it was nothing more than a churned up, muddy area that bore testimony to the pounding received from the firemen's feet and the water from their hoses. He stood gazing at the ruin for a moment and then, stepping through the mud, made his way round to the back and looked up at the roof and the bedroom window from which Tess and Laura had made their escape.

Moving closer to the sitting-room window he peered through the glassless frame into the smoke-blackened shell. It was hard to believe such devastation. He thought back to Mrs. Salmon's words regarding the stated cause of the fire: the storm, in possible conjunction with the electricity system in the house. Tess and Laura—they might have died.

He had stepped around the side of the building and was just moving on towards the front when he came to a halt. He turned and stepped back, then stooped to look at something lying in the mud. He could so easily have passed it by. He looked closer. He felt sure he recognised the colour and pattern of the fabric; dark blue, flecked at the edges with gold. Reaching down, he took a corner of the material and pulled it free. Surely it was the scarf that Tess had sent to Madeleine on her birthday. She had been wearing it that evening in the restaurant.

When Madeleine awoke she didn't immediately remember what had happened the night before. She lay there for a little while with the realisation slowly dawning that something momentous had occurred. And then, seeing her Burberry hanging up behind the door the memory came back to her.

Yes. She had been to Devonshire. To Bridcombe. To the little cottage where Matt and Tess were staying. She lay there, thinking back, seeing the scene in her mind as she had waited on the edge of the woods. She saw Matt drive away in his car, saw the light in the downstairs window go out, saw the cottage looming larger as she approached, saw the interior, the flames . . . She remembered afterwards her rush through the woodland to where her car was waiting, and then the drive home. She had got back this morning just before one.

She got up, had her breakfast and prepared to leave, all the while with a strange kind of excitement that made her tremble slightly. When she was all set to go she put on her Burberry. It was still a little damp. And where was her scarf? She searched in her pockets but it was nowhere to be found. She didn't care. All she could think of was the fire. What had been its outcome, and how could she find out?

She thought about it all the while she

sat on the train, and it was still on her mind when she arrived at the office. She had to find out. She had to know. She thought of Tess, picturing her in the burning house. She felt no remorse for her at all. Whatever had happened to Tess she had brought it on herself.

On the way back to the hotel Matt stopped at an outfitters and with his Access card bought some underwear, socks, two shirts and a pair of jeans.

Arriving at the hotel he found the room key was still at the desk; obviously Tess was still out shopping. There was a message for him from Edie, the PA, asking him to call her in her room. When he talked to her on the intercom a few moments later he learned that he would be required that afternoon, and that in order to try and catch up on lost time, filming would probably go on quite late. Just before Edie hung up she asked Matt whether there was any good news about Laura. No, he told her; she was just the same.

Upstairs in his room he sat on the bed and deliberated as to whether or not to go to the hospital. He decided against it. He would wait for Tess and they would go together. In the meantime there was plenty to be done. For one thing there was the insurance to be sorted out for the things lost in the fire. He should make a start thinking about that . . .

He didn't, though, but continued to sit there on the bed. After a while he put his hand to his jacket pocket and took out a paper bag. From inside the bag he took the silk scarf, now almost dry from the heat of his body. If it *was* Madeleine's scarf then it meant she had been at the cottage.

Questions swarmed in his mind, but forcing them aside he picked up the phone and gave the girl on the switchboard the Kinsells' number. When Dot came on the line he told her briefly of Laura's accident and gave her the hotel's number. After Dot had expressed her sympathy she said that Robbie had just come in and would like to speak to him. Robbie's voice came over the line a moment later and Matt told him also of Laura's accident, though playing down its seriousness. Afterwards Robbie told him of the things he and

Kevin had been doing. Then, as the conversation was drawing to a close, he asked, "Daddy, did you hear from Aunt Madeleine?"

"Aunt Madeleine? No, why?"

And then Robbie told him—how Madeleine had been to the house and how he had given her the address of the cottage in Bridcombe.

Afterwards, when the conversation was over, Matt continued to sit there. So he had been right. It *was* Madeleine's scarf. There couldn't be any possible doubt of it now. Madeleine had been at the cottage. And after she left it had burned to the ground.

He turned the scarf over in his hands. It was evidence of a sort, evidence he could take to the police.

After a while he wrapped the scarf up again and put it into his briefcase. The briefcase already held several items that had come from Madeleine: the pen she had given him, and the ring . . .

As he sat there Tess returned from the shops with the items of clothing she had bought for Laura and herself, and a little later she and Matt left for the hospital.

There was no change in Laura. They sat beside her bed in the darkened room and talked to her of Susie and Robbie, of her dolls, her friends, her favourite songs—but nothing drew any response.

When they left her side some time later they stopped in the hospital's little cafeteria where Matt bought coffee which they drank at one of the tables overlooking the parking lot. He tried to persuade Tess to return to the hotel later and meet him for lunch, but she said no, she wasn't hungry; she would stay where she was. She was silent then, gazing from the window, while Matt wondered whether to tell her of his discovery, the discovery that Madeleine had been to the cottage shortly before it had been destroyed. Also, if he did tell her, then exactly how should he do so—and when? Was there a right time for such news? And what should he say?

As he thought of the best way to tell her he studied her while she, unconscious of his eyes upon her, continued to gaze out. And then, in that moment, seeing her there in the hard, bright light of the morning, he saw how altered she was. The sudden realisation almost took his breath away. It seemed to have happened in just weeks, the change in her. His mind went back to the time just before their return from California. How different she had been then. Then she had been relaxed and happy, and it had shown in her face and her body, and in her voice, too, and in the very way she had moved. It had been apparent in so many ways.

He watched her now as, preoccupied, she sipped at the coffee. The movements of her hands were fluttery and nervous, and there was the slight hesitant jerkiness of agitation in the way she moved her head. He saw the vertical lines that creased her forehead between her eyebrows and saw again the circles, deeper now, beneath her eyes. Recalling how tanned she had been when they had returned from California he thought that she now looked unnaturally pale. Also, he suddenly realised, her skin seemed to have lost some of its firmness and he was all at once aware of the time that had passed since they had first met.

One of the things he was most conscious of, though, was her weight loss and he wondered how he had not noticed it before. He looked at her hand as she nervously toyed with her paper napkin, and saw how thin it was, the skin on the back of it stretched taut over the knuckles. *Oh, Tess*, a little voice in his head cried out, *how could I have been so blind?*

He found himself thinking back to those times when she had been short-tempered, irritable or unresponsive. He could begin to understand so much better now. And how much more was she to go through? How much more before she could relax and begin to enjoy life again? One thing was certain, it couldn't be while Madeleine posed such a threat. Madeleine: she had done it all.

Madeleine. She had to be stopped.

But how? He thought of the silk scarf in his briefcase. Was that the answer; to go with it to the police? He had thought it was, but now looking at Tess he knew it was not. She had gone through so much distress in the past where Madeleine was concerned. And apart from that she was still suffering from the effects of losing her mother. Now, also, at this moment her daughter lay unconscious in a hospital bed. There was a limit to what Tess could bear.

It wouldn't take much, he was sure, to push her over the edge, and a prosecution of Madeleine, with all that it involved, could just about do it.

The more he looked at her, the more certain he was that the police were not the answer. There must be some other way. There *had* to be. One thing he was certain of, though; it couldn't continue. He had said such a thing to himself in the past, but now he meant it as never before.

He left Tess in the hospital. She would go back to sit with Laura while he tried to work on his lines for a while and then have lunch. After that he would go off to the location.

In his hotel room he opened his briefcase and took out his script. Then he reached back into the case and brought out an envelope. It contained the letter Madeleine had written to him just before she had made her suicide attempt. If she had succeeded life for Tess, himself and their children would have been so much easier.

He read the letter and as he sat there an idea came into his mind. If it were possible

. . . if Madeleine were here . . . if he could get to meet her somewhere . . . No. He tried to thrust the idea from him. There had to be another way.

The idea stayed, though, turning over in his mind.

Madeleine had recalled something that Robbie had said when she had talked to him outside the house in Ashford Barrow. He was staying with his friend, Kevin Kinsell, he had told her, and had vaguely gestured in the direction of a house a little further along the street. Now with the information she called Directory Enquiries and asked for the Kinsells' telephone number. A minute later she was contemplating the number on the pad before her, then she lifted the receiver and dialled.

A woman answered, and on Madeleine enquiring for Mrs. Kinsell the woman said, "Yes, speaking." Madeleine went on to introduce herself and then said she was trying to find out when Tess and Matt would be returning from Devonshire. She'd been given the address of the place in Bridcombe, she added, but she wanted to telephone them.

A few minutes later when she replaced the receiver she had been given the hotel's telephone number and the story of what had happened. There had been a fire at the cottage where they were staying. Matt and Tess were safe, but Laura had been injured in a fall and was at present lying unconscious in a Bridcombe hospital.

It was Laura who had been hurt. Madeleine found she was trembling. She groaned, leaned forward over her desk and put her head in her hands. She hadn't known Laura was with them. Robbie had said his sisters were staying in Wiltshire. Clearly, though, that hadn't been so; Laura had been with Matt and Tess, and now she was hurt.

Laura. Tears streamed down Madeleine's cheeks. *God, what have I done?* she silently cried out.

When she had regained some of her composure she picked up the phone and dialled the number of the hotel.

18

WHEN she heard Matt's answering voice she hesitated for a moment and then said, "Hello, Matt. It's me, Madeleine."

Silence, and then his voice came again, now guarded, measured. "Hello, Madeleine. This is a surprise, hearing from you."

"I had to call," she said. "I just found out about Laura. Your neighbour told me. I just had to call. I hope you don't mind."

"—No, of course not."

"Poor little girl. Oh, Matt, I do hope she's going to be all right."

"Yes, I'm sure she will be. We're waiting to hear."

"Your neighbour—she said Laura was unconscious."

"She still is."

"—Oh, God . . ." As Madeleine thought of the child lying in the hospital bed, tears came to her eyes. "Matt," she said, "if there's anything I can do, please let me know. Please."

"Yes, I will."

There was a little silence then she said, "You know—I can hardly believe I'm talking to you like this."

"Oh? Why not?"

"Oh, Matt, you *know* why not. What I did. You know."

"What you did?"

"The puppy." She could hardly bring herself to say it.

"Oh . . . yes," he said, "the puppy."

"Can you ever forgive me for that?"

"I haven't given it much thought lately," he said. "I've had other things on my mind."

"Yes, of course you have." Then she burst out, "Oh, Matt, I don't know why I did it! What a terrible thing!" She began to cry, saying through her tears, "I don't know why I do these things. Something gets into me and—" She lost the words in a spate of sobbing, and then taking a breath she said brokenly, "Forgive me, please. Will you? I know I've asked you the same thing before, but I mean it. This is the last time. I'll never, *never* do anything to hurt you again."

Silence at the other end but for the faint sound of his breathing. "Please," she said.

"Yes, Madeleine. I forgive you." He paused then added, "And don't cry. There's enough sadness already without that."

The touch of warmth in his voice touched her so deeply that her sobbing burst out again and she had to struggle to bring herself under control. When she was calmer she said, "I'm sorry for being a fool, but this has been on my mind. I didn't dare hope you would ever say that you—you forgive me." She wiped her eyes and nose with a tissue, paused for a moment then asked, "How is Tess?"

Somehow she could almost feel him tighten up at this and there was a brief silence before he answered. Then he said, "She's very low. She's taken some bad shocks. First Ellen, and now Laura's accident."

"Yes, but at least she's got you."

"I guess so."

"Oh, Matt, if you only knew what that means, to have someone near at such a time. When Mummy died I was completely alone. And how I envied Tess then—having you and the children. I had nobody to offer *me* a shoulder. I had to get on as best I could."

"Yes, it must have been very hard. I can imagine."

"Can you? I don't think anyone can imagine what it's really like, to be totally alone. I've lost everything I ever had. Everything."

"Madeleine, don't say that."

"It's true. I've lost *everything*: my mother, your affection, and that of Tess." She shook her head, vaguely aware of a wild, shrill note coming into her voice. "And apart from losing Mummy I didn't even have her affection towards the end."

"Madeleine, your mother loved you. You know that. She was always your ally. Always."

"No!" She burst out sobbing again, and cried out desperately, "Oh, once, yes, she was my ally, but not at the end. At the end she *hated* me. She *despised* me." She went on, the words pouring out in a torrent as if nothing could stop them. "I always had Mummy," she cried, "if no one else. Until that last morning. And that was the end of it." Into her mind came a picture of her mother's face as she had looked at her in the cottage. "Oh, Matt," she cried brokenly, "why did *she* have to know about it? I was so sorry for what I'd done, and I *needed* her. That's why I went to see her, because I needed her. And she turned away from me. She turned away."

Matt was silent on the other end of the line. She went on, her words gathering momentum again. "I'd have done anything to undo what I'd done. And how could I have known she'd be at your house when it was found?"

Matt's voice came then. "You mean the puppy," he said.

"Of *course* the puppy!" she cried out. "What else do you think I'm on about! I did a terrible thing and that *she* should know about it!"

"How could she not know?" he said. "She'd be certain to have learned of it at some time."

"Yes, of course, but—oh, God, Matt—the way she looked at me. I shall never forget that look in her eyes. She was the only person I had left, and to have her look at me like that, as if I were a stranger!" She was weeping again now, uncontrollably, while on the other end of the line Matt remained silent.

When she was a little calmer he said, "It's over now, Madeleine. You must try to put it all behind you."

"Yes."

"And try to forget it."

"Yes." She would never forget the sound of his voice, gentle, understanding. "I want you to remember one thing, Matt," she said.

His voice came back, now a little guarded but still warm. "Oh? What's that?"

"I just want you to remember that you can depend on me, for anything. Anything at all. Remember that. All you have to do is let me know."

And the warmth was still there in his voice as he answered her. "Thank you. I won't forget."

When she had hung up she dried her eyes and then sat at her desk feeling the aching sadness slowly draining away and a faint warmth growing in its place.

Matt sat staring out of the window. The phone call had come while he sat thinking on the idea that had sprung into his head, coming like an answer to a prayer, and because of it he had gone along with her, listening to her tears and her pleas for forgiveness, saying the things she had wanted to hear. Her call was disturbing, though. In his head he could still hear the sound of her wild, tearful voice. Some of the things she had said were bewildering. He didn't understand . . .

He sat there, thinking back. She had spoken of going to see Ellen after the puppy had been found. *I needed her*, she had said. But she'd never mentioned it before. At the inquest she had said nothing of having seen Ellen that morning. Had he misunderstood? No. Although she had sounded almost hysterical there had been no mistaking her words. She had been to West Priors on the morning of Ellen's return from Ashford Barrow. There was no doubt at all.

He found himself growing tense as he

became more and more aware of the revelation. Why hadn't she told anyone that she had seen Ellen that morning? And what had taken place at their meeting? Obviously whatever had happened it was still very much on Madeleine's mind. He went back over the telephone conversation again, remembering the things she had said and trying to discover any significance they might have. In his mind a scenario took shape, built on the things she had told him.

And the clearer it seemed to grow, the more certain he was that it was true.

After Madeleine had killed the puppy she had been stricken with guilt and needed Ellen's comfort. Yes; *I needed her*, she had said, *that's why I went to see her* . . . And so she had gone that morning to West Priors, obviously arriving there after Jane had left. And Ellen, knowing about the puppy, had withheld her affection, her love. He thought of Madeleine's words: *She turned away from me. She hated me. She despised me.* Yes. The words rang in his brain now. Yes. There had obviously been a scene. Yes, yes. And afterwards? Afterwards Ellen had been found dead at the foot of the stairs; she had apparently fallen . . .

He sat very still. Madeleine had been the last one to see Ellen alive. Why, then, had she never admitted it? Did she have something to hide? And the answer came at once: *Yes*. It was the only possible explanation.

Now his thoughts went from Ellen's death at West Priors to the fire here at Bridcombe. He was certain Madeleine had been responsible for the latter. Could it be, then, that she had been responsible for Ellen's death in some way?

It was quite possible. The things Madeleine had unwittingly disclosed to him on the telephone; they all pointed to her involvement. He felt certain of it: in some way she had been responsible for Ellen's death. He had no proof and he couldn't imagine how it happened, but he was sure that it *had* happened. Also, whether it had been by accident or design he couldn't guess. He only knew that he was sure, and the more he thought about it the surer he became. He knew it just as surely as he knew that she had tried to kill Tess.

And with the thoughts of the attempt on Tess he realised suddenly that Madeleine wasn't likely to give up. Not now. In earlier days he had hoped that she would stop her scheming, and he had given her so many chances to do so. All for nothing. She had merely taken the hope and trust invested in her and used it to further her schemes. And now her scheming had led to Laura lying unconscious in a hospital bed—let alone the attempt on Tess's life and what he thought she might have done to Ellen.

And if she wouldn't stop of her own accord, then, as he had said to himself earlier, she would have to be stopped.

The idea that had sprung in his mind shifted and became the beginnings of a plan. Still vague and embryonic, it flickered on and off like some faulty light bulb. For all its uncertainty, though, it remained there, constant. Not long ago in the face of her distress, the idea and his half-formed resolve might well have weakened and died. Now, with the revelation that her words had brought to him, they grew stronger.

He turned his head and looked down at

Madeleine's letter where it lay on the bed. He picked it up, read it once again and then carefully replaced it in its envelope.

Madeleine, sitting at her desk, kept thinking of Matt. This had been the first time she had really let go to anyone since her mother's death. She was a little disturbed to recall how tearful and distraught she had been, but it was too late now to change anything. Besides, it had had a cleansing effect on her; she felt better for it.

And she felt somehow that Matt had been warmer towards her. Yes—so different from those other times of late when he had been so cold, so unapproachable. She thought again of how, at the end of their conversation, she had told him that he could depend on her. And she remembered so well the sound of his voice when he had answered her. "Thank you," he had said, "I won't forget."

And was it Laura's accident that had done it? Perhaps. She didn't know. Perhaps the shock of it had opened his eyes to other things around him. Who knew? That was a matter for the psychologists. All she knew was that he seemed, somehow, to have changed. Could it be? Time would tell.

After lunch Matt went to the hospital. There with Tess he sat at Laura's bedside for an hour and then left to drive out to the location.

He was to be in several of the shots; first of all in the tiny graveyard at the edge of the village, in a lane nearby and then in front of the farmhouse. He went through the hours in a kind of daze, the minutes passing like drops from a slowly leaking tap. Somehow, though, he did all that was required of him and at last his final shot of the day was finished and he was free to go. As he came off the set, eager to change and get back to the town, Edie came hurrying up to say there was a phone call for him.

Aware of his heart beating, he went with her, entered the trailer that was a mobile office, took up the receiver and heard Tess speaking his name.

"What's the matter?" he said.

"It's Laura—" and as his heart lurched she added, "Matt, she's all right."

383

He was so sharply aware then of the relief in her voice, the gladness that took her tone up a notch and gave it a slightly hysterical touch. "She's all right," he repeated, and his own spirits soared. "She really is?"

"Yes. She came round just a few minutes ago. Oh, Matt, she's conscious again. And she knew me. She knew me at once, as soon as she came round."

When he had put the phone down he just stood there. Then he became dimly aware that one of the girls was setting a chair for him and he sat down and felt the warmth of the tears that spilled down over his cheeks.

Edie stepped closer and asked, "Are you okay, Matt? Can I get you something?"

He turned to her and shook his head, hardly trusting himself to speak, and all the while the tears kept coming. She went away and reappeared before him holding a cup of coffee and he looked up into her plain, good-natured face, took the cup and grinned. "Thanks, Edie. I'm an idiot. But my little girl, she's going to be okay." He hugged himself. "She's regained consciousness." And then his grin welled up and spilled over and he sat there laughing while the tears streamed down his face.

A few minutes later he was out of his costume and back in his own clothes and leaving the farmhouse. Heading back in the direction of his car he had to pass by the set where the crew were setting up for the next shot.

As he drew near, Dan Callow, the director, searched his expression and said, smiling, "I hear from Edie that everything's all right," and with his words it seemed that everybody stopped what they were doing and listened. Then the grin that spread over Matt's face became reflected in the faces around him.

"Yes," Matt said, "she's fine. She's conscious now and she's going to be all right."

There was a brief moment of silence and then, as one man, everyone cheered and began to applaud.

In the hospital Matt went into the dimly lit room where Tess sat at Laura's bedside. Laura was sleeping. Without speaking, Matt drew up a chair and sat down next to Tess. He reached out, took her hand and held it in his own.

As he sat gazing down at Laura's peaceful face he reflected again on her recovery. It seemed so much a miracle. It *was* a miracle. They had her back again, and she was going to be all right. With the realisation his resolve strengthened still further. Never, *never* would he allow her to be at risk again. Whatever happened, whatever it cost him, from now on he would make sure that his children were safe.

With the strengthening of his resolve the germ of the plan in his mind stirred and took on a more positive shape.

An hour later, when they had left the room and were moving back along the corridor, they saw coming towards them the young doctor whom they had met on the night of Laura's admission. He raised a hand to them as they approached and came towards them. "Just the people I wanted to see," he said. Then, as they came to a stop he added quickly, with a little smile, "Don't look so worried. All I want to say is that you're going to need to be patient for a while longer. Although

Laura's come out of her unconsciousness she's by no means recovered from the blow that caused it. That may take a while longer yet."

Tess frowned. "How much longer?"

The doctor shrugged. "Recovery is generally good in such cases but, as I say, you'll just have to be patient." He paused. "I wanted to let you know so that you don't build up your hopes too soon. I'm afraid for a while yet she's going to need a good deal of rest and careful nursing."

"And she won't be able to come home yet?" Matt said.

"When did you have in mind?"

"Well, we were hoping—tomorrow?"

The doctor shook his head. "No, I'm sorry. We shall have to keep her under observation for two or three days yet, to make sure there are no complications."

"But she *is* going to be all right?"

"Oh, yes, I'm sure. She's showing every sign of making a very good recovery." He put a hand on Matt's shoulder. "Now," he added, "you go on home. She'll sleep and sleep, and it's what she needs." He looked into their faces. "*You* go and get some rest, too. Both of you. It's what you need as well. Come back and see her to-morrow."

Back at the hotel Matt ran a bath while Tess got ready for bed. When he was in the bath he called out to Tess, asking her to bring his script to him so that he could study it for a while as he soaked. When she brought it into the bathroom and handed it to him a minute later he looked at her expression and said, "What's up?"

"Nothing." She turned away and went out of the room, and he gazed after her with a slight frown on his face and then tried to give his attention to his lines.

Twenty minutes later he had finished his bath and, drying himself off, went into the bedroom where he found Tess lying in bed, wide awake.

"You should be asleep," he said.

She said nothing for a moment, then without looking at him said, "What are you doing with Madeleine's scarf?"

"What?"

She sat up in bed. "The scarf I sent Madeleine. It's in your briefcase, covered in dried mud. I saw it when I got your script."

He just stared at her.

"Tell me," she said, "please."

He gave a little laugh. "Oh, that," he said. "What makes you think it's Madeleine's?"

"Please, Matt. I should know. I gave it to her. What's it doing in your case?"

He knew then that he had to tell her the truth. He couldn't keep it from her, and now, even if it were possible, he would not. "I found it," he said simply.

"Where?"

"By the cottage here in Bridcombe." He gestured with a thumb. "The morning after the fire."

She looked at him, her face set. Then, after long seconds she said, "Madeleine was there."

"It seems that way."

Another silence then she said, "We could have been killed, Laura and I."

"Don't think about it."

"I can't stop thinking about it." She shook her head slowly and gave an ironic smile. "They said the fire was probably caused by some electrical malfunction or something due to the storm . . ."

"Yes."

She nodded. "But we know better, don't we."

A little later Matt lay in bed beside her. In the dark she said, "When will she give up, Matt? When will she be satisfied?" He didn't answer and she added, "It makes me so afraid."

"Yes. But don't worry about it any more." He put his arm around her. "It won't be long till we can go back home."

"And then?"

"And then?"

"The whole thing will just continue, won't it? With Madeleine. It will just go on and on . . ."

"No—it's going to be all right."

"Is it?" Her voice was heavy with scepticism. "We've been through all that before. How can I believe it any more?"

"Trust me. This time it will be."

"What can you do?"

"Just trust me."

He held her, and she nestled into his warmth. "I want it to be all right," she said. "Oh, Matt, I want it so. It's *got* to be all right."

"It will," he said. "It will." He held her closer. "Sleep now. Go to sleep."

She awoke in the night. She sat bolt upright in bed and cried out. There were no words; just a loud, animal-like cry. Matt sat up beside her and put his arms around her. At first she fought him off, but then her dream faded and she became aware of reality. She wept then, wrapped in his arms, and he held her until her tears stopped. She felt thin and fragile in his arms. After a while she lay down again, and lying beside her he listened to her breathing. She wasn't sleeping, he could tell. He lay on his back, staring into the dark.

At the breakfast table next morning he tried unsuccessfully to persuade Tess to eat more than the slice of toast she nibbled at. No, it was enough for her, she said. When they had finished he saw it was still only half-past nine. On an impulse he got up. "I thought I'd run round to the shops and get something for Laura," he said, and Tess nodded and said she'd see him over at the hospital.

He left her then and walked off briskly in the direction of the shopping centre, there finding a toy shop where he picked out a doll with dark curls and wide brown eyes. Emerging into the air again he stood for some moments on the pavement then went into a stationers and bought writing paper and envelopes. After that he went into a small café where he bought a coffee at the counter and carried it over to a table near the window.

Setting the doll down on the next chair he sat down and took from his briefcase the pen that Madeleine had given him. This would be the first time he had used it. After writing a few words on a sheet of the paper he addressed an envelope, then, delving into his briefcase again he took out the ring she had given him, wrapped it in a piece torn from a paper napkin and placed it in the envelope along with the letter.

When he had stamped the envelope he sat for some moments just looking at it lying before him. Then, leaving the cup of coffee untouched, he picked up the letter, his briefcase, and the box containing the doll, and walked out. At the corner pillar box he posted the letter and continued on back to the hotel. There, finding that Tess had already left, he got into the car and drove off to the hospital.

This time when he went into Laura's room he was greeted by the smile she gave him. It was the first time she had responded to him in any way since the accident, and glancing at Tess he saw his own gladness reflected in her eyes.

Leaning down over the bed and looking at Laura's smiling face he felt that his emotion could choke him. "How are you, baby?" he said after a moment. "Are you okay?" And she mouthed a yes and he took her hand and held it between his two. Her hand was so small and he was aware all over again of her vulnerability.

Laura didn't stay awake long. In just over an hour she was asleep again. He got up to leave for the location soon after, at eleven-thirty. "Take the car," Tess whispered. She didn't plan on going anywhere, she said, and she'd be able to manage perfectly well without it.

"Fine." He nodded, leaned down and planted a light kiss on the cheek of the sleeping child, then with Tess behind him he quietly left the room.

In the corridor he kissed Tess and was just turning away when she said, "Matt, what's the matter?"

"The matter?"

"Yes—and I don't mean that—that business we talked about last night . . ."

"Oh, come on, Tess." He frowned, irritable. "There's nothing the matter. Come on now. I haven't got time for all this."

She waved his words aside with a sweeping movement of her hand. "Don't give me that. I know you too well to be put off by any such feeble denial. You're keeping something from me. What is it?"

"I'm not keeping anything from you. What makes you say that?"

"I just know. At breakfast and now: you're so—preoccupied. Why? What is it?"

He shook his head. "You're imagining things." He took a step away. "I must go or I shall be late."

Back in Laura's room Tess moved to the window, pulled up the blind a little way and looked down. After a few moments she saw Matt appear below and walk off in the direction of the car park. When he had vanished from sight she lowered the blind and sat down again at the side of Laura's bed. In her mind she could see Matt's face so clearly. His eyes. The set look to his mouth. He had looked haunted.

There were several scenes being shot that day in which Matt was not involved and he was left with plenty of time to himself. He had a paperback whodunnit with him, but on finding, after several attempts, that he couldn't get past the first few pages, he gave up and put it back in his case.

The time dragged by, and all the time one question went over and over in his mind. How would Madeleine respond to his letter when she received it the next morning?

19

ON Friday morning Madeleine came downstairs to leave for work and took up the few items of mail from the hall mat. There was something for her; an envelope with a small firm shape inside it. She put the few things for the other residents on the small table and studied the envelope addressed to herself. It had a Bridcombe postmark. It must be from Matt. It had been addressed, she noticed, in violet ink . . .

After a moment she turned, went upstairs again and let herself back into her flat. There by the window she stared down at the envelope. Why was he writing to her? Her fingers trembling slightly she tore open the envelope, took out the little padding of paper, unwrapped it and saw the ring. It was the ring she had given him; the half of her Marie Antoinette ring she had found at West Priors that day. And now he was returning it. Why? As a gesture of disdain? A calculated insult? It was the final blow. As she gazed at it tears sprang to her eyes and ran down her cheeks. She sat down on a chair, put her head in her hands and wept.

After a while she lifted her head and took the folded piece of paper from the envelope, spread it out and read the brief message he had written: *I must talk to you. Please call me between six and seven. M.*

And she suddenly realised what the ring was for. It was the sign that she had waited for, what she had longed and prayed for for so long. All at once all the despair and unhappiness of the past were just melting away. Matt needed her.

After a hectic day, the last one on the location, a final wrap was called just after five-thirty and Matt, so relieved to be free, got back into his own clothes and set off for his car. As on previous days he had parked it at the end of the unmade road and followed the rough path—the short cut—that ran along the cliff-top towards the Needle. Now, on the way back, he halted for a while on the path and looked out at the sea. Then, edging forward, he gazed down at the rocky floor below at the foot of the cliff. Only for a moment, though, and then he was on his way again, hurrying along the path.

It was after six-fifteen when he got back to the hotel. As he expected, Tess was not there. She'd be over at the hospital and expecting him to join her. He couldn't go yet, not yet. He looked at the telephone. The anticipation set his heart thudding. This was no time to back out, though, and anyway, perhaps she wouldn't call.

The waiting was unbearable and he eased it by pouring himself a scotch and then getting ready for a shower. He had just put on his dressing-gown when the telephone rang. He stood quite still. All of a sudden he was afraid. What had he begun? He wouldn't answer it. He would stop now—now, before he was drawn irrevocably into something from which there would be no return. The telephone went on ringing. Ignore it, he told himself, just let it ring. But it probably wasn't Madeleine anyway; it was probably Tess or Robbie or Susie; or maybe Edie with his call for Monday at the studios . . . He stepped forward and lifted the receiver.

"Hello?"

"Matt? It's Madeleine."

He sat down on the bed and caught his breath. "Hello, Madeleine."

"I got your message." Although her voice was soft it had an intensity about it. "You wanted to talk to me."

"Yes. Yes, I did. I do. As—as soon as possible."

"What about?"

"No. Not now. We can't discuss it now."

"When? And where? When are you leaving Bridcombe and going home?"

"Not yet. Laura's still in the hospital." Then, lying, he went on, "And I still have a few days' work to do here. We won't be returning until some time next week."

"I see. So—would you like me to drive down there to see you?"

"Could you?"

"Of course, Matt. Anytime. I told you —if you ever need my help you have only to let me know."

"It's a lot to ask, I know, but—"

"No, it's not. It's not a lot to ask. I'll be glad to." She paused, then, "I love you, Matt. You know that."

He said in answer, "Oh, Madeleine . . ."

Then there was a moment of silence and she said, "Right. I'll come down tomorrow, shall I? Just tell me where to meet you. And at what time."

"Have you got a pencil?"

"Yes. Go ahead."

When Madeleine had replaced the receiver she looked at the piece of notepaper on which she'd written down the directions Matt had given her. Under his instructions she had also drawn a little diagram. She would set off first thing in the morning.

At last it had happened, Matt had come to her. But she had known that one day he would.

Matt had gone to the hospital after his conversation with Madeleine, there joining Tess at Laura's bedside. Laura's progress continued sure and steady, and the doctor said that all being well she could leave the following day, right after lunch.

Laura's condition and the doctor's pronouncement should have brought Matt all the relief he needed. It did not, though.

Now that his brain was freed of worry over Laura all his thoughts were taken up with Madeleine.

She would be there tomorrow . . .

That night he again lay sleepless beside Tess in the hotel bed and, staring into the dark, tried to picture his meeting with Madeleine the next day. In his mind he enacted the scene, trying to imagine the looks and the words that would be exchanged. One thing he was certain of, though: whatever happened it would be the last meeting they would ever have.

As he lay there he felt as if one part of his mind had detached itself from his darker side and its involvement and, rising up and away to some distant vantage point, listened to the words and read the thoughts that went through his brain. And it gazed at him in horror.

First thing Saturday morning Tess called Geoff and Stella to say they'd be leaving Bridcombe early in the afternoon, right after Laura was discharged, and would be picking up Susie as soon as they could get there. After that she called the Kinsells and gave them an idea of the time they'd be returning to Ashford Barrow. With that done it only remained to pack their belongings (very few since the fire), and wait for Laura to be discharged. To save unnecessary expense they would check out of the hotel that morning, and put their things in the car until they left.

Tess was on tenterhooks when she and Matt arrived at the hospital, fearing that Laura might have suffered some setback during the night that would necessitate her remaining where she was for a while longer. She needn't have worried. Laura was brighter than on the day before, and impatient to be out. The good news was added to by the Sister saying there shouldn't be any doubt about Laura's discharge and that she would come to no harm on the car journey as long as she was comfortable.

Promising Laura that they would be back soon to take her home, they left the hospital, Tess saying she wanted to do some shopping in the town, and Matt saying that the car had proved troublesome and that he wanted to get it looked at before they set off. They parted outside the hospital gates.

As Tess made her way to the shopping centre she pulled up her raincoat collar against the chill wind that swept in off the sea and quickened her pace.

Thirty-five minutes later her shopping was finished, and standing on the pavement she went over the list in her mind to see whether she had forgotten anything. There was nothing she could think of. Apart from the necessities she had bought, among them food for the weekend, she had also bought little gifts for the children: a dress for Laura's new doll, a space ray gun for Robbie, a book for Susie. As she stood there heavy drops of rain splashed onto her hand and, glancing up, she saw that dark clouds had gathered. Turning, she saw close by a cafeteria and she hurried inside. There, after placing her shopping on a chair by a vacant table she joined the queue at the counter. Then it was that she saw ahead of her a familiar figure. Madeleine.

Involuntarily she came to an abrupt halt and the woman behind clicked her tongue in impatience. As if coming out of a trance Tess collected herself and pushed her tray along on the chrome rails, at the same time watching her sister who, now level with the till, was paying the cashier for coffee and a pastry. As Tess continued to watch, Madeleine, her tray in her hands, moved away and took a seat right next to where Tess had left her shopping.

Tess felt sweat break out on her forehead and she reached up and loosened the collar of her coat. Then, in another minute, she was facing the surly girl behind the cups and saucers, mechanically ordering coffee, paying for it and taking her change. As she turned from the counter she was aware of a little pulse that began to beat nervously in her temple. Seconds later she was moving to the table and Madeleine, glancing up, was meeting her eyes.

For a moment neither spoke. Then Tess gave a nod. "Hello, Madeleine."

"Tess . . ." Madeleine stared at her, eyes wide, while a little frown creased her brow. Then her mouth moved in a faint smile. Tess just managed to return it as she put down her coffee. Then she took off her coat and placed it next to her shopping. As she sat down Madeleine got up and moved to the same table, taking the chair opposite Tess's.

"This is quite a surprise, seeing you here," Tess said. "What are you doing in Bridcombe?"

Madeleine paused then said, "I thought I'd come and see how you were. I heard from your neighbour that Laura had had an accident. Is she all right?"

"Yes, she's going to be all right." Tess didn't believe any of Madeleine's words about the reason for her visit. There was something else; there had to be. "What are you here for, Madeleine?" she said.

"I told you the reason."

"I mean the *real* reason."

Madeleine frowned. "I told you, I came to see you. I was going to call your hotel a little later. I've only just got here."

Tess nodded. "All right, so now you've seen me."

"I—I don't understand . . ."

"Oh, I think you do. You said you came here to see me, and now you have. So you've fulfilled your purpose. You can go away again."

Madeleine stared at her. "I can hardly

405

believe this is you talking, Tess. This isn't like you a bit."

"No, maybe not." Tess shook her head then calmly went on, "I got wise to you, you see. After all this time. For so long I refused to believe what was right in front of my eyes. But now my eyes are open, Maddie. Wide open. So I say again, now that you've seen me you can go home. And I hope that this meeting between us, now, is the last we shall ever have."

She had never spoken to Madeleine like this before. In the past she had always turned the other cheek. Not any more. "Go home, Maddie," she said. "You might have come to see me, but I don't want to see you. Ever again."

Madeleine continued to gaze at her, then raising one eyebrow she said coolly, "And supposing I tell you I lied to you."

"Well, that wouldn't be anything new, would it?"

Madeleine's eyes narrowed and she nodded. "Yes, I lied." She paused. "Well, don't you want to know what I lied about?"

Tess refused to be drawn. "Not particularly."

"I didn't come to see *you*. I came to see *Matt*." Madeleine smiled. "Did you hear what I said?"

Tess shrugged, trying to show a calm she was far from feeling. "So what?" she said. "What makes you think he would want to see you? Go on home. He doesn't want to see you, any more than I do." She was surprised at the hardness and the coldness in her voice. She leaned forward across the table to give added emphasis to her words. "Go on home, Maddie," she whispered intensely. "There's nothing for you here."

"No?" Madeleine's reply was equally quiet. "Well, what's happened to you, Tess; you're not as sharp as I thought. You don't really think I'd be here on some wild goose chase, do you? Credit me with a little intelligence, do." She smiled coldly into Tess's face. "I said I was here to see Matt, and I shall be seeing him, and there's nothing you can do about it. Nothing at all."

There was something in Madeleine's eyes and voice that gave Tess some feelings of doubt. But Madeleine couldn't be speaking the truth. She couldn't be. It was just another of her lies. "I don't believe you," Tess said.

Madeleine shrugged. "It doesn't matter to me whether you believe me or not. The only important thing is that *I* know it and that *Matt* knows it."

"Well," Tess gave a hollow-sounding laugh, "that's nice for you. Does Matt know about the meeting, or are you keeping it as some cute little surprise for him?"

Madeleine remained calm. "No, Tess, it's no cute little surprise for him, as you put it. He knows all about it. It's all arranged."

Tess stared at her. She felt she'd had the upper hand. Not now. "No," she said. "I don't believe you. You're lying, as usual."

"I'm not lying. Look, I'm here in this one-horse town. Doesn't that tell you anything?"

Tess shook her head; she couldn't accept that Madeleine was telling the truth. "I don't believe you," she said. "I just don't believe you."

Madeleine gazed into Tess's eyes. "You're really pathetic, Tess. You know that?" She sighed and looked at her watch. "I shall have to go soon, to meet Matt."

Suddenly Tess knew she was speaking the truth. She couldn't admit it, though. She said, "Matt said nothing to me about any meeting with you."

"You think he tells you everything?" Madeleine said. "It wouldn't be the first time he's kept quiet where he and I are concerned—and you must be well aware of that." She paused. "When I leave here I'm going to meet Matt. It's as simple as that."

"How did you do it?" Tess tried to put scorn into her voice. "How did you trick him into agreeing to a meeting with you?"

"I didn't. It was his idea."

Tess laughed. "Now I know you're lying."

With Tess's words a flash of anger sparked in Madeleine's eyes, and she reached out, dipped into one of her coat pockets, fumbled for a moment and brought out a piece of paper. "There!" With a flourish she held it up and Tess saw words there in Matt's handwriting. *I must talk to you*, he had written. *Please call me between six and seven.* And then the familiarly scrawled initial: *M*. Below that she caught a brief glimpse of writing in Madeleine's hand, words and figures and also a diagram. Travelling directions? More than that, she couldn't tell, for Madeleine, with another flourish, took the paper back again. "Perhaps now you'll believe me," she said as she put it back in her coat pocket.

Watching her, Tess suddenly felt an overwhelming tiredness. She turned in her chair and briefly put her hands up to her face. What was happening? Into her mind came a picture of Matt's face as she had seen him that morning. *You're keeping something from me*, she had said to him. *What is it?* She realised that her hands were trembling and she lowered them and wrapped them around her coffee cup, and all the while she could feel Madeleine's eyes upon her. Raising her head slightly she looked across the table and saw the sardonic smile on her face.

And as she looked at her and saw the smile, Tess felt the rage within her swell and rise up; rage that had been inside her for years, and for all those years subdued. Not any more, though, and now as it flared up she gave in to it and, lifting the full cup, threw the hot coffee into Madeleine's face.

Madeleine screamed and jumped up from her chair as the coffee hit her and ran down on to her sweater and skirt. "Jesus Christ!" she cried out, clutching at her face. "Oh, God—Tess. . . !"

Tess said nothing, but just sat there, aware of the eyes of the other patrons upon her. She didn't even look round as Madeleine, wiping at her face, turned and moved away towards the counter. Tess was no longer concerned with her. She was thinking of Matt. Was he keeping something from her? Had he made arrangements to meet Madeleine? And was that why he'd said the car needed attention? But why should he lie? What did he want to hide from her? And why did he want to see Madeleine?

Dully raising her head she ignored the mutterings and disapproving stares in her direction and looked over to where Madeleine took some tissues and a cloth from a girl behind the counter and began to dab at her face and clothes. Tess turned away. Then, a moment later, with purpose in her eyes, she was getting up, all weariness gone. The action that followed took only moments. Quickly, so quickly, she dropped her coat onto the seat next to Madeleine's and took up Madeleine's coat and put it over her arm. Then, picking up her shopping bags, she turned and, without a backward glance, stepped smartly away towards the door. She was tense, expecting at any moment to hear Madeleine cry out and come running after her. But there was no sound. And then the next moment she was moving out onto the pavement. And she was safe.

It wasn't raining now, though the pavement was wet. She hurried on through the crowds of Saturday morning shoppers until she came to a narrow side street. Here she turned and moved along to a doorway where she set down her bags and put on Madeleine's Burberry. In one pocket she found a handkerchief and a hat. In the other she found some cigarettes and the piece of paper. Taking out the latter, she unfolded it and read what was written there.

Beneath Matt's words was Madeleine's writing. *11.30 to 11.45* she had written and beneath that, *Bridcombe Needle*, then *Cliff Lane* and *footpath*. And at once she recognised the directions as applying to the location for Matt's past week of filming. Near the foot of the page was a roughly sketched little diagram, obviously drawn by Madeleine under Matt's guidance.

Pushing back the cuff of the coat Tess looked at her watch and saw the time was just after eleven. She pocketed the piece of paper, took up the shopping bags and moved back towards the main street. As she emerged she looked about her for some sign of Madeleine. There was none, and she stepped to the edge of the kerb and cast her eyes about in search of a taxi.

Matt sat on a large stone on the cliff-top, surrounded by shrubbery and keeping well back out of sight of any casual walkers. Not that he expected many people to be out on such a wild day as this and in such a cold, bleak spot. It wasn't the day for sightseeing. The ground was wet under his feet, a keen cold wind was blowing, and the clouds above threatened more rain at any moment. On the way along the cliff-top his feet had sunk into the soft earth—a legacy of the week's filming. What with all the rain that had fallen and the many pairs of feet belonging to the film company, the ground had been churned up into mud.

He looked at his watch. Eleven-thirty-two. Madeleine should be here at any minute—if she was going to appear. His legs were getting stiff from sitting on the stone and he got up and stretched. Craning his neck to peer over the brambles he looked over to the left where the footpath led up from the end of Cliff Lane. The spot he had chosen in which to wait was a deep hollow in the ground, almost completely ringed by the dense bushes. Even the tower was out of sight at this point. He turned, stretching up to gaze around him. Would she come?

At the thought of her arrival his heart started to beat wildly again and he began to hope, desperately, that she would stay away. But hoping, wishing, did no good. He had to take action, and he had determined to do so and he had come too far to back out now. He touched a hand to the pocket of his jacket where Madeleine's note lay, and pictured the words she had written there, words he now knew by heart:

Matt,
You leave me no choice but to do what I have to do. Being left with no self-respect, and no future at all where you are concerned I've got no reason now to go on living.
I would have given you everything— while you have given me nothing— nothing but unhappiness and, now, the determination to end it all. Which I am about to do.
Remember me. Madeleine

He would have to put the note in one of her pockets. At the thought he began to tremble and his teeth began to chatter. Hugging himself, he sat back on the stone again and tried to keep from shaking.

Tess got out of the taxi in Cliff Lane, waited till it had turned and driven out of sight again then made her way along to the other end of the lane where there were no houses. Here the lane came to a dead end and only a stile indicated a continuing way

415

of any kind. There was no sign anywhere of Matt's car. As she hurried towards the stile the smell of the sea was so much stronger. And the wind was stronger, too, and colder, and now she felt the spitting of rain on her face.

On the other side of the stile she found a sheltered spot under a hedge and she placed the shopping bags there. They were too heavy to carry and were a hindrance she didn't need. She would pick them up on the way back. Unencumbered, she stepped out more quickly, following the footpath according to the instructions on the paper. To her left the sea lay spread out, grey and uninviting to the dark horizon, while some distance ahead of her she could see the shape of the Needle pointing up at the dark, lowering clouds. The further along the path she walked the muddier it became, and the going was becoming increasingly difficult. To make it easier she tried to keep to the side where the ground was a little firmer. As she walked she peered about her, trying to catch some sight of Matt. She had no idea where he would be waiting. *And for what purpose was he there? What did he want to see Madeleine for?* She had no idea. All she knew was that she was afraid and that she must get to him soon, before something happened that was irreversible. She moved a little faster, but with care, for the way was getting more slippery with every step she took and the old wall that ran along the side of the path was crumbling away in places.

Raising her head she looked up at the sky. It seemed almost black now. Suddenly a flash of lightning lit up the storm-darkened scapes of land and sea around her and she flinched as thunder cracked with terrifying nearness. Then as the rain began to pour down even harder she pulled up the collar of Madeleine's Burberry, reached into the pocket and pulled out the yellow hat.

In the darkening of the gathering storm Matt had waited, every so often peering through the shrubbery. And then, at last, he had seen her, moving along the footpath some fifty yards away. She was wearing the familiar Burberry and was pulling on her yellow hat against the sudden downpour of driving rain. She seemed to move in her own silence, all sound drowned by the noise of the storm. Thunder cracked and he saw her cower slightly from the edge of the cliff. Out over the sea the lightning played and in the flashes her slim figure stood out sharp and clear, brilliantly illuminated against the darkness of the hills beyond. She was so much closer than he was prepared for and he cursed himself for not keeping a constant watch. Also, he was suddenly aware of her slightness and her vulnerability. He thrust such unnerving emotions from him, and instead reminded himself of the things that she had done. She had tried to murder Tess; and would surely do so again if ever given the chance.

With such thoughts going over in his mind he crouched, watching as she drew nearer. Without the brilliance of the lightning, the rain and the darkness blurred and shadowed her figure. He waited while at the same time he tried to still his thudding heart and quell the trembling of his body. Ten yards . . . nine . . . He tensed . . . eight . . . seven . . . She was coming closer . . . six . . . five . . . He took a deep breath . . . four . . . three . . . A step forward . . . another deep breath and then he moved.

He came up behind her, swiftly and stealthily, and she heard no sound of his approach, becoming aware of him only at the very last moment. Then, turning her head and seeing him there, the terrifying, looming shape of him, she opened her mouth to cry out. But, in the same moment that his right arm curled around her body, so his left hand was there, clamping roughly down over her mouth and shutting off her cry. Then, still behind her, with his body pressed against her back, he lifted her off the ground. The next moment he was bearing her struggling to the edge of the cliff.

She fought desperately in his grasp as he dragged her through the churned up mud of the pathway, but he held on. Before, in his imaginings, it had all been over so fast; one second she was there on the path and the next she was plunging down onto the rocks. In reality it was not like that. With her struggles and the slickness of the rain it needed all his strength just to hold her. Her slim body writhed and jerked wildly in his grasp and her head twisted back and forth to escape the pressure of his hand.

Finally, though, he reached the edge of the cliff and, with his feet slipping and sliding in the mud, fought his way to a gap in the old stone wall. There, making a swift effort to change his grip, he took a breath and made to swing her out over the edge.

It was the rain and the mud that hampered him. Apart from the slipperiness of her rain-wet body he could get no purchase with his feet for the final effort needed, and as he tried to throw her from him he slipped in the mud and fell. He went down heavily, slightly winding himself on one of the stones from the wall, and when he struggled upright he saw that in the fall she had gone over the edge and was lying on a narrow out jutting of rock some four or five feet below. He stared down at her. Her eyes were closed and she lay quite still. He searched around nearby and at last found in the shrubbery a stout piece of a broken branch. With it he could push her off and . . . His resolve only needed to be strong for a few more moments and it would be done.

As he made to get down on all fours he suddenly began to retch and, turning back to the shrubbery, he vomited. He turned his face up to the driving rain. *Dear God, what am I doing?* a voice within him cried out. *What have I done?* Then, looking at the broken branch that he held, he drew back his hand and threw it far out, out into the wind and saw the wind take it and fling it inland again so that it fell in the fields beyond the shrubbery.

Getting onto his knees again at the edge of the cliff he looked down through the gap in the wall where she had gone through. Below, the spur of rock formed a small, sloping ledge, just a few feet down from where he now knelt. She lay in exactly the same position, her eyes closed just as before. She hadn't moved at all. She must be stunned, he thought.

"Madeleine . . ." he called down, and when she didn't respond he called louder. "Madeleine . . . *Madeleine. . . !*" She still made no answer. All his hatred for her had gone now, and all he could think of was getting her back to safety. Whatever she had done in the past it didn't matter. They would work it out somehow. All that mattered for now was that he get her back up, to safety.

With the thought he lay flat, prone on the wet, muddy earth and stretched down his right hand to her. He wasn't able to reach her, though. The next moment she opened her eyes and, finding where she was, gave a cry of fear. "It's all right, it's all right," he said, and in spite of the noise of the wind and the rain she heard him and lifted her head slightly and looked up at him for a moment, and then the fear overcame her once more and she shut tight her eyes and clung to the rock. In the moment of lifting her head, though, the yellow rainhat slipped from her head, slithered off the spur and fell, and with the hat falling, Matt saw her hair. And he saw at once that it was unlike Madeleine's in its style. He stared at her.

"Tess." Awed, he spoke in a whisper which was at once lost on the wind. And then he shouted her name: *"Tess! Tess!"* What was she doing here? It was a nightmare, and all of his own making. "Can you hear me?" he yelled.

She answered without looking up, "Yes, yes, I can."

"See if you can reach me," he shouted. "See if you can reach my hand." And as he finished speaking he stretched his right hand down to her once more and then watched as she slowly shifted her position a little on the wet, slippery surface and raised her hand to reach up. A moment later, though, she had withdrawn her hand to clutch at the rock again.

"I can't," she cried out. "I can't. Oh, Matt, I'm afraid. Help me!"

"I will! Just hold on!" The fear that drenched him like the pounding rain brought his body out in a cold sweat, while at the same time his throat felt so constricted that it was almost painful to speak. He called out again to her, trying not to give away his own fear. "Just hold on. I'll run into the village and get some help." As he finished speaking he got to his feet. "No!" she screamed out. "*No!* Oh, God, don't leave me alone!"

Distraught, he turned full circle on the cliff-top, helpless and wondering what to do. And then suddenly a small black dog appeared from the shrubbery and came sniffing at him. Matt's initial reaction was to drive him off but then he realised that the dog might not be alone. With the thought he cupped his hands to his mouth and shouted as loud as he could: "Help! Help! Help!" He waited, listening, while down below on the spur Tess clung on. He called down to her, "We'll get some help soon. Somebody will come by. Just hold on . . ."

And then a voice was calling to him above the sound of the storm, and turning he saw a man come hurrying, the black dog running to join him. Short and middle-aged, the man wore an oilskin and wellingtons. "Was that you shouting?" he asked as he drew nearer.

"Yes," Matt said, the tears starting again in his eyes. "Thank God you've come. There's been a—an accident. My wife—" he gestured down the side of the cliff, "she's fallen. I can't get her up."

"Oh, Jesus!" The man's face paled. Hurrying forward he stood beside Matt at the cliff-edge and looked down to where Tess lay on the spur.

"I fell," she said pathetically. "Please, help us."

The man nodded. "I'll run back to the village to get rope and bring some help.

I'll only be a minute." Even as he spoke he was turning and moving away, and seconds later he had pushed through the shrubbery and was out of sight.

"Matt! *Maaaaaaaaatt!*" The sound of Tess's screams rang out and Matt leapt back to the cliff-edge and peered over. "Matt, I'm slipping!" she cried out. "I'm slipping down!"

He saw to his horror that she had slipped further down on the spur. "Keep still!" he yelled. "Don't move." He couldn't wait for the man to get back. Something had to be done now—or it would be too late.

"I'm going to find something," he yelled, and dashed away. He ran through the shrubbery and up into the field beyond, to where he thought the piece of branch had fallen. He saw it almost at once, and rushing to it he picked it up, then turned and dashed back to the cliff path.

Christ! Just in the minute he'd been gone she seemed to have slipped further down on the spur. With all the rain, though, it was no wonder. Without hesitating he threw himself down in the mud and stretched out the branch. The end of it was within a foot of her.

"Here . . . take it. Take it and I'll pull you up."

All the time the rain was beating down, lashing them with what seemed an unexpendable fury, and through its screen he watched as slowly, slowly she moved on the spur and reached out a mud-smeared hand towards the branch. He saw her fingers close over it, then grip tight and hold on. He saw the relief that swept over her pale face, the momentary closing of her eyes as salvation came into her grasp.

"Good!" he yelled. "Now hold on with your other hand as well. And don't let go!

Holding on to the branch he set his right foot against a large, firmly set stone in the earth and braced himself as she gripped with her other hand. Then he began to pull. And slowly she began to rise up from the spur, holding on to the branch tightly while her feet sought for purchase on the face of the cliff. She was close, so close now. Another foot, one more, one more . . . Inch by inch she came nearer and nearer the top, nearer to him where he stood holding the branch, leaning back with the wind and the gale in his face, his arms straining at their sockets.

He became gradually aware as he stood there slowly pulling her up, that someone else had come upon the scene and was standing watching, and he half expected another pair of hands to be offered, to help him in his efforts. No one came forward, though, and now the task was almost done. Almost, just another few moments . . .

And then, suddenly, he felt a jolt run through the branch and up to his shoulders and saw that the relief and the hope in Tess's face were replaced by abject fear. His heart lurched as she cried out, "I can't hold on! My hands are slipping!" He saw that her hands, slick with the rain and mud, were further down on the branch, and getting lower all the time. With every second that passed she was losing her hold.

"Hold on tighter!" he screamed at her, and pulled harder, lifting her higher, higher. And she was almost there, almost there at last; almost on a level with him, her right foot coming up, scrabbling desperately to find one last foothold, her hands at the very end of the branch.

And then, just as her foot found a purchase, he saw her hands slip off the end of the branch.

Suddenly released from the strain that had been pulling against him he staggered back, while at the same time Tess screamed, the sound ringing out into the air, and fell backwards, her eyes and mouth wide in horror. And then she was gone and he was standing there, holding the branch and hearing nothing but the sound of the wind.

After a few moments he became aware of people there. The man in the oilskin was back, and with him other men carrying ropes. The man in the oilskin came to him, put out a hand and touched his shoulder. "I'm sorry," he said. "We came as fast as we could . . ."

Matt looked at him vacantly then shrugged and turned away.

It was then, through the screen of his tears, that he saw another figure, and realised that it was she who had been there in the background. He frowned. *"Madeleine . . ."* Vaguely he noticed that she was wearing Tess's coat.

As he stood there she came to him,

stopped before him. "You're wet through," she said. She reached up and touched a gentle hand to his cheek. "Oh, Matt, my poor, poor Matt."

THE END

GUIDE
TO THE COLOUR CODING
OF
ULVERSCROFT BOOKS

Many of our readers have written to us expressing their appreciation for the way in which our colour coding has assisted them in selecting the Ulverscroft books of their choice. To remind everyone of our colour coding—this is as follows:

BLACK COVERS
Mysteries

★

BLUE COVERS
Romances

★

RED COVERS
Adventure Suspense and General Fiction

★

ORANGE COVERS
Westerns

★

GREEN COVERS
Non-Fiction

MYSTERY TITLES
in the
Ulverscroft Large Print Series

FICTION TITLES
in the
Ulverscroft Large Print Series